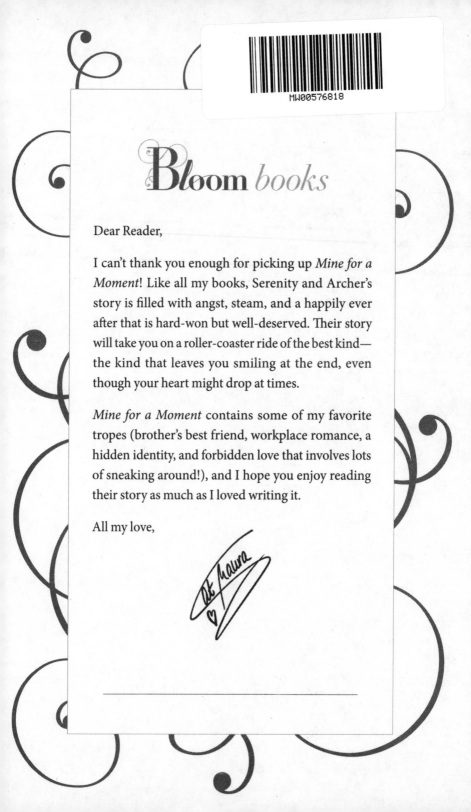

Bloom *books*

Dear Reader,

I can't thank you enough for picking up *Mine for a Moment*! Like all my books, Serenity and Archer's story is filled with angst, steam, and a happily ever after that is hard-won but well-deserved. Their story will take you on a roller-coaster ride of the best kind—the kind that leaves you smiling at the end, even though your heart might drop at times.

Mine for a Moment contains some of my favorite tropes (brother's best friend, workplace romance, a hidden identity, and forbidden love that involves lots of sneaking around!), and I hope you enjoy reading their story as much as I loved writing it.

All my love,

ALSO BY CATHARINA MAURA

The Windsors
The Wrong Bride
The Temporary Wife
The Unwanted Marriage
The Broken Vows
The Secret Fiancée

MINE *for a* MOMENT

CATHARINA MAURA

Bloom books

This one is for anyone who's ever tried their best to be worthy of real love, only to be found lacking. You are enough. Sometimes, things simply aren't meant for you—not because you don't deserve them but because better things are on their way. You will never be *the one* for the wrong person, but you will be *everything* to the right person.

Published by Bloom Books, an imprint of Sourcebooks
P.O. Box 4410, Naperville, Illinois 60567-4410
(630) 961-3900
sourcebooks.com

Cataloging-in-Publication data is on file with the Library of Congress.

Printed and bound in the United States of America.
PAH 10 9 8 7 6 5 4 3 2 1

One

SERENITY

The soft rattling of the spray can in my hands steals away my every thought, momentarily dulling the heartache that led me to these deserted streets in the first place. My heart thunders in my ears, quietening everything else as I put the final touches on my latest artwork.

My stomach tightens as I step back to take in the final result—a realistic depiction of a girl leaning against the wall of the old apartment block I'm standing in front of, her head thrown back and her eyes squeezed closed as tears stream down her face, leaving mascara tracks on her cheeks. To her side, the walls look broken up to reveal a couple in their living room, dancing as they smile at each other like nothing else exists.

It won't take my fans long to realize that there are countless photos in the background, some of the three of them, but most of them just of our crying girl and the man that's now holding tightly onto someone else. They'll look at it, and maybe they'll feel my pain, but they won't understand—they won't know that this is the very same building, the same apartment I thought I'd live in with Theo. This is the culmination of years of unrequited love, of waiting too long, only to watch my last chance slip through my fingers.

People will walk past, and perhaps they'll pause and stare, but they won't realize the significance behind my piece. They won't know that I've stood here with those same tears in my eyes, pretending it doesn't hurt to watch my best friend love one of our friends the way I wish he'd love me.

"Hey, you!"

Fear rushes through me in the moments before I look over my shoulder, my mind not quite capable of deciphering what I'm seeing. It's all wrong—the time and place, the desperation written on his face as he charges toward me, his breathing labored. *Archer Harrison.* My brother's best friend and the one man I can't get caught by.

I jump into action and throw a second glance at my supplies, my heart aching at the thought of leaving them behind. The mere cost of it all makes me hesitate for a moment too long before I turn and attempt to run, giving Archer the chance to catch up and wrap his hand around my wrist.

"Please," he says, his voice so familiar yet so foreign all at once. I've never heard him sound so beguiled, so frenzied. "I've been looking for you for over a year."

I look over my shoulder, more relieved than ever that I'm not just wearing a face mask and a crimson wig but a hoodie too. There's no way he could recognize me in this getup, but Archer has always been oddly observant. He's perhaps the only person other than my brother who truly sees me, without judging, never allowing his prejudices to distort who I am. If I linger too long or say the wrong thing, he'll know.

"I only have one question," he says, his voice softer now, placating. "I won't ask you who you are or why you keep your identity hidden. I'm not after your work or trying to profit off you like so many others have. So will you please hear me out?"

I know I should pull my wrist out of his warm hand. I should turn and run, and never look back, but when he looks at me like that, I can't deny him. Archer has always been steadfast and confident, an unshakable force in my life, so to find him standing here like only I hold the answers to questions that keep him up at night leaves me shaken. Against my better judgment, I nod.

He breathes a sigh of relief and steps closer, his gaze searching. Something crosses his face, and I hold my breath. It isn't quite recognition, but it's familiarity, like some part of him realizes he knows me, but he can't quite place me. He shakes his head almost imperceptibly, and I draw a shaky breath.

"*The Ballerina*," he whispers. "It was your first piece, about eighteen months ago. She looked just like someone I used to know, and I have to ask…who is she? Why her, and why then? Did you know her, or have you seen her?"

His voice breaks, and my heartache takes a new form, spreading from my chest to every single nerve ending. My breathing becomes shallow, and I look down, unable to face him. I never stopped to think that my attempts to alleviate my own pain would in turn inflict it upon him.

Eighteen months.

It's not me he's been looking for.

It's her. Still.

The plea in his eyes is evident, his grip tightening as silence stretches between us. I can't tell him that both he and my brother, Ezra, are the reason behind that piece—not without him figuring out who I am. I remember the day I painted her across one of the walls in our hometown; it was the first time I ever did street art, and I haven't dared to paint on any of the buildings so close to home again for fear of giving away my identity.

I'd come home from college for my mother's birthday, about a year after Tyra disappeared without a trace, and both Ezra and Archer were pretending she wasn't on their minds despite the devastation written all over their faces. It hurt to watch them avoid so much as mentioning her when it was the first time in years she wasn't with us on Mom's birthday. She deserved to be missed, to have her memory be honored.

So I painted her dancing across a stage in the Swan Lake costume she used to dream of wearing someday. Because that's how I needed to remember her: as the shining light she was in our lives. Tyra wasn't just Archer's girlfriend—she was Ezra's best friend and the big sister I never had. She was my biggest supporter, and the only one who truly believed my art was valuable and worth pursuing. Painting her felt like honoring her, and though it didn't close the gaping hole in my heart, it took away the edge of my pain.

It'd been an act of rebellion, and I'd known painting her in such a highly visible spot would force Ezra and Archer to face her every single time they drove home, but I did it anyway. I didn't want her disappearance to be her legacy, but I never meant for my mural to keep haunting Archer for so long. It isn't what she would've wanted.

"I'm sorry," I murmur, my voice barely above a whisper. "She's gone. All we have left are memories and dreams that won't come true." None of us want to admit it, but the fact that she's been missing for over eighteen months means we likely won't ever see her again. We lost her, and we're all just trying to avoid acknowledging it.

His eyes widen, and I realize I said the wrong thing, giving away that I knew her, that the ballerina I painted was Tyra. "Who are you?" he asks, his voice terse.

I shake my head and yank my wrist out of his grip, wishing I hadn't said anything at all. I look back once before I rush away, grateful he doesn't follow me.

Two

ARCHER

I lean back in my office chair as my thumb brushes over the ridges of the silver paintbrush charm left behind by the artist known as The Muse. By now she must have realized that she lost it last night, but according to my security cameras, she hasn't come back to look for it.

"Who are you, Muse?" I whisper, unable to figure out why she seemed so familiar. It's clear she knew Tyra, and though I couldn't see much of her face, those dark eyes of hers held secrets—secrets I suspect relate to Tyra and her disappearance.

I clench my jaw and tighten my grip around the bracelet charm, wishing I hadn't let her go. I should've questioned her, should've demanded answers. Muse has no idea how long I've been looking for her, how close I've gotten several times before our paths finally crossed last night by sheer coincidence. The building she'd chosen to bless with her art was one I own, and had one of my residents not reported her, I'd never have found her.

"Archer, you fucking missed our meeting."

I'm snapped out of my daze as Ezra, my best friend and business partner, storms into my office, pure fury written all over his face. Muse's charm slips between my fingers, hitting my desk just as he reaches it.

"You've been harping on and on about this expansion opportunity for months now, and you miss the fucking meeting?"

I run a hand through my hair, guilt crashing through me as I stare at the charm on my desk, sunlight reflecting off it in a mystic kind of way, almost as though it's taunting me. "I found her."

Ezra tenses, and the pure hope I find in his eyes when I look up completely guts me. "*Muse*," I'm quick to correct, my heart wrenching painfully. I'm a fucking idiot. If he'd said those same words to me, I'd have reacted the same way, but our hope only ever turns into devastation.

"*Muse*," Ezra repeats, his shoulders slumping, pure bitterness in his voice. My guard is instantly up, knowing he hates it when I mention her. Ezra considers her street art vandalism and doesn't see the value of it, doesn't understand her notoriety and fame, let alone my appreciation for her work. He doesn't understand that Muse gave me something to look forward to throughout one of the hardest periods of my life, when darkness threatened to consume me.

Something about her art made me feel like she understood what I was going through, like she too just wanted someone to see and acknowledge her pain, her grief. I've watched her art develop, watched her tell a story I doubt anyone else could decipher, and because of it, I feel connected to her in the strangest way.

Ezra knows it, and he hates it. He'd never admit it, but I suspect he feels like my admiration for Muse is a betrayal of Tyra when it's nothing like that. Until a few days ago, I wasn't even sure of Muse's gender.

"She was just a few blocks away from our office over the weekend, spray-painting a building I own. I asked her about the ballerina mural,

MINE FOR A MOMENT

and it was clear she knew Tyra, but I can't figure out if she knows anything about..." *about Tyra's disappearance.* I run a hand through my hair and swallow hard, unable to finish my sentence.

Ezra looks down, his gaze conflicted, almost like he wants my words to hold weight, but he's as tired of having hope as I am. We've both been searching for clues as to what happened to Tyra, only to come up empty every time.

"Muse said something I can't get off my mind. She told me Tyra is gone, that all we have left are memories and dreams that'll never come true. There was a finality to her tone, as if she knew what happened. I've just been replaying her words over and over in my mind and—"

"Archer, where did you get that?" he asks, cutting me off midsentence, a hint of shock in his eyes as he reaches for the charm on my desk.

I raise a brow and rise to my feet, swiping it out of his hand in one smooth move before hiding it away in my suit pocket. "It's Muse's," I murmur, feeling defensive. "She lost it last night." I don't tell him that I'd been holding her wrist and that the charm came loose when she pulled her hand away. I'm not sure why I feel the need to hide that, but something about that moment, the way she looked at me...it seemed private for reasons I can't quite convey.

Ezra looks up and slowly buries a hand in his curly hair, squeezing it the way he does when he's stressed out. "Fuck," he whispers. He clears his throat and shakes his head. "Muse...you've been fucking obsessed with her art from the moment her murals appeared." His voice is soft, and for once, he doesn't sound irritated when speaking of her. "And they started to appear about a year after Tyra disappeared, didn't they? Did you see Muse's face last night?"

"Art," I huff. "That's the first time I've heard you refer to her work as *art* and not as *plain vandalism.* And no, I didn't see her face. She

was wearing a mask—all I could tell was that she's a woman, likely around our age or younger."

Discomfort crosses his face, and I frown.

"What's wrong?" I ask, surprised by his reaction. Normally he'd have jumped on even the vaguest clue related to Tyra's disappearance, but this time, he's more focused on Muse. I brace myself for the inevitable tirade he launches into every single time I mention her art, telling me she's nothing but a glorified criminal, but it doesn't come. Instead, he just stares ahead, looking forlorn.

"It's nothing," he says belatedly, raising his hand to his hair again. "Her latest mural—what is it?"

I raise a brow and stare at him, feeling oddly defensive when it comes to Muse. "It was a piece that seemed to convey unrequited love," I tell him, and then begin to describe it. For once, he listens patiently, and it completely throws me off.

"Do you have a photo of it?" he asks, his tone urgent.

I nod and show it to him. He takes my phone from me and just stares at it for several moments. "I guess you saw something I didn't want to acknowledge, but I can't deny her raw talent, the pain in her work," he says eventually. "I just didn't recognize it for what it was."

"And what might that be?"

He shakes his head before handing my phone back, his expression grim. "A cry for help."

Three

I draw my legs up on my bed as I stare at the paintbrushes I hid away in my childhood bedroom, knowing full well that I can't use them without upsetting my mom. It's why I turn to street art every time I'm home for more than a week—because I can't imagine not being able to paint at all. I didn't think I'd ever get caught, but I did, and I'm not sure where that leaves me.

Painting is the only thing that's ever truly allowed me to stop overthinking—it's the closest thing to peace I've ever found. Without my brush or a spray can in my hand, I feel vulnerable, an unwilling participant in the real world and all its accompanying worries. I can't stand the idea of having to give it up entirely, but if Archer had recognized me, I'd have been in a world of trouble. It would've been even worse had it been someone else—someone who would've had me arrested.

My phone rings for the fifth time this morning, a photo of Theo with his arm slung around me lighting up my phone, and the urge to paint skyrockets. I can't avoid him much longer, but I don't know how to be around him anymore. I can't face him and pretend I don't know what he's keeping from me.

My thoughts have been a mess since I saw him kiss our mutual friend, Kristen, through the window of our favorite diner. I know he's been trying to find a way to tell me about them, but I don't want to hear it. Not yet. I'm not ready to let go of the idea of us. I thought that if I just waited long enough, he'd finally see that I could make him happy, that I could be the one. Not just his best friend but the person he shares the rest of his life with. I'm not ready to smile like it doesn't hurt or wish them well when I don't mean it as much as I should.

"Serenity?"

My head snaps up at the sound of Theo's voice, and my heart skips a beat when he walks into my bedroom, pure concern written all over his face. My gaze lingers on his soft, light brown curls and those green eyes that have visited me in my dreams almost every night for years now. He smiles, and my stomach flutters.

"Hey," I murmur, trying my hardest to force a smile. I should've known he'd come find me if I ignored his calls. It's rare for us to go more than a handful of days without seeing each other, after all. When I told him I wanted to move back in with my parents during my job search following college, he moved back in with his parents too, just so I wouldn't feel alone here. In hindsight, I wish he hadn't. Maybe then he wouldn't have fallen for Kristen.

Theo's gaze roams over my face, as though to assess whether I'm okay. His eyes eventually settle on the phone on my bed, his expression hardening. I ignored his last call seven minutes ago, the exact amount of time it'd have taken him to get to me. "I couldn't reach you," he says as he sits down next to me, his shoulder brushing against mine. "I was so worried, Ser. Did you even realize internship emails have gone out?"

I look up at him and inhale sharply as I reach for my phone.

I'd been so focused on Theo and Kristen that I've been avoiding my phone altogether, not wanting to see their texts, either in our group chat or individually.

"I came straight here when I got mine. Should we open them together?" he asks, his voice soft and sweet.

My heart wrenches painfully, and I let my eyes flutter closed briefly. This is exactly why I fell for him—because he always makes me feel so special. He made me feel like I was his person, the way he is mine.

I bite down on my lip as I unlock my phone, my stomach tightening. Until a few days ago, this internship ranked highest on my list of things I wanted to accomplish this year, and it hurts to have the shine of it dull the way it has. Theo and I were meant to move in together if we both got internship positions, and I was finally going to take a chance on us.

"What if I didn't get in?" I ask, my voice soft, and it kills me to realize that a small part of me hopes that's the case. Not getting in means not having to face Theo as often, and I hate that my dreams are tainted by my broken heart.

"Impossible," Theo promises. "There isn't a thing in this world that you can't accomplish. This is nothing. Just a few moments from now, you'll get to cross another accomplishment off your list. I just know it."

He looks at me like he genuinely believes there's nothing I can't do, and I can't help but wonder how I misread the signs as badly as I have. I was so certain that the way he looks at me meant he had feelings for me too, and I'm not sure what's worse: the fact that I was wrong or the knowledge that I simply didn't know him as well as I thought I did.

"Okay," I whisper. "Let's find out if we got in."

He nods and reaches for his phone. "Ready?"

I take a deep breath, my stomach taut with nerves. "I'll count us down."

He grins, an indulgent look in his eyes. "You're intent on delaying the inevitable for just a few more seconds, aren't you?"

Inevitable. I'd hoped that's what *we* were. "Fine, I'm starting my count down right now!" I tell him, earning myself a chuckle that normally would've made me smile back at him. "*Three,*" I murmur, opening my email app to find that there is, indeed, an email waiting for me.

"Two."

"One."

We both click on our emails, and almost instantly, we both begin to smile. I reach for him wordlessly, and he chuckles, his arms wrapping around me. "We did it," he says, holding me so tightly that we fall backwards onto my bed. He just laughs and squeezes me a little harder.

"We did it," I repeat, my nose pressed against his neck. His hugs never failed to lift my mood, but now they just fill me with guilt. The thought of him being with Kristen, and of her ever seeing us this way, makes me feel sick. I guess that's part of why I've been avoiding both of them—because I knew things would change, and I wasn't ready.

"I can't wait to see your brother's face when you tell him," Theo says, pulling away to look at me, his eyes twinkling with pride. I smile as I imagine Ezra's incredulous expression. He might very well be happier than I ever could be to hear that I'll be interning at the company he founded with Archer. Ezra has never put any pressure on me, but he always made it clear that he'd love for me to work for Serenity Solutions someday.

"I bet you already have dozens of to-do lists for us," Theo says, sitting up. His smile slips a fraction, and my stomach dips. "I've never met anyone who loves lists more than you do."

I sit up too, my heart racing as I cross my legs, wishing we didn't need to have this conversation. "It's good to have some direction, and honestly, it just feels amazing to cross something off a list," I tell him, my voice trembling. "Makes me feel accomplished. You'll probably hate me when you see the long list of things we'll need to do in the next couple of days, but you'll thank me when it's all done."

He looks away, regret flashing through his eyes before he manages to hide it. He stares at me for a moment, his expression foreign. I've never seen him look at me like that. "Serenity," he says, his tone hesitant. "I don't think we'll be able to move in together like we planned. There's something I need to tell you."

Four

ARCHER

I frown when my phone alerts me that my best friend's silent alarm system was triggered, and for a moment I'm certain that can't be right. Ezra's penthouse and mine take up the entire top floor of this building, and just getting past the receptionist is a challenge.

I sigh as I push off my sofa and head to the hallway, irritated. It's most likely just one of the building attendants delivering his mail for him, but once the alarm is triggered, no one but Ezra or me can turn it off.

My temper instantly dissipates when I pull my door open to find Ezra's little sister standing in front of his door, just a few steps away. She turns, her long, dark, curly hair swaying, and I freeze when I see tears in her eyes.

I take a step forward without thinking, and then another, until I'm cupping her face, my thumbs swiping at her tears. "*Archer*," she says, her voice breaking as a sob tears through her throat.

"What happened, Serenity?" I ask, my voice harsher than intended. I study her face, taking in her red eyes and the pure despair in her gaze. "Who did this to you?"

MINE FOR A MOMENT

She shakes her head, and it fucking guts me to see my best friend's little sister like that. I wordlessly pull her into my arms, holding her tightly, and she begins to cry in earnest.

I push my fingers through her hair in response, cradling her head as she presses her forehead to my chest, hiding herself away as her small body rocks from the force of her sobs. "Please," I whisper, my heart aching. "Tell me why you're crying, sweetheart. Tell me how to make this right."

Serenity shakes her head again, and I pull away just a touch to lift her into my arms. She gasps, her tear-filled eyes finding mine for a moment as I carry her into my home. Her arms wrap around my neck, her nose brushing against my throat as she holds on to me like she wants consolation but doesn't want me to witness her sorrow, and fuck, I'm all too familiar with that need.

I kick the door closed and carry her to the sofa, sitting down with her in my lap. She tightens her grip on me, almost like she's scared I'll let go, and I hold her a little tighter, my hand roaming over her back soothingly as she tries her hardest to inhale through her sobs, her breathing ragged. The sounds she makes fucking devastate me, and my own eyes fall closed as I bury a hand in her hair.

"Was it Theo?"

She flinches, and my blood runs cold. Neither Ezra nor I ever liked her best friend, and if he hurt her, I'll hold him down myself while Ezra makes him pay for each and every tear Serenity has shed— before taking a turn of my own.

"A-Are my f-feelings t-that obvious?"

I tense and shake my head slightly. "No," I murmur, even though Ezra and I have both known for years. I always hated standing back as Theo seemed to take Serenity for granted. "The way you looked just now is near identical to the way my little sister has looked for years. You look heartbroken."

She clutches at me and holds me tighter, her face pressing against my neck. I sigh and push my hand deeper into her hair, my other hand settling on her lower back. No one should have the power to devastate her like this. "He didn't touch you anywhere, did he?" I ask with barely controlled rage. "Are you hurt?"

She shakes her head, and I relax a fraction. "It's not like that," she reassures me, her breathing evening out just a touch. "I'm not physically hurt."

I sigh and lean back on the sofa, moving both of us into a more comfortable position. "You wanna know what I used to tell my sister each time she'd cry over a broken heart?"

She nods and balls her hands into my T-shirt.

"You'll find someone who will see your worth, Serenity. You'll occupy his every thought, and you'll be everything to him. The kind of love you're after is out there, and you'll find it—with the *right* person."

She raises her head to look at me, not quite realizing the position we're in as she sits in my lap, her arms still wrapped around me. "Has your sister found that kind of person?" she whispers, her voice tinged with hope. She looks at me like the mere thought of ever loving someone that isn't Theo, and being loved the way I just described, is preposterous.

"She's getting married next week," I tell her, the words bittersweet. "It's an arranged marriage, but that marriage will fix what time couldn't."

"How can you be so sure?" she asks, sounding skeptical. I grin at her, relieved to find some luster back in her voice. It's ridiculous how beautiful she still is despite the tears that stain her face. Her pain hasn't dulled her gorgeous hazel eyes at all.

"Because the man she's marrying truly loves her as much as she loves him, even though they both claim to hate each other. Someday, you'll find someone who loves you the same way—*unconditionally*, despite the odds, despite the obstacles life might throw your way." What I don't tell her is that the man Celeste is marrying is also the one that broke her heart in the first place. The last thing I want to do is encourage Serenity to keep waiting for Theo, like she's so obviously been doing.

"If she's getting married next week, you'll have to see your grandfather, won't you?" she asks, concern for me crossing her face, despite her own devastation. I've always loved this about her—the way she cares so deeply. Not even her own pain is enough to push aside her instant concern for me. She's so fucking precious, and she doesn't even seem to realize it.

"Yeah," I whisper, my heart aching at the thought of having to face the man that disowned me nearly a decade ago purely because I refused to follow in his footsteps and pursued a career that didn't involve me becoming a hotelier like he expected me to. I've barely spoken to him in years, and my parents have done all they could to ensure I wouldn't have to see him, but there's no getting out of it this time.

Serenity's hand wraps around the back of my neck, and a thrill runs down my spine. She has no idea how long it's been since I last had someone in my arms like this. I didn't even realize how badly I'd been craving that kind of connection. "It'll be fine, Sera. More than anything, I'm looking forward to seeing my sister walk down that aisle. Someday, that'll be you too, you know? Someday, you'll meet someone that'll make you see how wrong Theo would've been for you."

"Someday," she repeats, her hands sliding to my shoulders as she sits up, balancing her weight on my thighs. "I used to think that someday, Theo and I would be like my parents. They were best friends before they got together. I'm not sure if anyone ever told you, but Mom divorced Ezra's dad because he cheated on her, and personally I always thought that was fate. I thought that Ezra was meant to be my brother and that everything happens for a reason. I thought I'd just have to wait for Theo to realize that I'm the one for him, just like Dad waited for Mom, loving her quietly."

I sigh and push one of her curls out of her face, unsure what to say to that. I don't have it in me to discourage her, to break her heart any further. Her eyes fall closed as she draws a shaky breath. "I think I'm tired of waiting for *someday*, Archer," she whispers. "For years I've been trying to suppress my feelings for someone who never even saw me the same way, and all the while, I let life pass me by. There's so much I never experienced simply because the idea of him was always better than any man I met in real life. I want everything I missed out on— coffee dates, talking until the sun rises, making out in the backseat of a car, being truly *wanted*, all of it. I can't keep waiting for the right person when I should be *living*. I never should've put my happiness in the hands of someone else."

The thought of her doing any of that with anyone doesn't sit particularly well with me, and I can't quite figure out why. "Does it have to be the backseat of a car?" I ask, my gaze roaming over her face. Her eyes widen a fraction, like she's suddenly aware of how close her face is to mine. "I rate it one out of ten. It's cramped and uncomfortable, and you'll probably get elbowed at some point."

A startled laugh leaves her lips, and I grin at her, glad I was able to ease some of her dejection. Her eyes trail over my face, settling on my mouth for a moment, and all of a sudden I find myself wondering what she's thinking when she looks at me that way. That expression… it's not one I've ever seen on her before.

I bite down on my lip and move my hands to her waist, knowing I should move her off me and entirely unable to. I tear my eyes away and take a steadying breath. "I agree that you shouldn't let anyone hold you back, Serenity. You don't want to look back someday and regret not doing things because of someone who never deserved your devotion, someone who never returned it. If you feel like there are things you're missing out on, you should take control of your life and your own experiences." I pause, struggling to find the right words. "However, don't let him be the reason you rush into something you aren't ready for."

"But I am," she says, her voice tinged with desperation. "I'm ready, Archer. I'm twenty-two, and I've never—" Serenity shakes her head, her expression conveying sudden shyness. "I'm tired of feeling like I can't control my feelings, of letting them deprive me of a chance at something real of my own, when the person I'd been waiting for never wanted me and never will."

"I get it," I murmur, my heart squeezing painfully. I haven't quite been living my life either. Guilt keeps me trapped in the past, tied to someone who's no longer here. "Just promise me you won't do anything risky or impulsive, okay?"

She pushes off me and rises to her feet. Even with her hair a mess and red eyes, she looks like a fucking goddess. She's effortlessly beautiful, and I'm not sure why I never noticed it before. "I won't do anything risky, Arch," she promises, crossing her arms. "On the contrary."

I raise a brow, and she grins at me, her smile finally fully restored. Her eyes twinkle as she stares at me for a moment, seemingly making up her mind about something.

"I'm going to make a list."

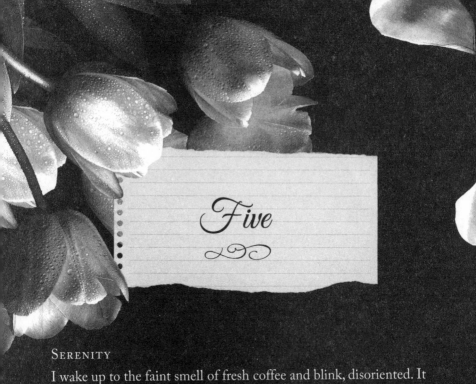

Five

SERENITY

I wake up to the faint smell of fresh coffee and blink, disoriented. It takes me a few moments to remember that I'm in Archer's guest room, and I draw a steadying breath as my mind begins to replay Theo's words. Fresh waves of something that can only be described as grief wash over me at the thought of Theo with Kristen, and I squeeze my eyes closed, wishing I could fall back asleep and escape the thoughts that torment me.

I turn over in bed, my mind torturing me with images of the three of us together—except he'll be holding her hand, and each time he thinks I'm not looking, he'll lean in to steal a kiss, all the while wishing I wasn't there at all. Things will never be the same again, and I'll have to pretend I'm happy for them while silently mourning everything I thought I'd have with Theo, everything I waited so patiently for.

I knew it'd hurt to hear him admit he's dating Kristen, but I underestimated how badly. There's only been one other occasion when my grief ran so deep that not even painting could dull the pain—when I found out Tyra had been missing for a week and no one knew how to tell me. It's a jarring feeling to be so disappointed in myself for feeling the way I do. Losing her the way we did was far worse than what's going on with Theo, yet it hurts nearly as much. It makes me feel pathetic, and self-loathing rapidly consumes me.

I throw the covers off and sit up, my heart squeezing painfully as I reach for my phone, finding dozens of messages from Theo waiting for me, most of them requests to let him know I arrived at Ezra's house and that I'm fine. I bite on my lip as I scroll through them, only to pause when I notice that there's one more message—from Kristen.

KRISTEN

I'm sorry. Please, can we talk?

I tighten my grip on my phone before throwing it onto my pillow, welcoming the sudden flames of anger that ignite deep in my gut. She knew about my feelings for Theo, and though I wasn't entitled to him in any way, I can't help the tinge of betrayal I feel.

I'm shaking as I walk to the en suite bathroom, finding a towel waiting for me. *Archer.* I bury my face in my hands and draw a steadying breath as I recall the way I cried my heart out last night and the way Archer just held me, offering me quiet support. I can't believe that I admitted as much as I did. What was I thinking, telling my older brother's best friend that I was tired of waiting? That I wanted to be kissed in the back seat of a car? My heartache must've temporarily made me lose my mind.

Mortification keeps my dejection at bay as I get ready, unsure how to face Archer after everything I said last night. I don't want him to pity me, but how could he not after the way I fell apart in his arms? I should've gone to Ezra's house after Archer offered to let me in last night, instead of letting him persuade me to stay in his guest room. I squeeze my curls and stare at myself in the mirror for a moment, trying my best to find one single positive in this situation. *At least he didn't realize that I'm The Muse.* The way he behaved last night made it clear that he didn't even suspect me, and that's a definite win.

My cheeks are still burning by the time I walk into the hallway, following the smell of coffee to the kitchen. I freeze when I find my brother leaning against the counter, a mug in his hand. The wrinkled suit he's wearing makes me suspect he came straight home once he realized I was here, and fresh guilt hits me right in the chest.

He looks up when I walk in, his eyes filled with concern. "Serenity," he says, putting down his coffee to offer me a hug.

"I'm sorry," I murmur, hugging him tightly. "I didn't mean to worry you."

Ezra pulls back to look at me, his gaze searching. "I'm just glad Archer was home. I change my door code every few months and didn't think to tell you. Are you okay?"

I nod and force a smile, despite the way my fragmented heart bleeds. "I'm fine. I just…I just don't really want to talk about it if that's okay?"

Ezra sighs, but thankfully, he nods. "You know I'm here if you ever need anything, don't you? Anything at all. You'll never be alone so long as you have me, Serenity. I know I haven't been around as much as I should've been, but I'll work on that."

My eyes widen at his serious response, and guilt settles in my stomach. Truthfully, Ezra was never meant to know I'd gone to his house in tears. I knew he was on a business trip, and I went to his house because I needed to be alone. I never meant to make him feel bad for not being there last night when I didn't even expect him to be.

I begin to reply, only to pause when I spot Archer standing in the corner, gray sweats hanging low on his hips, paired with a white tee. His eyes meet mine, and he throws me a sweet smile. The pity I'd expected is nowhere to be found, and I smile back, relieved to find him looking at me the way he usually does.

"I made you pancakes," he says as he grabs a plate and loads it up. "Sit down and have some food."

I nod and welcome the change of topic gratefully, my eyes widening when he hands me a plate of fluffy pancakes topped with chocolate and strawberries. It looks like the kind of thing you'd get in a restaurant, and I glance up at him gratefully. I'd forgotten how good of a cook he is. He hasn't stayed the night at my parents' house in nearly two years now, after all.

Ezra joins me at the breakfast bar quietly, concern etched into his face. It's clear he has questions, but I'm not sure I can answer them without bursting into tears all over again.

"Part of the reason I came here is because I have some good news to share," I murmur eventually, staring at the creamy color of the latte Archer gave me. I never realized he knew how I like my coffee.

"Oh yeah?" Archer says, his expression kind and encouraging. I never told him specifically what made me cry last night, and I wonder if he knows how grateful I am that he didn't demand answers beyond making sure I was physically unharmed.

My gaze moves between the two men, and I try my best to smile. "In two weeks from now, I'll officially be an intern at Serenity Solutions."

Ezra blinks in surprise, and then the biggest grin lights up his whole face. "No fucking way," he says, chuckling. He looks up at his best friend, pure disbelief in his gaze, and I follow his line of sight to find Archer looking at me with the most incredulous expression. I watch as his disbelief makes way for pride, and he shakes his head.

"Serenity," he says. "Thousands of people apply every year, and HR selects *ten*."

I shrug, unable to hide a hint of smugness. Ezra wraps his arm around me and squeezes, pure glee radiating off him. "I'm so proud of you," he says, smirking. "But you know we'd have given you a job if you wanted one."

I nod. "I know, but Theo and I…" My smile slips, and I force it back into place. "Theo got in too, and it was important to us both that we made it because we deserved to."

I note the way Archer tenses in my peripheral vision, and Ezra's expression sobers too. "He got in too, huh?" Archer says, something akin to irritation sparking in his eyes.

"Does that mean you're moving here?" my brother asks, his voice filled with excitement.

I nod hesitantly. I spent so much time trying to find places Theo and I could potentially rent, but I can't afford any of them on my own. My heart wrenches as I imagine Theo doing with Kirsten what I thought I'd experience with him—viewing places together, decorating and turning a tiny flat into a home.

"I'll clear my guest room for you," Ezra says. "I handle all of the company's implementations, so I'm hardly ever home. I'm gone for weeks at a time. You'll mostly have the place to yourself, but Archer will always be next door if you need him."

I look up and begin to shake my head, but Ezra shoots me a stern look, shutting me up before I've even had a chance to object. "You know Mom would worry about you endlessly if you lived anywhere else, and honestly, I don't want you living in some kind of shithole when I have a perfectly good room for you."

"He's right," Archer says. "Besides, if you don't enjoy living at Ezra's, you can always move out. Give it a try, Serenity."

I nod hesitantly, and my brother grins, clearly pleased. "It's settled then," he says, his voice brooking no argument.

Six

SERENITY

"I'm so proud of you," Mom says as she helps me pack, her gaze lingering on the painting supplies I set aside to bring with me. "I was worried you'd let your intellect and your degree go to waste, you know?"

I glance at my variety of acrylic paints, hearing the words she won't say. She was scared I'd insist on pursuing a creative career, even though she's reminded me over and over again that stability matters above all else. I once suggested that I'd love to paint professionally, and it upset Mom so much that I ended up moving all my painting supplies to the attic, where she wouldn't have to see any of it. "Of course not, Mom," I tell her, smiling weakly. "I'm excited to work with Ezra and Archer."

Education was a gateway to my parents—law school and their resulting careers as lawyers allowed them to build an amazing life for Ezra and me, even though they immigrated here with nothing to their name. I get it, and I truly appreciate everything they did for us, everything they sacrificed. I just wish she wouldn't be so dismissive of my art. I know chances are low that anyone would ever want to pay for my work, but I wish she hadn't tried to shut my dreams down so desperately.

I wish she'd believed in me, even if that belief came with a sincere wish for me to choose a safer and more predictable career path. If I didn't think she'd prosecute me herself, I'd have told her I'm The Muse, the street artist the entire country seems to love and hate in equal measure, just to see how she'd react.

Mom tapes a box closed and looks up, hesitating. "Serenity Solutions has grown into a huge company," she remarks, her tone cautious. "Are you sure you don't want anyone to know Ezra is your brother? It'd be much easier if people knew, sweetie."

I shake my head and remind myself that she has the best intentions. "Mom, we've spoken about this," I tell her, my voice soft. "I never even told Ezra or Archer about my application because I wanted to do this by myself. I'd always feel like a fraud if I got in any other way, and I'm concerned people would just pander to me if they knew I'm the CEO's little sister. I wouldn't learn a thing because everyone would just go easy on me all the time."

Mom looks down, her expression conveying barely hidden frustration. "I don't want you to have to work twice as hard as everyone else, Serenity. Without the protection Ezra can provide, you will have to. It's not like at college, where grading is anonymous and your work truly speaks for itself. At work, they'll take one look at your curly hair and the color of your skin, and they'll judge you harder than your peers. Despite my education, I've had to work twice as many hours as my peers for the same promotions, the same opportunities, the same *salary*. The same goes for Dad. It's so rare to have an advantage, and I promise you, anyone else in your position would leverage it."

I grab her hand, my thumb drawing circles across the back of it. "I'll ask Ezra for help if I need it," I promise her. "Let me try this my way first."

She sighs and gently pushes my hair out of my face. "All right, honey," she says, her gaze filled with uncertainty. "Just remember that you're not alone. I know Ezra travels a lot for work, but you have Archer too. He will be there for you if you ever need anything, you know that, right?"

I nod, my mind drifting back to the way he held me last week. "I know," I murmur, feeling oddly conflicted. Throughout the years, Archer has become more than just one of my brother's friends—he's part of our family. Except, he really didn't feel like family when he wrapped his hands around my waist. "Honestly, if I ever actually needed help, I'd probably go to Archer first. Ezra would blow up at the mere thought of someone not treating me fairly, and he's just far too petty."

Mom bursts out laughing and nods. "Well, don't let your brother hear that," she says, her eyes sparkling with amusement. She looks me over, seemingly satisfied with my attempts to reassure her, and begins to pack a new box.

I'd be lying if I said I wasn't scared to start my first real corporate job, and I *am* grateful that I'll have both Ezra and Archer nearby if I need them, but I don't want the first career steps I take to be laden with nepotism. I'd like to believe in my own abilities. That has to be enough.

I sigh as I pick up a frame, my heart wrenching at the sight of Theo's smiling face, his arm wrapped around me. I haven't seen him in the few days since he told me he's dating Kristen, but not for a lack of trying on his part. He's called me a few times, and he's texted me every single day, apologizing over and over again for not telling me sooner and for not being able to move in with me like we'd planned. I know I should reassure him and tell him it's fine, that I understand, but I don't have it in me to pretend my heart isn't breaking. It's why I haven't replied to any of Kristen's texts either—I don't want to have to lie and pretend I'm okay for her benefit.

I should leave the photo here, in my childhood bedroom, where I keep memories of the past. I know I should, but I can't help myself as I carefully place the photo in the box I'm packing, my heart aching.

"Honey, I'm not sure why Theo and you aren't moving in together anymore, but perhaps it's for the best," Mom says, her tone hesitant. "You've been so fixated on the idea of Theo that you never even bothered to give anyone else a chance. He's a great guy, but I never thought the two of you would make a good couple. He never challenged you, and it always seemed like you treated him more like a brother than anything else."

I grimace, realizing that I hadn't been as sly about my feelings as I thought I'd been. Archer knew, and as it turns out, so did Mom. Who else knew? If it was obvious to them, then surely Theo must've known too. Perhaps he knew and hoped I'd get over it. Maybe he wanted to be with Kristen all along and held off because he knew how I felt. What if I was the one standing between them?

"We're no longer moving in together because he's dating Kristen and they want to live together."

Mom's gaze snaps to mine, and the pity I see in her eyes undoes me. It unravels the bandages around my tattered heart, my wounds reopening. Despite that, I smile in the most sincere way I can manage.

"It's fine," I tell her, my mind drifting back to the notebook I keep on my nightstand and the brand-new to-do lists I wrote down in it, each of them designed to help me get over Theo. "I have my whole life ahead of me, and it's time I start living it."

She smiles at me so reassuringly that I almost begin to feel guilty for the contents of one of my lists.

Almost.

Seven

SERENITY

"I'll miss you, Serenity," Dad says, and it hits me right in the heart. He looks forlorn, his gaze roaming over the boxes that Archer and Ezra have started to move from my bedroom to Ezra's car.

"I'll miss you more," I tell him as I bridge the distance between us, rising to my tiptoes to press a kiss to his cheek.

"Don't be like Ezra," he warns. "Come home more often than he does, okay? I know it's a long drive, but maybe you could come home on the weekend every once in a while?"

His arm wraps around me, and I rest my head on his shoulder. "I will. I'll drag the boys back home with me too, as often as I can."

Dad grins at me, his eyes filled with a foreign kind of sorrow. He looked at me like this when I graduated high school too, and then again when I got my degree. It's almost like he thinks I'm no longer his little girl, when nothing could ever change that.

"I'll drive her down whenever she wants to come home," Archer says, leaning in the doorway. "I'll take any excuse to have one of Malti's amazing home-cooked meals."

Dad smiles at him, something passing between the two of them. "Malti and I miss having you here, Archer. It's been a while since you spent the weekend with us. You should come home more often too, son."

Archer's expression falls, and I look down, my heart wrenching. I know exactly why he no longer comes over as much as he used to—because everything here reminds him of Tyra. It's where he first met her and where their relationship developed one summer. Mom and Dad might not see it, but I notice his haunted expression and his strained smile every time he steps foot into this house.

"Archer, when Ezra is on one of his countless business trips, you'll keep an eye on her, won't you?" Dad asks, his tone pleading, and it catches me off guard. My dad is a fearless criminal lawyer—he doesn't cower, doesn't plead.

"Always," Archer promises, his expression solemn.

"Dad," I murmur. "Please don't. Ezra and Archer are unbearable as it is. Don't give them an additional false sense of responsibility."

Dad shoots me one of those chastising looks that used to shut me up instantly. "Nothing false about it," he says as he grabs one of the last few boxes.

I sigh, my eyes meeting Archer's as Dad walks out with it. He grins at me reassuringly before looking over the room, to make sure we didn't miss anything.

"I'll never forgive you if you tattle to my dad about anything I do," I warn him, thinking back to the way he caught me spray-painting a building a few blocks from his office. If he'd realized who I am, would he have told my parents? My mother would be heartbroken if she knew.

Archer chuckles and walks over to my bed. "The way I see it, you have two options. Either don't do anything worth tattling about or bribe me."

"Bribe you with what?" I ask, intrigued.

"Those cornstarch cookies you make would be a good start."

He reaches for the notebook I left on my nightstand, and a hint of panic rushes through me as I think back to what it contains. "I've seen you write in this before. Did you want to bring it?"

I rush over to him just as he turns to face me, and I end up crashing into him. Archer stumbles and wraps an arm around me, steadying me, his eyes wide.

"Give me that." I reach for my notebook frantically, and he raises a brow, amusement flickering through his amber eyes as he keeps it out of reach, above his head.

"What the hell is in here that has you so panicked?" The curiosity in his eyes doesn't bode well for me, and when his expression turns mischievous, I know I'm in trouble.

"I'll bake you the cookies you like," I rush to tell him, rising to my tiptoes to reach for my notebook, my body pressed against his.

He looks down at me, his gaze roaming over my face. "I'm not new to negotiating with people in this household. How many cookies? When will you bake them? Will they taste as usual? You can't purposely burn them."

"Damn it," I mutter under my breath. I absolutely was going to make him pay for blackmailing me, but sadly, he knows better than to settle for a first offer with the daughter of two illustrious lawyers.

Archer chuckles and shakes my notebook, far too pleased with himself. "Two dozen cookies," he demands.

I roll my eyes and step on top of my bed in an attempt to get to my notebook, but Archer is too fast. He steps back, and I narrow my eyes as I leap up. Archer laughs as he catches me, holding me up against him with his arms behind my knees, my notebook falling onto the floor in the process.

"Tell me you'll bake me cookies and I'll let you go," he says, his eyes twinkling, clearly trying his luck. If I'd known he loved those cookies so much, I'd have made them for him more often.

"Let me go or I'll bite you," I warn, only half joking.

His gaze roams over my face, and his smile melts away as his eyes settle on my lips. "Bite me, huh?" he murmurs, his voice different than usual. My stomach flutters, and all of a sudden I realize how close we are, how hard his abs and chest feel against my soft curves.

"Don't test me," I whisper, my lips so close to his that I could reach out for a taste—if I wanted to. Would he let me? Ever since he held me in his arms that night, I've wondered what he might taste like. The thought came suddenly, and I haven't been able to get it out of my mind.

Archer's breathing accelerates, and he carefully lowers me to the floor, his eyes on mine. "I wouldn't dare," he says, his voice soft, and for a moment, I wonder whether his words are double-edged.

He reaches down, only to freeze, and I'm instantly reminded of my notebook. I glance down to find it opened on the page I'd bookmarked, the title of my list clear in a pretty, pink, *large* font.

"What the fuck is this?" Archer says, snapping up my notebook before I can.

I try to snatch it out of his hand, but it's too late. His grip tightens, and his expression shifts into something I've never seen on him before. My arm falls to my side, mortification washing over me. "It's nothing," I whisper. "Please, Arch. Pretend you didn't see it."

His jaw tics and his breathing quickens. "*People I'd want to lose my virginity to,*" he reads out, his eyes flicking over the grand total of two names on the list. Theo's name is crossed out, and then it reads *Archer Harrison*, right underneath. Damn my habit of naming lists in obvious ways so I don't forget what they're for.

My cheeks are blazing, and my heart is pounding wildly. I don't have it in me to face him, to witness him judging me—or worse, to see disgust in his eyes.

"Why is my name on this list, Serenity? What the fuck is this list?"

My jaw snaps shut as I grab my notebook and hold it to my chest. "I'd argue that it's pretty self-explanatory." My tone is defensive, despite the shame that eats at me.

Archer places his index finger underneath my chin. "Look at me." I'm tempted to refuse him, but then he sighs and steps closer. "Please, Serenity."

I raise my eyes, my heart beating wildly. There's no judgment in his expression, just confusion, and something else...something I've never seen before. "You were never meant to see that," I admit. "I've just been creating all these lists to help me get over Theo, and I told you that there are certain things I wanted to experience, didn't I? This is just one of them. I know you would never want to...do *that*...with me, but I just—"

"Then you must know me better than I know myself."

My eyes widen, shock crashing through me when his words register. His hand falls away, something akin to regret taking hold of his features, almost like he just realized what he said. "Serenity," he begins to say, only for footsteps to sound nearby.

I hear Ezra call my name and glance at the door Dad left open furtively. "You won't tell him, will you?"

Archer stares at me and runs a hand through his hair. "I ought to," he murmurs. He sighs and steps back, his gaze traveling to the notebook I'm still holding on to for dear life. "I won't tell him, but you and I *will* talk about this."

Eight

ARCHER

"Don't worry so much." I tell my father as I straighten his golden *Father of the Bride* pin, glad it's just the two of us in the room. Mom and Dad have done all they can to keep my grandfather and me apart while trying to be discreet about it, and I appreciate it more than they'll ever know, but it wasn't necessary. As it stands, Serenity's list has occupied all my thoughts to the extent that seeing my grandfather hardly even registers. All I've been able to think about is the way she's been avoiding me and the way she felt against me on the sofa—and then again in her bedroom.

"What if we're just condemning Celeste to even more years filled with pure unhappiness?" Dad asks, his expression torn. "Have you seen her lately? I barely recognize her."

I shake my head, my gaze drifting to the whiskey bottle on the dresser in his hotel room. "We're not," I reassure him. "Haven't you noticed how she's regained that fire in her eyes? She's no longer listless, going through the motions aimlessly. Just being around Zane again makes her come alive. I'd take an infuriated Celeste over the version of her that wasn't truly living."

Dad nods and reaches for the bottle, staring at it for a moment, seemingly lost in thought. I can pretty much guess what he's thinking. Zane, my sister's fiancé, gave him that priceless bottle the first time he came over for dinner, many years ago.

Neither of us had been accepting of Zane and Celeste's relationship, in part due to the years-long rivalry between our families and the resulting feud between Zane and Celeste growing up. They went from hating each other and continuously attempting to sabotage each other in high school, to falling in love shortly after Celeste returned from college overseas, and neither Dad nor I could quite understand it.

In hindsight, those years were the happiest I've ever seen either of them. If I could go back in time, I'd have been accepting of them sooner, and I'd have questioned them both a little harder when their relationship went up in flames.

"Let's go have a chat with Zane before the ceremony," Dad says, tightening his grip on the bottle before handing it to me. I nod hesitantly and put the bottle back in the bag Dad wrapped it in.

He seems conflicted as we walk to Zane's room in his hotel, and truthfully, I feel the same way. I won't admit it, but I'm just as scared we made the wrong choice when we pressured Celeste into this arranged marriage. After all, neither of us knows why they broke up. All we saw was the aftermath, the mutual destruction.

I take a deep breath before knocking, my mind made up. Celeste might hate us for this, but I'll take that over watching her waste away.

Zane pulls the door open swiftly, both his movements and his expression betraying his irritation, only for shock to take over his features. It's clear he was expecting his four brothers. Even after all these years, I can still read him the way I used to. After all, throughout the years that Zane and Celeste dated, he became my best friend. I was closer to him than I was to Ezra, and I always thought he'd become my brother-in-law. He was family. Still is.

"Can we come in?" Dad asks.

Zane nods and stands aside to let us in, and I hesitate before following Dad to the small seating area in the corner, not quite sure what to do or say. Zane hovers by the door for a moment, and then he follows us, sitting down next to Dad. "I didn't expect…this," he says, his voice softer and kinder than I'd anticipated. It's clear he wants no part in this marriage either, but I suspect that, deep down, he knows he'd never walk away from a chance to make Celeste his wife.

Dad smiles and leans over, startling Zane as he straightens his bow tie and the rose boutonnière on his suit. "You're about to become my son-in-law. It's not so odd that I'd want to have a word with you beforehand, is it?"

Zane shakes his head, and I straighten in my seat, a tinge of hope settling in my chest. God, I hope he makes my sister happy. I hope he saves her from herself. No one but him can do it, and fuck, between the two of us, she deserves happiness most. At times, it's like we're both cursed, and there's nothing I wouldn't do to take on her pain, to see her smile again. "The day Celeste introduced you as her boyfriend, we took you out to the garden," I remind him. "Do you remember what you promised us then?"

Something flickers in Zane's eyes before he looks away— something that looks a lot like the love he used to look at my sister with. Back then, he promised us that he'd love her with all he has and that someday, he'd make her his wife. He promised us that he was going to make her happy, despite everything standing in their way. It's a promise I need him to keep, now more than ever.

"I remember."

Dad reaches for the bag we brought with us and pulls out the bottle of whiskey. The way Zane looks at it tugs at my heartstrings. It's a bottle that belonged to his late father, and I know it wasn't easy for Zane to part with it.

"I've been saving this for today," Dad says, and the edges of my lips turn up slightly as I reach for the glasses Dad put in the bag for this moment.

Zane is quiet as Dad pours him a glass, clearly more overcome with emotion than he cares to admit. "It won't come as a surprise to you when I tell you that you've let me down," Dad says, and Zane instantly tenses. "I don't know what happened between you two, Zane, but I know my daughter isn't blameless. For years, I watched you try to hurt each other, and I know it won't stop anytime soon. The only question I have for you today is this: Do you, underneath all that hatred I now see in your eyes, still love my daughter?"

I raise a brow, having expected that question about as much as Zane had. Zane remains silent and runs a hand through his hair, pure conflict crossing his face. He takes a deep breath before raising his face to look my father in the eye.

"Yes."

This time, I can't suppress my smile. Relief washes over me, and I lean back in my seat. I'd known he still loved her, but hearing him admit it is still reassuring. I nod at him and hand him a glass.

"Then this is what we'll do," I tell him, placing my full faith in him once more. "Each time we see you, we'll share a glass. By the time this bottle is empty, you'll need to have fulfilled your promise, or I'll do what my sister doesn't have the heart to—I'll fucking annihilate you, consequences be damned."

He nods slowly, clearly not wanting to make a verbal promise. I know what he's like, and I know how much Zane and Celeste have hurt each other. He might think there's no way forward, but I know he's wrong.

Dad sighs and taps his glass against Zane's, and I follow suit. "For real this time," I tell him, reciting the same words I once told him. "Welcome to the family, asshole."

Zane grins, no doubt remembering the first time I said those words. I just hope I won't come to regret saying them this time.

Nine

ARCHER

I stare at my phone as I take my seat at the front of the aisle, where Zane's four brothers have already gathered. It's odd just how much Serenity and that damn list of hers have been on my mind. She's single-handedly taken away all my worries about facing my grandfather, and she doesn't even know it.

I barely notice him sitting one row over when, normally, I'd have been anxious, worried about every word I say. This time, I'm a lot more concerned about how short Serenity has been in her text messages. It's clear she feels awkward about the whole situation, and fuck, I don't know how to handle this. Do I pretend I never saw her list, like she asked me to, or do I acknowledge it so we can talk about it?

All of a sudden, an unwelcome thought infiltrates my mind, showing me images of her in bed with some nameless man who won't give a damn about her. Something I've never experienced before settles in my stomach. It's not quite protectiveness, but it's something close to it. Whatever it is, it fucking infuriates me.

I don't snap out of my thoughts until Zane enters the room,

reluctance written all over his face. His brothers all collectively breathe sighs of relief, clearly having thought he might not show at all. I put my phone away as Zane's youngest brother reluctantly hands one of his older brothers a fifty, and I can't help but smile. I suppose some things never change—including their penchant for placing bets amongst themselves.

Music begins to play, and we all rise as the doors open. Everyone turns to watch Celeste enter on Dad's arm, but I keep my eyes on Zane, praying I wasn't wrong about him. He swallows hard, his eyes widening. Every last shred of reluctance and hatred melts away, until all that's left is that same expression he used to wear around my sister—utter devotion.

Something about it reminds me of Serenity and the conversation we had. This kind of unwavering devotion…that's what she deserves, and Theo will never give it to her. He doesn't deserve to have her to himself when he doesn't appreciate her the way he should.

For one single godforsaken moment, I wonder what it'd be like if I truly did take her virginity like she wants me to, taking what he doesn't deserve. I push the thought away as quickly as it came and clench my jaw, refocusing my attention on my sister. That fucking list. It completely messed me up, and I'm starting to think I'll never quite forget about it.

Dad places Celeste's hand in Zane's, and he takes it carefully, like he's scared the moment will break. He hasn't taken his eyes off her once, and the way he's looking at her makes me wonder if he's even aware of anything but her.

I sigh and run a hand through my hair, hoping this marriage truly will be the remedy I told Serenity it would be. It's been years since I last saw my sister smile genuinely, and fuck, I can't even remember the sound of her laughter. Her world is cast in shadows without Zane, but she'd never admit it.

I watch them carefully throughout the ceremony and draw a shaky breath when Zane says I do. Celeste's hand trembles as he pushes a wedding band onto her finger, and when it's her turn to say her vows, her voice breaks, her heartache bleeding into it.

Zane smiles at her so tenderly that I can't help but put my faith in him—a man that looks at my sister like that won't hurt her. He might pretend to, but her heart will be safe in his hands. The officiant tells Zane that he may kiss his bride, and his gaze drops to her mouth. He looks at her like he can't quite believe this is real, that they're standing at the altar together.

Zane leans in to kiss her, and Celeste rises to her tiptoes, deepening the kiss. I grin and cheer along with everyone else, snapping them out of the moment. The way my sister just kissed Zane back eviscerated all my remaining worries. It's clear their journey isn't going to be easy, but they'll walk it together, and I know exactly what'll be at the end of it: the same *happily ever after* that Serenity wants so badly.

Mom takes my arm as we're led into a large reception hall, her expression only barely disguising her concern. "She'll be happy, won't she?" Mom whispers, and I wrap my arm around her fully.

"Yes," I tell her resolutely. The love between Zane and Celeste is unlike anything I've ever seen before, and if they can't make it…*fuck*. Then what hope is there for the rest of us?

"What about you, sweetheart?" Mom asks, glancing over her shoulder at my grandfather, who's trailing behind with Dad. "Are you doing okay?" Mom worries endlessly, and I'm always scared something I do or say will keep her up at night. She struggles to keep the peace, and I hate that she feels responsible for doing that at all. It's been years, and I've made peace with the situation, but I know she hasn't. Grandpa made his choice, certain I'd fail without his support, and it just made me work harder, made me appreciate what I've built more.

I don't think we'll ever reconcile, and I've learned to accept that. I just wish Mom would too. "Weddings can be tough," she adds, and fresh guilt suddenly washes over me as realization hits.

It's not just my grandfather she's worried about—she's referring to Tyra too. Celeste's wedding should've made me think of her, but it didn't. For the first time since we lost her, she wasn't on my mind. "Mom, I have the most beautiful woman in the room on my arm," I tell her, my voice soft. "I'm doing more than okay."

She laughs, her whole face lighting up, and I grin back at her. "Are you sure you're okay? You were quite absent-minded last Sunday. I worry about you."

Mom insisted on doing weekly cooking classes shortly after Grandpa disowned me, and she's made both Celeste and me attend over video call every single Sunday for years now. It's her attempt to keep our family together despite everything, but I suspect it's also just to check in with Celeste and me.

"Tyra is gone, Archer," she reminds me. "You have to move on."

My heart sinks at the mention of her name, and my eyes flutter closed, guilt and pain tugging at me in equal measure. "I know," I murmur. *I know—but I can't. I don't deserve to.*

I haven't even gone on a single date since Tyra went missing—not any real ones, anyway. Some staged ones to keep the media and my friends and family off my back, but that's it. Each time I try to move on, guilt eats at me, reminding me that I don't deserve to be happy when Tyra might still be out there, waiting for me.

If I hadn't broken up with her days before we were meant to go on holiday together, she'd still be here. She wouldn't have gone overseas by herself, and she wouldn't have gone sightseeing only to never return.

I run a hand through my hair, my heart aching at the thought of her. At the very least, I wish I knew whether or not she's still alive. Not knowing eats me up inside. Is she out there, living her life happily? Did she disappear because she wanted a fresh start after we broke up, or did something far more sinister happen?

I've done all I could to find her, going as far as retracing her footsteps over and over again, only to come up empty every time. None of my contacts have any influence out of the country either, and all my leads have come up empty.

"You have to try," Mom says, squeezing my arm. "Please, Archer, at least try to be happy. It's breaking my heart to see both of my kids like this. It's been nearly two years, Arch. You can't keep living like this."

I look into my mother's eyes, the tears in them fucking gutting me. "I *am* trying," I tell her, but the way she looks at me tells me she knows I'm lying. The mere idea of pursuing happiness, of falling in love with someone while Tyra might be holding on to the memory of me, sickens me. I can't do it. I can't give up on her too—like everyone else has.

Ten

SERENITY

My steps are measured as I walk into Serenity Solutions' l
heart heavy. It kills me to have this moment taken from me b
insecurities. I should be filled with excitement on my first da
but instead, I'm dreading seeing either Theo or Archer.

I spent all weekend overthinking all of Archer's text
and counting my blessings that he was attending his sister's
so I didn't have to run into him. On top of that, Theo consta
texting me about his move, when the last thing I wanted w
anything about how moving in with Kristen went. It all left r
worn-out, stealing away the excitement I thought I'd feel.

"Serenity!"

My heart clenches painfully as I look up to find Theo
in the corner, two cups of coffee in his hands. He smiles at
approaches, handing me a cup. "I figured you'd be early," he
snuck out early to keep Ezra from bringing you to work, di

I look into his bright green eyes, pure sorrow spreading
chest. "No one knows me like you do," I murmur, hiding

behind the coffee he gave me—my favorite, an oat milk latte with a dash of hazelnut syrup. I've always loved the quiet intimacy that comes with knowing little details about someone that no one else does, but now it just hurts because it's this same level of thoughtfulness that made me think he had feelings for me too. "I really don't want the whole company to find out that I'm Ezra's sister, and it'd just start rumors if he drove me to work," I tell him. "It'd defeat the purpose of applying and getting in on my own merit, and he knows it."

It pains me to pretend I'm fine, to make small talk when all that's going through my mind is that he must've woken up next to Kristen this morning and that he'll go home to her tonight. It's all I've ever wanted.

He falls into step with me, his gaze roaming over my face in that way it does when he's got something on his mind. "Ser, is everything okay?" he asks, his voice soft. "I know the move was hectic and there's a lot going on, but you never pick up anymore when I call. Are you mad at me for not telling you about Kristen and me sooner? Or is this about us not moving in together like we'd planned?"

The thought of speaking to him while she's right there in the room with him doesn't sit well with me, but how can I possibly admit that? "I'm not mad at you," I tell him truthfully—I'm not mad. I'm *hurt*. "I've just been a little busy unpacking and settling in, that's all."

"If you aren't mad, then why haven't you spoken to Kristen once since I told you about us?" His voice is tormented, and my stomach twists when I find him looking at me like that, all because of her. "She misses you, Serenity."

I draw a shaky breath and try my hardest to force a smile, but I can't manage it. Does he truly not realize how I feel about him? How much pain he inflicts when he pleads with me on her behalf?

"Serenity Adesina and Theo Williams?"

I startle at the sound of my name and look up to find a blond guy walking up to us, a tablet in his hands. I nod hesitantly, and he grins. "My name is Mark Smith, and I'll be your mentor throughout your internship."

He guides us through the building, and I welcome the reprieve from having to answer Theo's question. I knew it was coming, but I wasn't ready. I'm not sure I'll ever be ready to deal with them as a united front when I was always the one he was closest to.

"This year, a total of ten interns were admitted, and everyone was lucky enough to be assigned to their preferred department, including the both of you. You'll join me in the design department, where we focus primarily on packaging the tech our brilliant CEOs invent in a user-friendly and aesthetically pleasing way."

We follow Mark as he helps us get registered, taking us through the HR process and getting us company IDs and laptops. Throughout it, I can feel Theo's gaze on me, but thankfully he doesn't attempt to continue the conversation we were having. Instead, he focuses on work, and I try to do the same.

Mark glances at my ID and grins at the photo as he leads us to our desks. "It's rare for anyone to photograph so well," he says, holding up his own ID. "It's almost a rite of passage, yet somehow, you seem to have been exempt."

His gaze roams over my face, and Theo tenses beside me. "Must be my unruly curls," I murmur, unsure what else to say. "My hair takes up half the photo." They're somewhat behaving today, and I hope it stays that way.

Mark chuckles. "Yeah, I've never seen hair like yours. Where are you from?"

I raise a brow and throw him a sweet smile, but it stings a little, that insinuation that I must not belong here because I don't look like him when I was born here just like he probably was. "I'm from a small town called Rivelle," I tell him, even though I know exactly what he means. He's curious about my ethnicity, but that isn't what he asked, so it isn't what I offer.

"It's about two hours from here," Theo adds. "We were both born and raised there. Serenity and I are actually childhood friends. We even went to the same college and everything."

Mark blinks in confusion, but then he forces a smile and nods. "Rivelle, wow. That's where one of our two CEOs is from. Have you ever met him before?"

I chuckle, unable to help it, and Theo grins. "Yes, we have, actually. Ezra Sterling is a bit of a celebrity in our town," he tells him truthfully, and I nod in agreement.

I always hated that my brother and I don't share the same surname, because it always made me feel like we aren't truly family. I didn't think there'd ever come a day when I'd be grateful for it.

"That's pretty incredible," Mark says. "We don't get to see Mr. Sterling frequently, but we do often have the honor of working directly with Mr. Harrison."

Mark leads us around the corner, and as if on cue, Archer looks up from where he's leaning against an empty desk, a beautiful, familiar-looking woman standing next to him.

My breath hitches, and Archer's eyes meet mine. He smiles smugly as he pushes off the desk, his gaze provocative. "There you are," he says, his voice gravelly. "At last." My heart begins to race as he keeps me trapped with his gaze, and heat rushes to my cheeks. He knows I've been running from him—and he knows he's finally caught me.

"Perfect timing, Mark," the woman says. "I want you and your interns to join Archer and me in our product design meeting."

"Isn't that Emma Evans? The company's COO?" Theo whispers.

Realization hits me hard, and my eyes widen. He's right. I should've recognized her from the company's website, and maybe I would have if I could've kept my eyes off Archer for more than a few seconds.

Archer grins as though he knows exactly how flustered I am, his expression far too pleased for my liking. Not in a million years did I think I'd actually work directly with him, and his amused smile makes it clear he's well aware of that.

Eleven

SERENITY

I can feel Archer's eyes on me as I take notes as quickly as I can throughout the meeting, barely able to keep up. There are only six of us in this meeting, and I'm more nervous than I'd care to admit. I've done extensive research on the company and its products, and in recent months I've tried to pay special attention to everything Archer and Ezra said. Despite that, I still feel a little lost as Dunya, a woman on Mark's team, gives a presentation on the feedback Serenity Solutions has received from the businesses that use our payment solutions.

Halfway through the presentation, Archer rises to his feet, and everyone falls silent. I follow him with my eyes as he makes his way through the room and takes a small remote control out of his pocket. He uses it to move a few slides back and sighs. "Payments failing is absolutely unacceptable," he says, his expression hard. "Design flaws I can live with, but this isn't one of them. This is a critical flaw. A payment failing immediately makes a retail customer uncomfortable, makes them wonder if our system is reliable. In turn, it just makes the businesses we work with lose faith in *us*. Hearing this is caused by a slightly too thick layer over the reader is simply ridiculous."

I'm transfixed as he questions Mark and Dunya on the quality control of the product before it was rolled out. I've never seen Archer at work, and it's like he's an entirely different person. He's always had a domineering aura, but it's even more prominent in this environment, and the navy three-piece suit he's wearing only adds to it.

I suck on my bottom lip and try my hardest to steer my thoughts in a different direction. When did I even begin to notice him that way? It was long before I added his name to my list, that's for sure. If I'm truly honest with myself, he occupied my thoughts more this weekend than Theo did. Him finding that list took the edge off my heartache, gave me something else to focus on. Over and over again, I replayed the moment that Archer told me I must know him better than he knows himself, effectively telling me I was wrong to think he couldn't want me. His words just ignited my fantasies, and all weekend, I kept thinking about what it'd be like to be with him. He kept my mind off Theo without ever even touching me at all.

"Recap the issue for me, Serenity."

My eyes shoot up to his, and his expression softens a little. His shoulders relax, and he leans back against the wall as he watches me. There's something different about the way he looks at me now, and I try my best not to read too much into it.

"There were three primary concerns the way I understand it. Our key concern relates to core usability, as payments have been failing more frequently than is acceptable in our latest model, causing harm to our reputation and our relationship with customers. This should be our primary focus. Secondly, there appears to be a design flaw in our chargers, making it so they no longer sit flush on customers' counters. This will be easier to fix, but I doubt there's a way to fix

50

this for customers who have already bought our point-of-sale system. Offering a new charger model could do further harm, since it'll seem like we sold them a less-than-ideal product, only to then charge more to make it more aesthetically pleasing. On the other hand, recalling products isn't really an option either. Lastly, we appear to have gotten a higher-than-normal amount of complaints about the battery life of our new POS system when used without its dock. It's heavily impacting those that primarily sell at conventions or pop-up stores, where they may not have access to a charger."

Archer glances at his watch and smiles. "Less than three minutes," he says, before turning to Dunya. "If our brand-new intern can summarize our issues in less than three minutes, why did it take you twenty?"

Dunya's expression falls, and he sighs as he runs a hand through his dark hair. "I need a summary and solutions on my desk by noon. I only attended this meeting because I expected you to have solutions for each problem you presented—so find them."

Archer's eyes meet mine as the meeting concludes, and some of the frost in his expression melts. My heart begins to beat a little faster when the edges of his lips turn up into the slightest smile. There's something oddly thrilling about the way we're hiding that we know each other, and it makes my thoughts turn to where they shouldn't go. My gaze involuntarily roams over his body, and I tear my eyes off him.

"Theo and you are so lucky," Mark informs me as we gather our things. "It's very rare that interns get to work directly with the CEO, but I've been involved with this project for a while now, and I'm glad Mr. Harrison is allowing Theo and you to join me on it. You'll learn so much."

I nod and force a smile, unsure what to say to that.

"He seems like a tough and unforgiving boss," Theo says, his tone

CATHARINA MAURA

conflicted. His gaze flicks to me, almost like he's trying to get a read on my reaction to that.

Mark raises a brow and smiles. "I guess it's his good looks that make people underestimate him. Honestly, between our two CEOs, Mr. Sterling is definitely the kinder one. I suspect that's why he leaves the company's management mostly to Mr. Harrison." He leads Theo and me to our new desks and smiles. "He tends to have high expectations, but every single time I'm in a meeting with Mr. Harrison, I walk away having learned something new. Sometimes it's about our products, but often it's things like today—like how you shouldn't walk into a meeting with your boss and present problems without proposed solutions."

I nod, unable to suppress a sliver of nerves. Seeing Archer in that room just now made me realize that he isn't just my brother's kind best friend, and I guess it's the same for Theo. We both seemed to have forgotten that Archer is a ruthless self-made multimillionaire who's likely well on his way to becoming a billionaire. He is clearly well-respected and well-loved, but more than anything, he's unattainable. What was I thinking, adding his name to my list? The more I think about it, the more mortified I feel.

I tuck a stray curl behind my ear and take a deep breath as I clear my mind and begin to tackle the list of things Theo and I were told to set up today, only for a notification to pop up from the company's instant messaging system.

ARCHER HARRISON

meet me in the garage at six. We need to talk.

Twelve

ARCHER

I lean back against the wall and watch as Mark hovers around Serenity while she puts her laptop in her bag. "We do quiz nights at the bar around the corner every Monday, and it's a great way to get to know people from other departments," he tells her.

She glances at Theo, and the way he looks at her grates on me. He's *never* looked at her like that before, so why now? Why the fuck is he looking at her like he finally realizes what he had? "I'll come with you if you're going," he says, his gaze filled with hope.

She looks into his eyes, clearly on the brink of giving in when I know she's done her best to draw and maintain boundaries between them. I told her to meet me in the garage five minutes from now, but it looks like she'd happily stand me up if it means spending her evening with Theo.

"You should go home," she says, surprising me. "Doesn't Kristen have a whole list of things she wants to do?" Serenity smiles shakily. "She should. I made a list for us and shared it with her."

"Right," he replies, his expression conflicted. "Yeah. I guess I should go home, huh?" He looks at her like he expects her to stop him, and I smile to myself when she nods and walks past him, leaving him sitting at his desk without a second glance.

"We'll just go together, then," Mark says, rushing after her. Something about the way he looks at her doesn't sit well with me either. It's clear he's rapidly developed a crush, and my need to nip that in the bud is near tangible, a force of its own.

"Mark, I need the design alteration we discussed on my desk by noon tomorrow," I say, knowing full well he'll have to work overtime tonight to make that happen.

He tenses when he notices me a few paces behind him, and he nods, barely able to keep his eyes off Serenity. Normally my employees jump at a chance to work authorized overtime, since we pay them triple for it, but it seems he'd still rather spend his evening with Serenity. Interesting.

I follow his captivated gaze, my eyes lingering. Damn, that cream dress she's wearing today and the way it highlights her curves... She's beautiful in sweats and an old ratty tee, but *fuck*, she's mesmerizing today, and it irritates me that I'm noticing it at all.

My eyes lock with hers as I walk past them, confident that she'll follow. I smile to myself when I hear her heels click behind me moments later.

"You haven't pressed the elevator button, Mr. Harrison," she says, her arm brushing against mine as she clicks the down button.

"I was waiting," I murmur, turning to face her.

"For what?"

"*You.*"

She bites down on the edge of her bottom lip, and something hot and heavy unfurls in my stomach. *Fuck.* I've tried my best not to notice how fucking sexy she is, but I knew it was a lost cause when I saw my name on that list of hers. Ever since, all I've been able to think about is what she'll taste like, how she'll sound when I make her come...over and over again. The feeling is almost always accompanied by guilt of different kinds, but even so, it's inescapable, all-consuming. It's been years since I've wanted a woman the way I want her, and fuck, I don't know what to do with that when I know I can't have her.

Serenity follows me into the elevator, both of us quiet all the way to my car. She hesitates when I hold the door open for her, and I raise a brow. "Ezra?" she whispers.

Hearing my best friend's name is jarring, an unwelcome reminder of reality. "He left early this morning and won't be back from a client site until tomorrow evening," I remind her.

"Still," she says, her voice soft. "We shouldn't be seen together like this."

"Then you'd better hurry up and get in."

She narrows her eyes for a moment and sits down, her gaze moving back and forth furtively.

"Don't worry," I tell her as I join her. "This isn't the first time I've given an employee a ride on my way out."

"Oh," she says, sounding relieved. "Of course, I'm sorry."

I throw her a smile as I drive us home, deliberately taking the longest route I can think of. We need to talk, but I'm not sure where to even start. "How was your first day?" I ask instead.

"Intense," she replies, her expression lighting up. "But so fulfilling. For years, I've heard Ezra and you talk about your company, and to now work there myself...it's surreal."

"Having our real-life Serenity work for Serenity Solutions is surreal to both of us too, you know. I'm pretty sure this is what Ezra always envisioned. He's happier than ever before, and he hasn't stopped talking about you joining us from the moment he found out."

I hesitate before parking on the side of a quiet road before turning toward her. "Which is why we have to talk about that list of yours and my name being on it."

"No," she retorts. Vulnerability crosses her face despite her firm tone. "We don't. Unless you're about to tell me that you'll do it, we don't need to discuss it at all."

My eyes widen a fraction when I realize that she truly does want this. *Me.* That list wasn't a drunken fluke. It was a real consideration. "Just tell me why, Serenity. Why me?"

She looks at me then, her gaze pained. "You're someone I trust, someone who'd never hurt me, and this…it's something I want to get out of the way, but I don't want to sleep with just anyone, and I just thought maybe you'd want this too. Not *me*, per se, but just being with someone you trust with no other expectations or pressure. I loved her too, you know?" She falls silent for a moment, clear agony crossing her face. "I would never try to take her place nor would I ever expect anything from you that you can't give. I just thought…I thought that maybe we could give each other what no one else can. I can see how hard it is for you to move on, and maybe…maybe I could help."

I reach for her and gently brush one of her long curls out of her face, my heart skipping a beat at the thought of having that with her. She's right. She's the only one I could ever be with that would understand what losing Tyra did to me, the only one woman that loved her just as much as I did. "I wish it could've been me, Serenity. I wish I could give you what you're after, but I can't. Not without risking my friendship with your brother and the company we share."

"I know," she whispers. "I never even should've… I'm sorry. I'll find someone else."

"*No.*" The word leaves my lips without conscious thought, and her eyes widen at my harsh tone. "Don't go looking for someone else, Serenity."

"W-What are you saying?" she asks, her gorgeous hazel eyes tinged with hope.

Longing hits me hard and fast when she looks at me like that, and fuck, I don't think I've ever wanted to bury my hand in a woman's hair this badly—pull her in, brush my lips against hers, feel her soft sigh against my mouth in the moments before I kiss her. "I—fuck, I don't know. All I know is that I can't stand the thought of you being with someone else."

She leans in and places her hand on my thigh. "No one would have to know," she whispers, and I raise my hand to cup her face, my heart pounding wildly. "It could be our little secret, Archer."

My thumb brushes over her lips, and she parts them just a touch. Goddamn. I desperately need a taste. "Do you understand what you're asking for? What we'd risk? We can't, Serenity."

She searches my face, and then she pulls her hand away, straightening in her seat. Her expression shutters closed, and she sighs. "I know," she whispers. "I'm sorry, Archer. Just…just forget about that list, okay?"

I run a hand through my hair, wishing I could and knowing I won't.

Thirteen

SERENITY

The words on my screen begin to melt together as I read the same report all over again, trying to ensure it's free from errors before I send it to Mark for review. Archer wasn't joking when he told me the working hours would be unconventional and the workload varies. In the week since Theo and I started, not a single day has been the same.

Just this week, we've worked with the design, implementation, customer service, and various engineering teams. I've learned more than I thought I would, and at the same time, I feel like I now know less than I did when I started.

"I'm exhausted and I've never been more glad it's finally Friday," Theo says, rolling his chair over to rest his elbow on my desk. "Wanna grab dinner together? Somehow I've seen you every single day yet we've barely spoken."

I hesitate, and he throws me a pleading look.

"There's a little bistro around the corner from the office that I've been wanting to try if you're up for it?"

"Sounds like fun," I lie. Work has kept both Theo and me busy enough for him not to complain about the lack of time we've spent together, but I think he's starting to realize that I've distanced myself. I've had to—I can't be in love with someone that's in a committed relationship with one of my friends, even if I'm not particularly happy with her right now. I need time to sort out my feelings and come to terms with our new relationship dynamics, so I don't do or say something I'll regret.

"You should invite Kristen to join us," I say as we walk out of the building together. The three of us haven't hung out together since I found out about them, but I know it's inevitable. I can't avoid her forever.

"It's *you* I want to hang out with," he says, his voice tinged with frustration. "You've barely looked at me since I told you about Kristen, and I just don't understand why. What did I do wrong, Serenity? Tell me why it seems like I'm losing my best friend."

We come to a standstill in front of the restaurant, and I look away. "You aren't losing me," I promise, unsure what else to say.

He takes a step closer and wraps one of my curls around his finger. "Are you sure?"

I nod, my heart aching. How do I explain to him that he'll always have me, but that I'm just trying to make peace with the fact that he'll never want everything I would've given him?

"Serenity?"

My entire body tenses at the sound of Archer's voice, and I take a step back before turning to face him. I stand rooted in place, captivated by the storm brewing in his eyes, and it takes me a moment to realize that Emma is standing behind him.

"Here for dinner?" she asks, a sweet smile on her face.

I nod and force a smile as she moves to stand next to Archer. Something about how close she's standing to him doesn't sit well with me, and something unfamiliar settles in my stomach.

"Wonderful," she says, beaming. "The two of you should join us. It's hard to get a table around this time, so we might as well share one." Emma looks up at Archer, and my heart wrenches when he smiles at her. "Every time Archer walks in here, a table magically materializes when everyone else is told they're fully booked. I still haven't figured out why they love him so much."

"Come on," he says, briefly placing his hand on my back as Emma walks in. Theo and I follow her silently, and just like she said, a server immediately materializes when Archer steps into the restaurant.

We're instantly led to a booth in the corner, and much to my surprise, Archer slips in next to me, placing me closest to the wall with him next to me, and Theo opposite me.

Theo hasn't said a word since Archer and Emma showed up, and something about his expression makes me wonder if he's upset we didn't get to spend any quality time together in the end. I should be grateful that he still wants to have dinner with me, just the two of us, but I'm glad we're not alone tonight. I'm just not ready to smile and ask him whether Kristen and he have settled into their place, only to then make up an excuse when he tells me to come over sometime.

Emma excitedly asks Archer what he's going to order, and the way he looks back at her makes my heart constrict in a way I'm not familiar with.

Theo runs me through the menu and tells me about every dish he thinks I'd like, but I can't focus on anything but Archer's indulgent tone as he bickers with Emma about their food choices.

"Why would you choose that when you're just going to eat mine, hmm?" he says, leaning in. The movement presses his thigh against mine, but he doesn't seem to notice—his entire attention is on Emma.

"I'll eat it!" she says. "But I do want a bite of yours too."

He chuckles, and something about their conversation makes me feel like an intruder in the worst way.

"Serenity?"

I blink, snapping out of my thoughts to find Theo looking at me. "Everything okay?"

Heat rushes to my cheeks and I nod as I begin to bounce my leg nervously, feeling entirely out of it. "Sorry, I'm just so tired. I'll have what you're having."

He nods, and I continue to move my leg rhythmically—until Archer places his palm on my thigh, the tips of his fingers grazing the hem of my skirt. My movements still, and I turn to look at him in surprise.

"I'd recommend the sea bass," he tells me, caressing my knee with his thumb before pulling his hand away.

"Oh," I murmur, flustered. "I'll try it, then."

He nods and smiles briefly before turning back to Emma.

"Tell us," she says, grinning. "How was your first week?"

"Felt like an eternity," Theo replies instantly, and I nod, eliciting a sweet laugh from Emma.

"It was fun, don't get me wrong," I add, "but it was also a bit overwhelming. I felt a little out of the loop most of the time, and I know that's what training is for, but I can't wait until I'm more up to speed."

She smiles kindly before glancing at Archer. "Remember when we were working from that garage we rented?" she says, her gaze filled with something that can only be described as intimacy. "It was exactly as Serenity just described back then, wasn't it? We had no idea what we were doing."

My leg begins to move again, something akin to jealousy tugging at me. The longer I observe them, the more it seems like Archer and

Emma are more than just close friends and colleagues. It makes me feel like a complete fool for thinking that Archer would even want someone like me when he has *her*. He may not have said anything, but he must've silently mocked me the moment he saw that list. I should've known he'd never have to look far for something casual, not with a face like his.

Archer places his hand back on my thigh and squeezes softly, startling me with his silent command to stop tapping my leg. I glance at him when he keeps his hand in place, but he's looking at Emma.

"I nearly forgot, but there's something I meant to ask you," Emma tells me, her cheeks rapidly becoming rosy. "I owe someone a favor, so I have to ask…are you by any chance single?"

"Very much so," I mutter. Theo's eyes shoot to mine, and for the first time ever, I can't read him at all. He seemed annoyed when we ran into Emma and Archer, and his mood just seems to worsen by the second.

"That's great," Emma says, but all I can focus on is the feel of Archer's hand on my thigh. My skirt rode up a little, and most of his hand is now on my bare skin. I thought he'd move it once I stopped moving my leg, but he hasn't. Instead, he's started to draw circles across my thigh with his thumb, making my heart race.

"Mo from IT seems to have fallen for you at first sight, and since he's a good friend of mine, I can't help but want to play matchmaker."

The mere thought of Mo asking Emma for a favor just to find out if I'm single makes me chuckle, especially because he's so straight-faced. "He helped me when my computer completely crashed on my second day of work."

"So…?" Emma says, her eyes filled with hope. "Is there any chance at all that you'd be willing to go on a date with him?"

I look up at Theo, my heart aching. I have to make a conscious effort to get over him or I'll end up ruining our friendship.

"No," Archer says before I can answer at all, his hand sliding farther up my thigh, his touch oddly possessive.

Fourteen

ARCHER

"Thank you for dinner," Serenity says, seemingly addressing both Emma and me moments after I sign for the bill. The way her eyes move between the two of us makes realization crash through me, and all of a sudden, I feel like a complete idiot. Surely she doesn't think there's something going on between Emma and me? Doesn't she realize that Emma is married—to a woman, no less? She'd never even be remotely interested in me, but I can see how it might seem that way.

Fuck. Is that why she nearly agreed to go on that damn date? I saw it in her eyes. She's determined to move on from Theo, and she seems convinced seeing someone else is the way to do it.

"I'll drive you home," I tell her, stepping away from Emma to move closer to her. I rest my hand on her lower back, and she looks up at me with an adorably bewildered expression.

Theo tenses. "I thought maybe we could grab a drink before we head home?" he says, his tone awfully desperate.

Serenity looks like she'll give in, and fuck, I don't want her to.

"Sera," I murmur. She lifts her head, our eyes locking. "Let me take you home."

I can't help but grin when she nods, sweet victory rushing through me. I don't know what she does to me, but whatever it is, it makes me feel more alive than I have in years. "You'll be fine making your own way home, right?" I ask Emma impatiently, eager to just get Serenity out of here and away from Theo.

Emma throws me a confused look, and I smile tightly. "I... Yes," she says hesitantly.

"Great. See you Monday, then," I murmur before leading Serenity away, keeping my hand on the small of her back.

"What are you doing?" she asks the second we're out of earshot.

"What does it look like I'm doing, Serenity? I'm taking you home."

"Why?"

"Why not?"

"*Archer.* You're being impossible. I told you I didn't want anyone to know I'm related to Ezra, and you just... God, that looked so suspicious."

I smirk at her as I hold the passenger door open for her. "Maybe, but not in the way you think. No one would relate the way I just behaved back to Ezra. They'd just think there's something going on between *us.*"

Her eyes widen, and my heart begins to beat a little faster when she becomes all flustered. Serenity rushes to sit down and pulls the door closed before I can do it for her, and I bite back a smile as I walk around the car to join her, amused by her reaction.

"You're surprisingly embarrassed for a woman who told me outright that she wants me," I tell her as I get behind the wheel.

Her head snaps toward me, but I keep my eyes on the road, trying my best to hide my amusement. "I didn't say that!"

"No?" I ask. "So you don't want me to spread your pretty thighs and fuck you?"

She inhales sharply, and I can't help but glance at her. She seemed serious about her list, but now I'm not so sure. "I do."

Fuck. Just hearing her say it makes my cock harden. I've spent days pretending that damn list didn't affect me when all I've been able to think about is the way she'd feel underneath me.

We both fall silent in the few minutes it takes me to drive home, the tension thick as I park in my garage. I turn to face her, an unfamiliar kind of desperation prompting my words. "I'll do it."

She raises a trembling hand to her hair, apprehension flickering in her eyes. "You'll do what?"

I reach for her and grab her hand, marveling at how small it feels in mine. "If you're truly serious about this, then let me be the one you put your faith in."

She stares at me speechlessly, and I smile, my heart overflowing with something I can't quite define. It feels heavy, desperate.

"Come on," I murmur, lifting her hand to my lips to press a soft kiss to her knuckles. Her breath hitches, and the sound sends a little thrill down my spine. "Let's go up and talk about what it is you want and what I want in return."

Serenity nods, and I step out of the car. She's silent as we walk into the elevator, her breathing a little uneven. Both of us tense when we reach the floor I share with Ezra, guilt threatening to make me change my mind. I push through it and lead her into my penthouse.

"Wine?" I ask, heading straight to my wine fridge.

"Please."

She sits down at my kitchen counter, and I push a glass toward her before pouring myself one. "Tell me exactly what you want, Serenity.

Do you just want to lose your virginity and sleep with someone once? What exactly did you envision when you created that list?"

She throws me a shy look and hides her face behind her glass for a moment. "I want to experience a bit more than that, with someone I trust. I don't want to have to date and wait for the right person, and then worry that I'm just not…good at it. I want to lose my virginity on my own terms, and I want to find out what I enjoy, how to bring someone else pleasure."

I nod, my cock fucking throbbing at the thought of having the honor of making her come. It's been so long since I've wanted someone this badly, and I forgot how thrilling it is.

"So more than once," I murmur as I reach for the notepad I keep in the kitchen. "Write down for me what you'd like to experience, Serenity. Tell me everything you've fantasized about, everything you want me to do to you."

"Are you serious?"

I nod. "Dead serious. If we're going to do this, I need to know what you hope to accomplish and what you absolutely don't want. Do you want me to eat you out and make you beg for my cock? Do you want something more clinical? Would you like me to call you my dirty little slut, or do you prefer to be praised? If it's something you've thought about, something you know deep down you want, tell me, and I'll do my best to provide it. You love making lists, don't you? So make me one."

She holds my gaze, not at all thrown off by my words. "I have one."

Serenity chuckles at my expression and reaches for the notebook she carries with her everywhere. "Tell me what you want in return before I show you my list."

I lean forward, my elbows on the breakfast bar. "I want you to paint me something."

Her eyes widen, a hint of panic flashing through them. Interesting. "W-what?"

"You loved painting more than anything when you were younger, and I never understood why you suddenly stopped. It wasn't until recently that I was reminded of your work, when Ezra hung one of your old paintings in his office."

She stares at me like she's trying to figure me out, something akin to fear in her eyes, and my heart begins to beat a little faster.

"What do you want me to paint you?" she asks, her voice soft, vulnerability shining through.

I look down for a moment, a thrill running down my spine. "There's a famous piece by The Muse that I'd like you to replicate for me. It's a ballerina standing on a stage, doing a pirouette in the role of Odette from *Swan Lake*."

Her breath hitches, and she wraps her arms around herself as she averts her face, her long lashes fluttering. "Maybe we shouldn't do this," she whispers, her voice breaking. "I…I didn't think this through, and I don't want to dishonor—"

"That's not what we're doing," I interrupt. "And it's one of the reasons why I agreed. I need this too, Serenity. I'd like to be with someone on my own terms, without guilt eating at me." I run a hand through my hair and sigh. "I haven't been with a woman since her, and I think this might just be what I need to move on."

I watch her as she clutches her notebook, my gaze roaming over her wild curls and her sexy full lips. It's odd, but somehow, guilt doesn't eat at me when I imagine her in my bed, her hair spread all over my pillows. The same guilt that kept me from dating anyone else is absent when it comes to her.

"No one can know about us," she whispers. "Ezra can never find out, and we'll need proper rules. I don't want this to turn into

MINE FOR A MOMENT

something it isn't meant to be. We can't...we can't do anything that'd hurt those we both love."

I nod in agreement. "How about we end our arrangement when you complete the painting? I think we'd both benefit from a time limit."

Serenity nods, her eyes filled with trust as she opens her notebook to the right page and pushes it toward me. I glance over it, a thrill running down my spine when I realize her fantasies and needs perfectly align with mine.

"Do you understand that if we do this, you'll be *mine*?" I ask, my tone harsher than I'd intended. "I don't want anyone else touching you."

"You're asking for fidelity?" she asks.

I nod, and she raises a brow.

"Are you willing to give me the same in return?"

"You won't have to worry about that, darling. I'm yours."

Fifteen

ARCHER

"*See* Ezra?" Mom says over video call as I separate egg yolks and whites absent-mindedly. "He was like that during our last video call too, and there was something off about him at Celeste's wedding."

Ezra glances up at me and raises a brow in question, having gotten used to my family and the madness that is our Sunday cooking class. He joins me most weeks, and over the years, he's pretty much become one of us. Sometimes he even dials in from overseas, just to catch up with my family. He hasn't said much, but I know he's been as worried about Celeste as I've been.

"He seems the same as usual to me," he says, before continuing to knead dough per Mom's instructions.

"No, he *is* acting a bit off," Celeste adds, peeking at me from behind Mom. "He's quieter than usual."

"So are we all just going to continue talking about me like I'm not here?"

My sister shrugs. "You might as well not be. You've barely said three words, and Mom has had to repeat the recipe three times. Seriously, what's up with you?"

I glance at Ezra, guilt settling deep in my stomach. He can never know that I'm silently counting down the minutes until he leaves for his next business trip, so I can invite his little sister over and finally kiss her, slide my hand underneath her skirt like I've been wanting to, and listen to her panting my name. I haven't been able to think about anything but her, and it's driving me crazy. It's been so long since someone occupied my mind like that, and I'm not sure how to feel about it.

"Nothing is up with me," I reply, irritated that she called me out. "What's up with you? How is married life treating you? Considering that I haven't seen an obituary for Zane yet, things must be going well enough."

Celeste's eyes flash with anger, and I grin to myself. It's been years since I last saw real emotions in her eyes. The irritation in her expression is a far cry from the listlessness I'd grown used to.

"Which reminds me," Ezra says. "I'm really sorry I missed your wedding, Celeste. If I could've rescheduled my trip, I would have, but it's just such a big client."

"I gave you little to no notice, Ezra. I completely understand." She throws him a sweet smile, and he glances at me in shock, his eyes widening just a touch. I nod subtly, trying my best not to chuckle. "That's something she does now," I whisper. "Smiling."

Obvious relief crosses his face, and it only heightens the guilt that's tugging at me. Ezra would never forgive me if he had the slightest inkling of the direction my thoughts continue to take.

I sit back as he chats with my family, making up for my silence and keeping them occupied with questions about the wedding ceremony as we finish the pie we're making. All the while, I try my best not to think about Serenity and the way she looked at me that night I had her in my lap. *Coffee dates, talking until the sun rises, making out in the back seat of a car, and being truly wanted.* This thing between us isn't supposed to be more than sex, but fuck, I want to be the one she does all of that with.

"So what's going on with you?" Ezra asks, snapping me out of my thoughts.

I glance at him only to realize that the call ended. I didn't even notice Ezra putting the pie in the oven. "What do you mean?"

He smirks as he walks over to my fridge and grabs a beer. "They're right, you know. You've been acting weird for a couple of weeks now."

"Weeks?" I repeat, confused.

He nods and takes a swig. "Initially I thought you didn't like having Serenity around, but in hindsight, you've been acting a bit weird since before she moved here."

I tense involuntarily and force a smile. *Things haven't been the same since the night I wrapped my arms around your little sister as she cried her heart out, and I realized how fucking beautiful she is.* "I'm just worried about the complaints we've been getting about the new point-of-sale system we rolled out," I tell him, the words feeling deceptive.

Ezra's relaxedness melts away, and he sighs as he runs a hand through his hair. "It's been a fucking nightmare," he admits. "I'm tired of having to troubleshoot setups at client sites, but I have to be there in person to show our clients how important they are to us."

"I'd go if I could, but I honestly just don't know the system as well as you do." Ezra has always loved the tech behind our products, while I've always loved running and growing our business. We complement each other perfectly, but it's hard for us to step into each other's shoes. Our business is one of many reasons why I never should've said yes to Serenity.

Ezra glances at me then, pausing. "I know," he says, sighing.

"Normally I wouldn't have minded, but I'm worried about Serenity. I'd hoped she'd join us today, but she's barely even left her room since she got here. I think Theo moving in with his girlfriend hit her quite hard." He takes another swig of his beer and grimaces.

I walk over to the fridge and grab a beer of my own, unease settling in my gut. The thought of her wanting Theo when it's my bed she's in doesn't sit well with me at all, but I knew what I signed up for. "She'll get over him soon enough."

Ezra throws me a look. "Did you forget that we had to watch your sister be utterly heartbroken for years? And then there's you. You haven't been yourself in so long either. Do you even remember the last time *you* laughed?" He sighs and looks down. "Fuck, I don't want to see Serenity lose that spark in her eyes."

I clench my jaw and lean back against the counter. "It's different. Zane never had eyes for anyone but Celeste, not even when they were kids. Theo never loved Serenity like that, and once she's experienced being with someone who genuinely sees and values her, she'll get over him. Hell, she'll wonder what she ever even saw in him in the first place." All the while, I don't point out that *he's* barely smiled since Tyra went missing. I don't think he even realizes that he, too, is a shell of the person he used to be.

"Maybe." He knocks back his drink, his gaze lingering on my face. "You'll look out for her, right? When I'm not here?"

My stomach twists, but still, I nod. "Of course," I promise, the words tasting bitter on my tongue.

Sixteen

SERENITY

"I hate having to leave you by yourself so often," Ezra says, his suitcase by his side. "I tried to stay most of the weekend, but I really need to go or I won't get there in time for my meeting tomorrow. Are you sure you're going to be okay?"

I smile shakily. He'd be so disappointed if he knew what I'm about to do. "I'll be fine," I murmur. "Besides, Archer is next door. If I need anything, I'll just go bother him. I doubt he'll mind."

Ezra nods. "I'll see you in three days, then. I'm sorry I haven't been here more, Serenity. I'd hoped to help you settle in and show you some of my favorite places in town, but work has just been so busy."

I brush my hand over his arm and shake my head. "I'm not a child anymore, you know. You don't have to worry about me so much."

He sighs and gently tucks a strand of my hair behind my ear. "I know, but to me you're still the baby I vowed to protect when I was ten. I don't think that'll ever change."

My heart wrenches, and I rise to my tiptoes to kiss my brother's cheek. Our age difference has always made him overprotective, and he's right, it probably won't ever change. "Have a safe flight. Text me when you land, okay?"

Ezra nods and walks out, seemingly reluctantly. I've never felt so conflicted. If he ever found out what I'm about to let his best friend do to me, he'd never forgive either of us.

I'm still second-guessing myself when I ring Archer's doorbell, but my doubts melt away when he opens the door wearing gray sweats and a tight black tee, a towel in one hand and drops of water running down his neck. Our eyes lock, and he steps aside silently to let me in.

"There's something I'd like to show you," he says, tipping his head toward the hallway. "Follow me."

I bite down on my lip as he leads me to his guest room, the same one I stayed in that night I showed up here unexpectedly, and all the while I try my best to keep my eyes off his muscular back. All of a sudden, I feel entirely out of place. I wanted to do this with Archer because I thought he'd make me feel safe and comfortable, but now that I'm standing here with him, I'm not sure I have the confidence to see it through. Someone like him…God, I could never live up to his expectations or even his past experiences.

"Here we are," he murmurs, pushing the door open.

"Wow," I whisper, my eyes widening when I take in the thousands of dollars' worth of art supplies—canvases, easels, incredibly expensive acrylics and brushes. "What is all this?"

I whirl around to face him, only to find him smiling at me sweetly. *This.* This is exactly why I chose him—because he'd never hurt me, would never even dream of it.

He takes a step closer to me, and my heart skips a beat. "I told you to paint me something, so it's only fair I provide you with what you'll need for it."

"Archer," I whisper, my eyes falling closed when he cups my face. "This would've easily cost you twenty grand. It's…it's too much."

"No," he tells me, stepping closer until I'm pressed against the doorway, his body brushing against mine. "It isn't enough, but it's a start. You've missed it, haven't you? Painting has always been an outlet for you, and I want you to have this, here, with *me*."

I stare at him wide-eyed, emotions threatening to overwhelm me. "H-How did you…"

I've missed painting on canvas more than he could possibly understand, but I promised myself I'd try to put it behind me. Every time I hold a brush, I'm filled with grand dreams and equally grand fears all over again, and I can't keep doing that to myself, and I can't take the disdain in my mother's eyes every time I mention my art.

"I haven't seen any paint stains on your hands since you went to college, no lingering acrylics smell in your hair. I know you, Serenity. I know you'll need to paint to ease your broken heart, so paint for me, darling."

My gaze roams over his face, pausing on his lips for a moment. "Thank you. For all of this, for…" My voice breaks, and he sighs as he brushes the back of his hand over my cheek.

"Go check out your new supplies," he tells me. "I know you're dying to."

I hesitate, my heart pounding wildly. "I thought we'd…"

Archer smirks, his gaze darkening. "Impatient, hmm?" he whispers, sliding a hand around my waist. I startle a little, and he chuckles. "Let's take it slow, Serenity. I want you dripping for me by the time I lay you down in my bed."

My breath hitches, and he grins as he steps back, tipping his head toward the easel set up for me. "Go on," he says. "I know you want to."

I can't help but smile as I step into the room, my fingertips grazing over everything Archer bought me. He just watches me quietly as I slowly but surely immerse myself in the one thing that soothes my soul.

I sigh happily as I drag a brand-new brush over the perfectly white canvas, marring it with my imagination. It's one of the things I love most about painting—it doesn't all make sense until everything is in place; then, all of a sudden, my organized chaos comes alive.

Archer pushes off the wall at some point, and my brushstrokes slow as he positions himself behind me. "Can I touch you?" he asks.

My heart begins to race, and I nod hesitantly. Archer wraps his hand around my waist and steps closer, until my back is pressed against his chest. I bite down on my lip when I feel how hard he is, my own body responding in kind. "Keep painting," he whispers, leaning in so his lips brush over my ear. "Don't mind me."

He kisses my neck, and a soft sound escapes the back of my throat, desire rushing through me. His left hand slides around me, until he's got his fingers splayed over my stomach, his touch warm even through my dress. "You look beautiful," he whispers, leaning in to kiss my shoulder. "This pretty black dress...did you wear that for me?"

"Yes," I admit. "What's underneath is also just for you."

That needy, guttural sound he makes has me squeezing my thighs together, my breath coming out in soft pants.

"I'm not sure why I thought I could be patient with you," he tells me as he cups the side of my neck and tips my face up. "You're all I've dreamt of every single night since I found that list, Serenity. Do you have any idea what I've done to you in my dreams? What I'll do to you tonight?"

I rise to my tiptoes, my lips only an inch from his. "I want you to show me, Archer. Let me be your living fantasy."

He pushes a hand into my hair and grips tightly. "You already are," he whispers, ånd then he kisses me, his touch slow at first, hesitant, until I respond. He groans, parting my lips to deepen our kiss, and for the first time in weeks, my mind quietens.

Seventeen

ARCHER

Serenity drops the brush she was holding, her arms sliding around my neck as she turns around, losing herself in our kiss as much as I am. I groan and pull her close, my hands roaming over her body hungrily.

She pulls away a little to look at me, her eyes brimming with a mixture of insecurity and need. It just makes me want to give her everything, do anything to make sure I don't lose the trust she's placing in me.

Serenity gasps when I reach down and lift her into my arms, her eyes on mine as I carry her to my bedroom. She doesn't say a thing as I lower her to the floor right in front of my bed, but the way her gaze roams over my body hungrily tells me everything I need to know.

She inhales sharply when I grab her hand and place it over my chest. "Undress me," I tell her, and fuck, the look in her eyes…I just know that'll be seared into my memories forever.

Her fingers wrap around the hem of my tee, and she pushes it up slowly, her eyes glittering as they trail over my abs. She's breathing as hard as I am, and damn, I'd forgotten what it's like to be lost in the moment, to give someone my full attention and let them drive away every other thought.

I grin as I help pull my T-shirt over my head, only to realize that her expression has suddenly sobered. She reaches for the silver chain around my neck—Muse's charm dangling off it. I hold my breath as she stares at it, her expression unreadable. "What is that?" she asks, her voice soft.

I glance down at it and shake my head. "It's nothing, baby," I whisper, before moving her hands to the waistband of my sweats. Something flickers in her eyes, and my heart begins to beat faster as her gaze travels between the charm and my face, but then she bites on her lip and pushes my sweats down, her breath hitching as she stares at my black boxers for a moment and the erection they completely fail to hide. "See something you like?" I murmur.

Her eyes shoot up to mine, and I chuckle, enjoying her bewildered expression. "I…um…"

I cup her face and lean in for another kiss, stealing away her thoughts. I know her well enough to suspect she'd overthink things if given a chance, only to beat herself up over it later. "My turn," I murmur when I pull away, my forehead dropping to hers.

She nods, and much to my surprise, she reaches for the hem of her dress and pulls it up herself, hesitating for a moment when she reaches her waist. Our eyes lock, and she smiles shyly as she pulls it up and over her head, until she's standing in front of me in the sexiest red lace set I've ever seen, complete with garters around her thighs.

"*Fuck.*" I raise my fist to my mouth and bite down on it, my cock throbbing at the mere sight of her.

"See something you like?" she asks, her voice trembling.

"I do," I tell her, wrapping one of her curls around my finger, trying my best to be patient and take things slow. "I *really* like everything I'm seeing."

She smiles, her shoulders straightening a little as she reads the adoration in my eyes. "Me too," she whispers, her hand trembling as she runs her fingers over my chest and abs, her lips parting when my muscles contract.

I keep my eyes on hers as I step back and sit down on my bed, holding my hand out for her. "Come here, darling. I want you in my lap."

She takes my hand, a hint of nerves crossing her face as she straddles me, sitting on my knees instead of my thighs. "Like this?" she whispers, her expression conveying shyness.

I shake my head and grab her waist as I pull her closer, until she moans at the feel of my cock pressing against her. "Like *this*." Her breathing quickens, and she rolls her hips a little, not realizing what it does to me to feel her grind against me like that.

"I probably shouldn't admit this," I tell her, "but I've fantasized about this since that night you showed up unexpectedly and I carried you to my sofa."

Her eyes widen, and the way she smiles fucking undoes me. "Really?"

I cup the back of her neck and nod. "Really," I whisper, tilting my head and kissing the edge of her mouth, before taking her lips fully. A thrill runs down my spine when she threads her hand through my hair, her tongue darting out carefully, hesitantly. I smile against her lips and part them, tangling my tongue with hers teasingly.

My fingers graze the back of her bra, and she tenses a little, pulling her lips off mine just as I undo it. I hold her gaze as I push the straps off her shoulders, and it falls away as she untangles her hands from my hair. She inhales shakily when my eyes dip lower, her arms moving over her chest instinctively.

"Don't," I plead. "Don't hide from me, darling."

She searches my expression, and it fucking kills me how she seems to anticipate rejection when the mere thought of any man having her in his lap and not wanting her is ludicrous.

Her arms fall away, and I swear every thought fades to dust. "*Goddamn*," I whisper, taking in the sheer perfection she's presenting me with.

Serenity gasps when I grab her hips and turn us over so she falls back onto my bed, her long, curly hair splaying over my pillows like a priceless piece of art.

The red lace panties and garters she's wearing complement her skin beautifully, and for a moment I just stare at her, unable to comprehend that I get to have her, that she's *mine*, even if only for a moment.

"Archer," she murmurs when I lift her ankle to my lips and kiss it, before moving a little higher, taking my time.

"Have I told you you're fucking breathtaking?" I ask as I kiss the inside of her knee, earning myself a little shiver. "That lingerie you're wearing for me? It's all I'll be able to think about for the rest of the week."

She smiles when I kiss her thigh, pleased with my words. Her list told me she thinks she'd enjoy being praised, and I have every intention of lavishing her with compliments. I'll show her what she deserves, how she should be touched, so she'll never settle for less again.

"Will you give me a taste?" I ask, kissing the lace between her legs. She gasps, her hips lifting off the sheets just a little when I spread her legs and kiss her pussy right over the fabric. I grin when I realize she's wet, my heart skipping a beat. Our eyes lock when I use my teeth to push her panties aside, revealing a perfectly smooth pussy. "Please?" I won't do anything she doesn't want me to, but fuck, I'm dying for a taste.

Serenity nods hesitantly, and I groan in delight as my tongue darts out. Never in a million years did I think I'd ever have my best friend's little sister in my bed, my face buried between her legs, and her soft moans filling the air between us.

"Oh God," she moans when I put her legs over my shoulders and tease her clit, taking my time circling it, depriving her of what she wants most. *"Archer."*

Hearing her say my name in that breathless voice of hers, her tone pleading...damn, I don't think I'll ever get enough of that. I reach for her red lace panties and rip them off impatiently, needing to get closer, and for a moment I'm certain I see outrage in her eyes, but then I drag my tongue over her pussy fully, and she instantly forgives and forgets the damage I did to her undoubtedly expensive lingerie.

"That's it, baby," I murmur as her pants come a little faster, her hips moving in line with the rhythmic movements of my tongue.

"I can't," she says, shaking her head. I pull back a little and smile as I coat my index finger in her wetness before pushing it in and curling it in a come-hither motion, pressing right against her G-spot.

"You will," I promise her, before diving back in and fucking her with both my fingers and my tongue. Her moans become a little higher-pitched, a little more uncontrolled, and I increase my pace, flicking her clit with my tongue until her legs begin to tremble, my name on her lips as she comes.

I smile to myself as I lay my head on her stomach while she catches her breath, feeling oddly pleased with myself. I can't remember ever taking such great joy in pleasuring a woman, but fuck, when it's Serenity, it just feels like such an accomplishment.

"That was...*wow*. I...um...Thank you."

I bite back my laughter as I lift my head to look at her, unable to keep my amusement from showing. I don't think anyone has ever thanked me for an orgasm before. "Darling," I murmur, pressing a kiss to her hipbone. "Don't thank me yet. I'm nowhere near done with you."

Eighteen

SERENITY

Archer slowly kisses his way up my body, entirely unaware of the wild beating of my heart. I've never felt anything like what he just made me feel, and it makes me regret missing out on this for so many years even more.

"Stop that," he murmurs, dragging his tongue over my nipple, eliciting another moan from me in the process.

"Stop what?" I ask, my voice unrecognizably husky.

He moves his attention to the other side, smiling to himself as he toys with me. "Overthinking," he answers. "When you're in my bed, I don't want you thinking about anyone or anything but me."

How did he know? It had never occurred to me that someone other than Theo knew me well enough to know what I'm thinking, but more than once now, Archer has proven that he knows me better than I ever thought he did.

"Promise me," he says, holding himself up on his forearms. "Tell me that you're mine, Serenity. For as long as this lasts."

There's something so thrilling about seeing Archer like this, showcasing vulnerability that makes this moment feel even more intimate than it already was. "I'm yours," I whisper, my voice shaking.

He nods and reaches for me, brushing my hair out of my face. "That's right," he whispers, his knuckles moving over my cheek. "You're *mine*." His hand trails down to my neck, caressing, his eyes cataloging all my reactions. "These are mine," he says, leaning in to suck down on the side of my breast, right next to my sternum. He leaves a mark, and he stares at it with such pleasure in his eyes that I can't help but squirm, my heart racing. "Every inch of your skin, every sigh, every moan," he murmurs, his fingers trailing down. "It's all mine, darling."

I reach for him, my hand threading through his hair, and he grins at me, seemingly pleased with the small amount of initiative I'm taking. Archer looks into my eyes as he drags his fingers down, eliciting a gasp from me when his index finger disappears between my legs. He bites down on his lip when I moan, his expression betraying his desire. I've never felt so wanted, and it's exhilarating.

"This pussy belongs to me, do you understand?"

I nod, my hips rotating just slightly as he begins to move his finger in slow circular motions, teasing me the way he did earlier. "I asked you a question," he says, pushing another finger into me.

"I understand," I answer, my body thrumming with need. I never knew it could feel like this, and that look in his eyes…I could easily become addicted to the power he's giving me.

"Good," he whispers. "Then give me one more, baby."

"*Archer*," I plead when he curls his fingers inside me and swipes his thumb against my clit.

"I love the way you say my name, darling. Drives me fucking wild, you know that?"

"I can't. I'm…I'm getting lightheaded." I'm so sensitive, my entire body feels electrified. Each touch feels like too much, and I can't tell if I want him to keep going or stop.

"Look at me," he commands, slowing down the pace as he moves closer, his face inches from mine. "You're doing so good, Serenity. *So good.* Do you have any idea how wet you are for me? You feel fucking perfect."

He sounds so proud of me, so appreciative, like I'm some kind of miracle he has the honor to witness, and it does something to me, makes me want to please him.

"Let go of that control you love so much, darling. Give it to me, let me take care of you."

"Oh God," I whisper as my body obeys his commands. My back arches, and his eyes darken as my moans become more incoherent, my hips moving with him involuntarily.

"Beautiful," he whispers. "You're so goddamn beautiful, Serenity. Look at you, baby." He increases his pace, his fingers moving faster, harder. "You're my every dream come true, you know that? Come for me, darling. Give me what I've been dreaming of."

My head falls back as my muscles contract around his fingers, the strongest orgasm I've ever felt washing over me, wave after wave, the feelings lingering. Archer smiles and presses a soft kiss to my shoulder. "Good girl," he whispers. "I knew you could do it."

Emotions suddenly overwhelm me, and I bite on my lip, unsure why I'm on the verge of tears when all I felt just moments ago was pleasure. I sniff, and Archer instantly tenses, his head snapping up. Something akin to fear flickers through his eyes, and he pulls his fingers away, eliciting a few final flutters as I involuntarily clench my thighs.

"Serenity," he whispers, his voice filled with concern. "Sweetheart, what's wrong? Did I hurt you anywhere? Was I too rough?"

I shake my head and reach for him, pulling him on top of me, my arms wrapping around his neck. "I'm fine," I whisper. His weight feels reassuring on top of me, and I inhale shakily when he presses his lips just below my ear. "I just... I'm not sure...I've just never felt anything this intense." I've never felt this wanted, this cared for.

"Was it too much? I should've...fuck, I should've taken it slower."

"No," I reply instantly, tightening my grip on him. "It was perfect, Archer. If anything...I want more."

He pushes himself up on his forearms to look at me, and I try my best to meet his gaze when all I want to do is hide. "More?" he repeats, his tone cautious now.

"I...I want *you*."

Archer bites down on his lip, and I revel in the way his cock twitches against me, the way his breathing instantly changes. "Use your words properly," he demands. "Tell me exactly what you want."

I look into his eyes as I move one of my hands between us, slowly sliding it down his abs, loving the way they tense at my touch. "Archer, I want you to fuck me."

He inhales sharply when I grab the waistband of his boxer shorts, his gaze searching—for a hint of trepidation, I suspect. He won't find any. I've never been more certain. I want this, and I want it with *him*.

"Give it to me," I whisper, throwing his earlier words back at him, and he groans, the sound needy and delicious. It fuels my confidence, makes me feel comfortable voicing my desires.

"Yeah?" he murmurs, pushing off me to sit on his knees between my legs. He smirks at me as he pushes his boxers down slowly. I gasp, and he looks up through lowered lashes, a pleased smirk on his face as he palms his erection. "You want this?"

I nod, and my heartbeat accelerates as renewed lust unfurls deep inside, blending with a hint of fear when Archer moves back on top of me and lines up his cock. When we came to an agreement, I also told him I'm on the pill, and the look in his eyes when I told him I didn't want anything between us is the same one he's wearing now. Pure possessiveness.

Our eyes lock as he pushes the tip in, his breath hitching. "*Fuck*," he groans, his chest rising and falling rapidly. "You okay?"

A sexy and entirely incoherent sound leaves his lips when I graze his scalp with my nails and tilt my hips just slightly. "Yeah," I whisper, grabbing hold of his hair.

He pulls back a little and then pushes deeper into me, and I tense, surprised by the feeling. I squirm underneath him, feeling overly full. "Relax, baby," he whispers, pausing, his gaze roaming over my face.

"It's... I'm not sure. It feels like too much, Archer." I'm too embarrassed to tell him that I can't take it when I know I physically can. I don't want him to think that I'm completely clueless, but right now, it truly feels like he won't fit, like he'll tear me apart if he pushes any farther into me.

Archer stills completely, his muscles straining as he reaches between us and grabs the base of his cock. I moan involuntarily when he drags it up, pushing it against my clit before sliding back into me just a fraction. "How's that, darling?" he asks, repeating the motion, until he has me panting.

"Oh God," I moan, tightening my grip on his hair. He grins, his gaze heated as he leans in and kisses me just below my ear, before moving to my neck, grazing my skin with his teeth before sucking down on it. All the while, he continues to tease me, the feel of his cock against my clit rapidly bringing me to the brink of another orgasm.

"I love these little sounds you make," he whispers into my ear. "I love that it's all for me, all mine. Do you have any idea how wet you are for me, sweetheart? How perfect your pussy feels?"

He pushes into me deeper, pulling out and dragging his cock against my clit with every single thrust, his movements faster now, in line with my racing heart.

"Please," I whisper, becoming lightheaded all over again. "Archer, oh *God*. I can't..."

He laughs, the sound sexy. "You can," he promises me. "You're taking my cock so well, baby. Just a little more. Can you take a little more?"

I nod, and he looks into my eyes as he pulls almost all the way back, before pushing into me fully, the sexiest sound escaping his lips when he bottoms out inside me. He's breathing hard, his entire body tense. "Serenity," he whispers, my name a plea on his lips. His forehead drops to mine, and he looks at me like I'm the most precious thing he's ever laid eyes on.

I keep one hand in his hair and move the other to his cheek, reveling in this connection between us. I'm not sure what I was expecting, but this is so much more. "Please," I whisper, unsure what I'm asking for. My body is humming with desire, and I moan when he begins to move slowly, carefully.

"Beautiful," Archer whispers. "You're so fucking beautiful, Sera. You feel incredible."

His nose brushes against mine, and I tighten my grip on his hair when he kisses me, his hand moving between us. "*Archer*," I whisper against his mouth when he places his thumb against my clit, trapping his hand between us.

He just kisses the edge of my mouth and smiles. "Let me try," he says, his tone cajoling. "I'm desperate for one more. I need to feel you come on my cock."

He keeps his eyes on mine as he moves his hips, his thumb slowly bringing me to the edge all over again. His pace increases, and the way his breathing changes makes my entire body sing. Watching Archer

Harrison lose control over me is something I suspect I'll never get enough of.

He thrives on my moans, his eyes lighting up each time he makes my hips roll, and before long, he's got my back arching and my legs trembling. "Yeah," he whispers, taking me harder, faster. "Just like that, baby. Come for me, beautiful."

And I do.

My muscles tighten just as he groans, his head falling to the crook of my neck as I come, taking him right along with me. "*Fuck*," he pants, rocking his hips gently as he kisses my temple. "That was fucking incredible."

He sighs happily, his body relaxing on top of mine for a few moments, before he pulls out and moves to his side, lying down beside me. He cups my face and turns my head toward him. "Feeling okay?" he asks, his gaze filled with worry.

I nod, suddenly self-conscious. I clutch at his covers and pull them up, not quite sure what to do or say. I hadn't thought of what the appropriate thing to do is *after*. "I, um, I should probably go."

He stares at me like I've lost my mind. "Go *where*?" he asks, a brow raised.

"Home?" My tone lacks the confidence I tried to infuse in it, and I squeeze my legs together, feeling a little uncomfortable and a whole lot of awkward.

Archer reaches for one of my curls and twirls it around his index finger. "Please stay," he whispers, surprising me.

"W-Would that be okay? I, um, I don't want to cling to you or do anything that would annoy you. I'm already asking for so much."

He chuckles and pulls me close, enveloping me in a tight hug. I relax into him, my nose pressed against his throat. "Stay," he murmurs, cupping the back of my head. "Right here, in my arms."

Nineteen

Serenity

"You've picked up CAD rendering very quickly," Mark says as he leans in to look at my screen. "I have a feeling you're going to end up becoming a permanent member of the design team when you finish your internship."

I smile up at him as Theo rolls his chair closer to take a look at my proposed changes to the POS system that's causing so many issues. "Damn," he says, smiling wryly. "This is a thousand times better than my attempts."

I grin at him as he moves back to his own desk, pleased with myself. I've fully thrown myself into the task we were assigned this morning, in an attempt to keep my mind off Archer and the slight sensitivity between my legs. I fell asleep in his arms last night, and everything just felt so much more intimate than I'd anticipated. He wasn't anything like what I'd expected in bed. His usual aloofness was entirely absent, and having his undivided attention was intoxicating.

I bite my lip as my mind replays the way he asked me if I'd let him take care of me before he grabbed a warm, wet towel, taking his time to wipe my thighs clean for me. Not even in my wildest dreams did I think he had that side to him, and it affected me more than he could possibly know.

The sound of the company's instant messaging system snaps me out of my thoughts, and my eyes widen when I see Archer's name. I look around furtively before opening the message, my heart pounding.

> **ARCHER HARRISON**
> why weren't you in my bed when I woke up this morning?

My breath hitches, and I sit up a little, a thrill running down my spine as I type a reply, trying my best to be both quick and sly.

> **SERENITY ADESINA**
> I had to get ready for work, and I didn't want to wake you.

> **ARCHER HARRISON**
> don't sneak out without a word again, darling. Just wake me up next time.

My heart skips a beat at the sight of the endearment, and instantly, my mind teases me with memories of him whispering *come for me, darling.*

SERENITY ADESINA

There won't be a next time! I can't stay over again. My hair was a complete mess this morning. It took me thirty minutes just to detangle it.

ARCHER HARRISON

I'm not following, Sera. What does that have to do with my bed?

SERENITY ADESINA

I have a silk pillow that makes my curls more manageable, and I really shouldn't sleep without it.

ARCHER HARRISON

I see...I wish I could've seen your messy hair this morning. I bet you looked beautiful.

I stare at my screen, my stomach fluttering. He says the sweetest things sometimes, and I don't think he even realizes it.

ARCHER HARRISON

how do you feel today?

SERENITY ADESINA

a little sensitive, but I'm okay. How are you?

My stomach twists as I begin to wonder if maybe he regrets what we did. He seemed to enjoy it, but then again, what do I know? Maybe it was too much hassle to be so patient, and maybe he didn't enjoy it as much as I did. I doubt he was able to truly let go when he was so concerned with my comfort.

ARCHER HARRISON

I'd have been better if I hadn't woken up all alone, only to then be thrown into back-to-back meetings. Come see me later. I'll be back in my office in thirty minutes.

I bite my lip again and glance around, making sure no one is looking at my screen.

SERENITY ADESINA

I can't. You know I can't. I don't want anyone to find out we know each other outside of work, and we shouldn't do anything that'll get us caught.

"Serenity?"

I gasp and quickly click my chat with Archer away, my heart beating out of my chest as I turn toward Theo, who's rolling his chair closer. "What's up?" I ask, my tone a little higher pitched than I'd like.

He frowns, his gaze searching. "I've been thinking about this all morning, unsure how to bring it up." He runs a hand through his hair, and my mind begins to run wild. Does he know? All morning I've wondered if he could tell that I feel a little different, and I'm not sure how I'd reply if he asked me outright whether something happened. There are very few secrets I've ever kept from Theo.

"What's wrong?" I ask, my voice trembling just slightly.

"Kristen wanted me to ask you if you'd like to come over for dinner sometime. She says you two have barely spoken in some time now, and she'd like to cook for you." He hesitates. "No pressure, of course. I just…I do feel like you judged her harder than me, and we both kept the same secret. It truly would mean a lot to me if you'd come over. Kristen…she thinks she lost you, and she's devastated. It's really hard to watch her agonize over text messages she wants to send you but can't."

I stare at him, my heart constricting painfully. He has no idea what he's asking of me—he won't ever know. The mere thought of visiting a home they share and having to watch them together pains me. How am I supposed to survive the reality of it?

"Please," he says, reaching for my hand. "Kristen keeps telling me that whatever is going on between you and her isn't as simple as I think it is, and I won't pry, but she isn't the only one who misses you. Please, come have dinner with us. Whatever happened between you two can't erase a decade of friendship, can it?"

I nod, pure agony spreading from my chest, numbing my senses. "Okay," I murmur. "How about sometime next month?" I ask, trying to buy myself some time. "I've been so busy with work, and honestly, I'm not sure I can fit it in any sooner."

He breathes a sigh of relief, not realizing how reluctant I am. Theo is my best friend, and he doesn't seem to realize that my heart is bleeding, that I'm forcing a smile as he beams at me. Or maybe he does, and he's just ignoring it in favor of making Kristen happy.

"We can leave together after work whenever you want," he says, his eyes twinkling. "I can't wait to show you our place. We chose it from one of your lists, and I think you'll really love it."

I pull my hand out of his, my stomach dropping when I realize that they're living in one of the apartments I imagined Theo and me in. He might not know what he's asking of me, but Kristen does.

Twenty

ARCHER

I hesitate as I stare at Ezra's front door, unsure how to navigate the new dynamics between Serenity and me. Do we still hang out together, or does she want certain boundaries between us? "Fuck it," I murmur, before ringing the bell.

She opens the door moments later, and a rush of something I can't quite define runs down my spine as I take her in. She looks fucking breathtaking in those tiny shorts and her sports bra, random paint streaks all over her body and her beautiful, long, curly hair cascading over her shoulders, to her waist.

"Archer," she says, clearly surprised to see me so early on a Saturday morning. "Hi!"

I grin as she steps aside to let me in. "Hi, darling," I murmur, the endearment slipping past my lips subconsciously.

She smiles in that adorably shy way, and my heart begins to beat a little faster as she leads me into the living room. Her eyes roam over my jeans and tee appreciatively as I sit down and lean back, and it takes all of me not to pull her on my lap and kiss her.

"I started the painting you requested," she tells me, plopping down right next to me, her thigh brushing against my jeans. "I didn't want to bother you unnecessarily, so I brought some of the supplies you bought back with me. Since Ezra isn't home this weekend, I figured I could work on it without being interrupted."

It's unreal how much her mere proximity has started to affect me. I've never experienced anything like this. The giddiness, the way my heart races when she looks into my eyes. It's all new, and it throws me off. I can't resist touching her and wrap my arm around her, pulling her closer, my face inches from hers. "So you planned to paint all day today? Bring it all back to mine later. I set up the spare room for you, so you'd have your own space for it. I *want* you in my home, darling. You're always welcome, even if I'm not there."

She nods, her eyes dropping to my mouth. I watch as she bites down on her lip, and my cock instantly hardens. The hold she has over me is unbelievable. "Okay, I, um, I will, and yeah, I was just gonna paint. Unless you had something else in mind?"

I reach for her and lift her onto my lap, my willpower entirely nonexistent when she looks at me like that. She gasps, her eyes widening when she feels my cock pressing against her ass, her gaze instantly becoming heated. Her breathing accelerates just a touch as she places one hand over my heart, the other moving around to the back of my neck.

"I did have something else in mind, actually," I murmur, holding on to the last shreds of my sanity with all my might as I grab her waist, loving the feel of her. "Knowing you, you probably have a list of things you want to do here, don't you?" I smirk, and she raises a brow. "Other than me, of course."

She laughs, and her head falls back in the most beautiful way. "You're ridiculous," she says, her eyes twinkling. "But yes, I do have a list."

"Let's do something on your list today, then. I'm free all day." It's not exactly true. I have mountains of paperwork to get through, but I don't give a fuck. It's been so long since I last took a day off, and one day won't kill me.

"Really?" She looks so bewildered, so hopeful, and instantly an unbidden thought comes to mind. *I'd do anything for her if she keeps looking at me that way.*

"Yep. Go get ready. I'll take you wherever you want to go."

She jumps off my lap excitedly. "Then I want to have brunch at the highest restaurant in the city. Can we?"

"Heritage Harvest?" I ask, raising a brow.

She nods, her gaze pleading. Sera looks like she's about to attempt to convince me with a thousand reasons why that's what we need to do today, and I grin.

"You got it, baby," I tell her as I grab my phone.

She does the cutest little jump before turning and rushing away to get dressed, getting ready in record time. Not even thirty minutes later, we're walking into the restaurant she wanted to go to, my hand on her lower back, a strange sense of pride rushing through me.

There's something thrilling about having her by my side. It makes me feel like I'm on top of the world to stand next to her, especially in that gorgeous red summer dress she's wearing, her lips a matching shade.

"Mr. Harrison," the restaurant manager says, his demeanor nervous as he throws Serenity a smile. "It's such an honor to have you here today. We prepared our best table for you."

I nod, and they lead us to a floral birdcage-style booth on the rooftop terrace. Serenity gasps, and I smile to myself as she scoots along the circular bench. It's been positioned to face an unobstructed view offering us a great deal of privacy. Even I have to admit it's pretty damn magical.

"Your favorite champagne," the manager says, smiling. All the while, Serenity just takes it all in, some of her initial excitement seemingly dimmed as she begins to tap her leg. "There's a set menu today, but if there's anything off the menu you'd like, we will of course make that for you."

I glance at my girl and place my hand on her thigh, a rush of possessiveness coursing through me when she looks at me. "Tell me what you want," I tell her. "Anything at all, darling."

She smiles shakily and shakes her head. "The set menu is fine."

I nod, and the manager walks away, leaving the two of us alone. "What's wrong?" I ask, slipping my hand underneath her dress to caress her thigh.

"Nothing," she says, looking away.

I reach for her and gently pinch her chin, turning her face back to mine. "Communication is important to me, Serenity. If we're going to be together in any capacity, I need you to communicate with me."

She looks into my eyes, insecurity flashing through them. "It's just…you've clearly been here before. It's silly, but my thoughts just began to spiral. I thought of you coming here with Tyra, and I just felt so guilty to be sitting here with you. It's not my intention to take her place. I'd never dare even dream of it, and I just…"

I cup her face, the same guilt she's feeling hitting me hard too. "I've never been here with her, but even if I had, it wouldn't matter. One of the reasons I agreed to this arrangement between us is because I want to make an active effort to let her go." I sigh and run a hand through my hair. "No one could ever replace her, but I don't want to live in the past anymore."

She nods, her expression solemn. "Me neither. When I added this place to my list, I thought that I'd come here with—"

I lean in and kiss her, cutting her off. She startles, and then she kisses me back, her hand wrapping around the back of my neck. My forehead drops to hers when I pull away, my heart racing. "I don't want his name on your lips when you're with me."

She bites down on her lip when I pull away, her gaze heated, and I can't help but smile. It's odd, how frequently I find myself smiling in her presence. I'm enthralled by her, and I don't snap out if it until our brunch is served by the chef himself.

"He seemed even more nervous than the manager was," Serenity says, taking a bite of her food, the sun shining down on her beautifully, illuminating her like some sort of goddess.

"Probably because I own this restaurant and he realizes that he'll lose his job if you don't enjoy his food."

She stares at me wide-eyed, and I grin.

"What?" I murmur. She's so fucking precious, and I don't think she even realizes it.

Serenity pouts in the cutest fucking way, and desire rushes through me. How the fuck does she do this to me? "I thought this was just a popular date spot for you and that's why they all knew you. I've seen photos of you with famous models and actresses in that gossip magazine, The Herald."

I grin as I cup her face, my heart beating wildly. "You're jealous." Her eyes flash angrily, and I chuckle. "What a beautiful fucking sight. Almost as pretty as when you come for me."

"I—I'm not!"

I smirk as I lean in to kiss her, taking my time to part her lips and tangle my tongue with hers, just the way she likes it. If there's one thing I've learned about her body recently, it's that her tongue is sensitive, and kissing her turns her on faster than anything else could.

"I'm yours," I promise her when I pull away, enjoying the way she pants for me, the way her eyes fill with desire, all for me. "I'm yours for however long this lasts, Serenity. I don't share, and I don't expect you to either. While we're together, you'll have all of me." I pause then, hesitating. "Besides, none of those dates were what you think they were."

She nods and pulls back a little, clearly flustered as she reaches for her fork and takes a bite of her truffle eggs. "Tell me about the restaurant," she says. "I never realized you owned anything other than Serenity Solutions."

I smirk as I grab her wrist and steal her next bite off her fork. She makes me act in ways I never have before. Somehow, being with her makes me more playful, more like a version of myself I thought disappeared over a decade ago.

"My mom loves cooking, and when my grandfather disowned me for refusing to follow in his footsteps and becoming a hotelier, she began to implement weekly cooking classes for my sister and me over video calls. I think it was just her way to ensure I stayed part of our family even after I moved out and began to spend less time with them, but it resulted in me becoming a huge foodie. I wouldn't want to be a chef, but I love the idea of having some input on menus and giving aspiring chefs a chance. Every time I find a new chef I love, I check if they'd like to run a restaurant for me." I point at her food and smile. "I found this chef through his social media videos. He'd been cooking at home as a hobby while working three different jobs, but he was meant for this restaurant, and hiring him was one of the best decisions I've ever made."

She looks at me with a hint of pride, and it does something to me, makes me feel vulnerable. "Why doesn't anyone know about this? I've never heard Ezra mention it."

I shrug. "He knows, but he also knows I like to keep these kinds of things low-key."

She nods, and we fall into easy conversation as we eat. I let her steal bites of my food, and she lets me steal kisses. Everything with her is so fucking effortless, and I never knew it could be like this. I feel so free around her. I didn't even realize how tense I was before I sat down here with her.

"What other hobbies do you have?" she asks eventually, genuine interest in her expression. "I feel like I've known you for half my life and I'm only just finding out that I don't actually know you at all."

I grin as I place my hand on her thigh and squeeze. "I'd argue that you know me better than most."

She bites down on her lip again and throws me a flustered look. *"Arch."*

I laugh and pinch her chin as I lean in for a quick kiss. I can't remember the last time I had so much fun just hanging out and chatting with someone. "I love art," I tell her. "Food and art are the two biggest loves of my life." I look into her eyes, my gaze searching. "I'm a huge fan of The Muse. Have you ever heard of her?"

Her eyes widen a fraction, panic clouding them for a second, before we're interrupted by the chef serving us desserts before she can answer. I watch her as she looks at the variety of pastries and cakes excitedly, and the way she moans when she takes a bite of chocolate cake fucking drives me wild.

"Come here," I murmur, pulling her onto my lap.

She gasps as I wrap my arms around her. "Archer," she whisper-shouts.

"No one can see us from here, and now that we've been served dessert, they won't bother us for a while." I lean in and kiss her just below her ear, earning myself a delicious little shiver. "I vividly remember you putting one interesting item on your list when I asked you what you wanted sexually." She wanted me to make her come in public, and that's exactly what I'm going to do.

Her breath hitches when I part her legs and slip my fingers between them, my cock twitching when I find her wet already. I suspected kissing her as much as I have been today would do it for her, but feeling it...*fuck*. Nothing makes me feel more powerful than knowing I have that effect on her.

"Eat your dessert, baby."

Her hands tremble as she does as told, taking another bite of her chocolate cake as I coat my middle finger in her wetness. Her hips roll when I slip two fingers into her and use my other hand to caress her clit. "You have no idea what you've been doing to me, sitting here looking so damn pretty, do you?" I curl my finger, teasing her, and she begins to rock in my lap. "And then you go and fucking moan as you take a bite of that damn chocolate cake, breaking down my willpower."

"It's delicious," she says, panting. "You should try it."

"Then give me a bite, darling."

She whimpers a little as I increase my pace, but even so, she picks up her fork and feeds me a bite, our eyes locking as she turns in my lap. She's such a good fucking girl, obeying my orders like that. This connection between us, the way she looks at me as she rides my fingers...it's fucking addictive.

"Kiss me."

Her fork clatters to the table as she pushes her hands into my hair and pulls me closer, her lips crashing against mine as I bring her to the edge and keep her there, loving the way she's trying not to moan.

"You're such a good girl," I whisper against her lips when her forehead drops against mine, her breathing erratic as she chases release. "You want to come for me, don't you?"

She nods, her pussy clenching desperately. *"Please."*

I grin, my heart overflowing with something I'm not quite familiar with. Protectiveness. Possessiveness. Desire. "Then come for me, baby," I whisper, giving her what she needs.

Her lips find mine as her muscles contract around my fingers, and I swallow down every single one of her moans. I never even meant to touch her today. This was supposed to just be a friendly get-together, it wasn't meant to be a date, but fuck, I don't think I can be around her anymore without wanting her.

Twenty-One

SERENITY

"How are you settling in, Ser?" Ezra asks me as he holds a beer bottle that he definitely stole from Archer's fridge. I wonder if he even realizes that Archer rarely drinks beer. I'm pretty sure Arch keeps his fridge stocked just for Ezra.

"Honestly, the biggest adjustment has been coming to terms with the fact that *you* are supposedly some big, fearsome, rich CEO," I tell him, my eyes trailing over the ratty superhero T-shirt and the black shorts with literal holes in them he's wearing. "You truly are a whole different person at work, and it's really shocking. You have no idea how tempted I am to take a photo of you and send it to the whole company."

He glances down at his clothes and bursts out laughing as he sinks down on the sofa. I join him and pull my legs up, a smile on my face. "I see you're doing just fine, then," he says, lifting his beer bottle to his mouth. "I was worried since I've been away so much, but you seem okay."

I nod, my thoughts turning to Archer. "Archer has taken me

sightseeing in my free time, which has really helped me settle in," I murmur, my mind drifting to all the places he's taken me to in the evenings and on weekends when Ezra isn't here. I didn't think I'd want to do anything that'd remind me of Theo, but Archer managed to turn the to-do lists I made with Theo in mind into something that's *ours*.

"I'm glad he's been there for you in my absence," he says, and I instantly begin to feel guilty for the secrets we're keeping. "And how has work been?"

"The workload is heavy but in the very best way. I'm learning so much, and I'm honestly having a really good time."

Though truthfully, a lot of that has to do with Archer too. It's the secret text messages and the way he's pulled me into an empty meeting room twice now simply to kiss me. I wasn't sure if I'd be okay working with Theo, but Archer makes it all bearable. I'm still dreading having dinner with Theo and Kristen, but even the thought of that doesn't torment me as much as it did when Theo first mentioned it.

"Serenity," Ezra says, his tone grave. I lift my face to look at him, my heart instantly beating a little faster when I find him looking at me with a conflicted expression. "I'm honestly really happy that you're enjoying working at Serenity Solutions, but I want you to know that I'd support any career you chose to pursue, no matter what it is. Mom might not understand, but I worked as hard as I did so you wouldn't have to. You can do whatever you want, and I'll have your back. If you want to pursue painting, I'll make it happen."

I stare at him in disbelief, my heart overflowing with tenderness.

"Think it over," he adds. "I'm serious. You're incredibly talented, so don't let Mom's words and opinions deprive you of your dreams."

I nod, my heart racing. What would he do if I told him that I'm The Muse? The few times I've heard him talk about my work, he's berated it and called it vandalism. If he realized I never truly stopped painting and which route I took, he'd be so disappointed in me.

"For fuck's sake," Archer says, startling me as he walks into our living room with an amused look on his face. My gaze roams over his tight white tee and lingers on the gray sweats he loves wearing at home. He knows I can't resist him when he's dressed like that, and when his eyes meet mine, there's a hint of provocation in them.

He yanks Ezra's bottle out of his hand and plops down on the sofa next to me, his thigh brushing against mine. "How the fuck do you keep getting into my house so unobtrusively? I didn't even fucking hear you." His arm wraps around the back of the sofa, the edge of his thumb resting against my shoulder.

Ezra simply grins and reaches over, stealing his beer back. "I'm a man of many skills," he says, shrugging as he knocks the bottle back.

Archer turns his face to look at me, his eyes lingering on my lips for a moment too long. He tears his eyes off me and drapes his free hand over his lap. "Do those skills include putting on the game?"

Ezra rolls his eyes and turns the TV on, his attention rapidly stolen away by the football game. All the while, the only thing I can focus on is Archer and how close he's sitting. Ezra didn't bat an eye at it, but my heart hasn't stopped racing.

I wasn't sure what it'd be like for the three of us to hang out since Archer and I started sleeping together, but everything seems the same, except for the way my body is responding to Archer's proximity.

I almost breathe a sigh of relief when Ezra gets up during a commercial, telling us he needs to check on something for work really quickly before disappearing.

The second we hear the door to his home office click closed, Archer reaches for me, his hand wrapping around the back of my neck as he pulls me closer. "Fucking finally," he whispers, before his lips meet mine. I whimper a little, my hand balling in his T-shirt as I kiss him back, my movements urgent, desperate. He parts my lips, and a soft moan escapes the back of my throat when he kisses me in that way that just steals away all my thoughts—deeply, leisurely, like I have his full attention, like there's nothing but me.

We're both panting when he pulls away, his forehead dropping to mine. "Couldn't resist," he whispers. "I can't have you sitting next to me looking so fucking irresistible without getting a taste of what's mine."

"The feeling is mutual," I whisper back. "You knew what you were doing when you walked in here wearing those sweats."

He grins as he grabs my hand and places it over his erection, making me feel just how hard he is for me from one single kiss. "And what's that?"

"You were tempting me."

"Did I succeed?"

I squeeze his cock, my breathing erratic. "Definitely."

He chuckles and leans in, kissing the edge of my mouth. "Good," he whispers. "Sneak back into my house later, darling. I need you."

I nod, and he grins as he turns his face to kiss me. "Ezra will be back any second," I remind him, pulling away a little.

He sighs and leans back moments before Ezra enters the room, and I pull my hand to my chest in a rush. Archer smiles as he throws his arm back over his lap, hiding his erection as my brother takes his seat in time for the game to resume.

He glances at us, but there isn't a hint of suspicion in his eyes. Even so, a new kind of guilt rushes over me. There's so much at stake if Archer and I ever got caught. We need to be more careful.

Twenty-Two

SERENITY

My heart begins to beat a little faster as Theo and I walk to his flat, each heartbeat heavier than the last as familiarity hits me. "It's so convenient that it's walking distance to work," Theo says as we walk up to the same building that now bears my artwork. "And it suddenly became more in demand just days after we signed the lease because The Muse was apparently here. Wild, isn't it?"

Wild, indeed. Me being The Muse is one of few secrets I've ever kept from him. Many of my pieces depicted my feelings for him and I never wanted him to figure it out. Now I'm more glad than ever that he doesn't know.

My stomach turns as we walk past my painting, and I begin to tremble as heartache threatens to overwhelm me. They're living in the place that was my top pick for Theo and me, the same one I told Kristen about so many times that she could hardly stand to hear any more about it.

Theo grins at me as we enter the elevator, and I glance around, my heart heavy. "It's nothing like your brother's place, of course, but it's charming in its own right."

I force a smile for him, trying my best to hide my conflicted feelings. I desperately want to be happy for him, but my heartache clouds my good intentions, until nothing but vague resentment is left. Does he even realize how many hours of research went into the list I created? Every single place on there was in budget, within walking distance, in a safe area, and nice enough inside. I did all that research for *us*.

"Here we are," he says, leading me to his front door. There's a cute sign on it with both of their names, and I take a deep breath before following him in, my hands shaking.

"Serenity," Kristen says the moment we step into the living room, her brilliant blue eyes filled with seemingly genuine hope. She reaches for her long blond hair, her movements betraying her nerves. "Hi, I... um...thank you for coming over."

My heart aches at the sight of her, and it hits me then. I missed her—more than I realized, more than I'd like to admit. She throws me a hesitant smile, and I nod at her, grateful that she hasn't tried to hug me like she would have in the past. "Hi," I murmur, looking around their living room. "This place is really nice," I force myself to say.

"Shall we?" Theo places his hand on the small of my back, and Kristen tenses just slightly. I step away from him instantly, but it kills me to do it. He and I have always been so close, and it hurts to now set boundaries that I don't want between us.

Theo throws me a startled look and drops his hand, gesturing toward the dining table instead. I nod and take a reluctant step forward, wishing I could just go home. It's not that I don't want to salvage my friendship with both of them, but I just don't want to do it tonight, when my wounds still feel fresh.

I'm well aware that I had no claim to Theo in that way, but I can't help but feel betrayed nonetheless. Kristen is the one I shared all my dreams with, the only one that knew how badly I wished that he'd finally see me. She knew I was too scared to risk my friendship with him, but I suppose it makes sense that she never encouraged me to make a move. I didn't even realize that she hadn't until now.

"I made that lamb ragout you like," she tells me, her hand trembling just slightly as she reaches for the pot on the table to fill my plate for me.

Theo jumps out of his seat and takes over from her, their eyes locking for a moment as his hand wraps over the one she's holding the spoon with. "Let me," he tells her, a sweet, intimate smile on his face, and it absolutely destroys me.

I look away, and Kristen seemingly snaps out of it, stepping back from Theo. "I, um, I forgot to grab the wine I bought." She rushes away, her cheeks bright red, and I watch Theo as he stares after her. I never even stood a chance, did I? He's never once looked at me that way, and I was foolish to hope he ever would.

"She's nervous," he tells me as he serves me some of the pasta Kristen made. "She's been texting me all day, second-guessing every single thing about this dinner." He hesitates, his gaze roaming over my face for a moment. "I've asked her what it is you two are arguing about, because I've never seen you go this long without speaking. She won't tell me, but she assures me it isn't about me or our relationship."

He sighs and fills Kristen's plate before his own, and all the while I wonder if she'll keep her silence. The last thing I want is for Theo to find out about my feelings from his girlfriend. Would our friendship even last if he knew? Or would he distance himself from me out of respect for Kristen? I thought I had so much to lose, only to find out that I might as well have taken my chances because I now stand to lose just as much, with far less to gain.

Kristen walks back in and holds up a bottle, trying her best to smile. "I bought you a cabernet sauvignon," she tells me, her eyes filled with hope.

"Thank you," I tell her. "I love a good cab."

"I know," she murmurs, her voice filled with regret as she pours me a glass.

I take it from her and stare at it for a few moments, trying my best to keep it together as I raise it to my lips, knocking back half of it.

Kristen tries her best to make small talk, and I try my best not to notice the way Theo wraps his arm around the back of her chair as he hangs on her every word. The worst part is that I'd normally have texted Kristen if I found myself somewhere I didn't want to be, and she'd call me giving me an excuse to leave. Now she's the one I want to get away from.

I sigh as I reach for my phone helplessly halfway through dinner, only to find a text message waiting for me.

ARCHER

have you had dinner yet?

I blink in surprise, the edges of my lips turning up into a smile. We've started to text throughout the day, and those little moments feel so intimate. There's something thrilling about knowing that I'm on his mind, even as he sits in important meetings.

SERENITY

I'm having dinner now

ARCHER

would you like me to come over? I know you don't like eating alone

My heart skips a beat, my mood instantly lifted. Things have been amazing between us. Most of the time, we're still *us*. We hang out, and occasionally he'll come over simply to watch TV with Ezra and me. But when we do those same mundane things while Ezra isn't home, he'll turn toward me with that look in his eyes I can't resist, and I inevitably end up in his bed. I'd been worried about being with him, but all of my fears have been unfounded. We've made it work perfectly.

> SERENITY
>
> that's really nice of you, Arch, but I'm not home

> SERENITY
>
> and don't worry, I'm not alone

I watch as text bubbles appear and disappear, a hint of impatience rushing though me.

"Serenity?" Theo says.

My head snaps up, and all of a sudden, I realize I'd just been staring at my phone for who knows how long. "Oh, sorry," I tell him, just as another message appears on my screen.

> ARCHER
>
> who are you having dinner with?

Theo raises a brow, a hint of confusion crossing his face. "Who are you texting?" he asks. "I've never seen you smile at your phone like that."

Kristen's gaze snaps to him, and I watch as she leans in. "Don't be so nosy, babe," she says, her tone sweet and placating, but I hear the hint of insecurity she tries to hide.

She places her hand over his, and he grabs it, entwining their fingers before he lifts their joined hands to his lips to kiss the back of hers, their eyes locked. All the while, I just sit there and stare at them, wishing it could've been me he looked at that way.

Twenty-Three

ARCHER

I glance at my phone as I wrap my towel around my waist, surprisingly annoyed Serenity left me on read. Who is she with for her not to answer my question? I'd have asked that even if we weren't sleeping together, so I doubt she'd think I'm overstepping.

I glare at my phone as I walk into my bedroom and throw it onto my bed moments before my doorbell rings, only to find Serenity standing in front of me. "Hey," I murmur, surprised.

Her eyes roam over my bare torso, and then she wordlessly steps forward, her hand wrapping around the back of my neck as she rises to her tiptoes and kisses me.

I freeze for a split second, and then I'm kissing her back. I pull her into my house and kick the door closed, my hands sliding down her body. She moans against my mouth, and I lift her up, loving the way her legs wrap around me instantly.

She gasps when I push her against the nearest wall, not quite able to make it to my bedroom before I begin to tug at her blouse. Serenity helps me take it off, and I groan as I palm her breast over the soft fabric of her bra, my thumb brushing over her hardened nipples. "Archer," she moans, rotating her hips against me.

I move my hands to her waist and continue to walk to my bedroom. "Where were you?" I ask, my voice rough and harsh.

She bites down on her lip, and for a moment, something akin to agony flickers through her eyes. "Theo and Kristen's house." She threads a hand through my hair, her touch carrying a hint of impatience. "She made me dinner."

I sit down on my bed with her in my lap, my gaze roaming over her face. "Tell me what you need, Sera."

"Help me forget," she pleads, placing her hand on my shoulders. "I need you to drown out the memory of him looking at her like she's his whole world."

She pushes against my chest, and my eyes widen as I fall backward onto the bed. Serenity smiles at me as she drags her index finger over my abs, her breathing erratic.

"I'll make you forget everything but my name, darling," I whisper, reaching for her bra. It comes undone, and her breath hitches as I pull it away.

I look into her eyes as I tilt her head and pull her in to kiss her, taking my time. I've learned that the easiest way to keep her from overthinking is to kiss her, slow and deep, until she's writhing in my lap.

Serenity gasps when I turn us over, throwing her onto my bed before covering her body with mine. She glances to her side, and I smirk when she realizes my sheets are now all silk. They took a while to arrive, since they were handmade just for her. "Archer," she whispers, only for her eyes to widen when my towel comes undone. I smirk at her, loving how honest her expressions always are.

"Lift your hips for me," I murmur, and she does as asked, letting me pull off her skirt. Her black lace panties follow, and I just stare at her for a moment, taking in her beauty.

She sighs and instantly wraps her arms around the back of my neck when I settle on top of her. "You're fucking breathtaking, you know that?" I kiss the edge of her mouth, and she hooks her leg around mine. "My gorgeous girl." I press my lips just below her ear, and she shivers. "All mine."

"*Archer*," she whispers, rolling her hips against mine.

"Yeah, baby? Tell me what you want."

She grabs my hair and pulls my mouth to hers, and I go eagerly, reveling in this connection between us. It's been so long since I felt this way—fully immersed in someone, my attention undivided. When I have her in my arms, there's no space for anything else. Only her.

Serenity parts my lips, her tongue darting out teasingly, and I groan as I kiss her back leisurely, loving the way she pushes her hips up. She's panting when she pulls away, her eyes filled with silent pleas. "I want you." Her voice trembles, like she's scared to admit it.

I smirk as I grab her hips and roll us over, so she ends up back on top of me. "Then take what you need from me, darling," I tell her.

She hesitates, her expression betraying her vulnerability as she sits up on my abs, her pretty legs spread. I reach for her waist, taking my time drinking her in. "It's like you walked out of my wildest fantasies," I whisper, my cock throbbing at the mere sight of her. She moans when I drag my thumb across her pussy, coating it. "Just look at you," I groan. "You're dripping all over my abs, and fuck if it isn't the sexiest thing I've ever seen."

"You're outrageous," she says, shyness overtaking her expression. It's clear she doesn't believe me, but she will by the time I'm through with her.

"Come here," I murmur. "I want you to sit on my face."

"W-What?"

I grab her ass and knead, loving how soft her skin is. "You can't present me with something so delicious and not even give me a taste. Come here, baby." She gasps when I lift her effortlessly, until I've got her right where I want her, her thighs on either side of my head.

"Archer," she groans when I tighten my grip on her hips, my tongue darting out to caress her. *"Oh God."*

"Don't hold up your weight like that," I warn, nipping at her thigh. "I told you to sit on my face, so *sit on it*. Ride my face, darling."

Our eyes lock as she lowers her body, giving me what I asked for. Fuck, I don't think I've ever wanted to please a woman as much as I do her. I want her to think of nothing but me—I want to be the man she'll always compare everyone else to.

"Is this okay?" she asks, rotating her hips just a little, her breathing heavy as she slowly but surely lets go and begins to guide my tongue. I moan my approval, and she reaches for my headboard. The way she moves her hips drives me completely fucking wild, and she doesn't even know it.

I watch her chase an orgasm, putting her own pleasure first as she rides my tongue, and it's the biggest fucking turn-on I've ever experienced.

She looks at me with so much faith, like I'm her lifeline, her escape, and *fuck*, I've never wanted to be someone's safe haven, but I do when it's her. I want to be the one she turns to, the one that takes away all her worries, replacing them with pleasure instead.

Her legs begin to shake, and I increase my pace, flicking against her clit harder, until my beautiful girl comes on my tongue, her eyes never leaving mine. She smiles at me as she comes off her high, and it does something to me, makes my heart skip a beat.

"I want more," she whispers, moving down, until she's sitting on my thighs, my cock right between her legs. She grabs it and looks at me, her gaze overflowing with desire.

I groan when she lifts her hips and lines up my cock, her head falling back a little as the tip slides in. "*Fuck*," I moan, reaching for her just as she lowers her weight on top of me, taking all of me.

She has no idea what she does—every single touch breathes life back into me, and it's fucking terrifying. My best friend's little sister was never supposed to affect me like this.

Twenty-Four

SERENITY

I sigh happily as Archer's arm wraps around my waist, his lips pressing against the back of my neck as he spoons me. "Wake up, darling," he murmurs, kissing me over and over again. "You need to get ready for work."

"I don't wanna go to work," I complain, still half-asleep.

Archer chuckles, and I blink lazily, only to freeze when I remember where I am. I fell asleep in Archer's bed again. It's been happening far more often than it should, but he doesn't look remotely annoyed to have me here. "So beautiful," he murmurs, his gaze darkening.

I sit up and reach for my hair self-consciously, the sheet falling away in the process. "Oh God," I murmur. "What time is it? I'm going to be late."

"It's still early, baby. Don't rush out just yet." Archer visibly struggles to tear his gaze off me, but eventually, he manages to nod at my nightstand. "Made you coffee," he tells me. "I've got your lunch packed and waiting for you in the kitchen too."

I pull the sheet up and reach for the mug, my stomach fluttering as I take a sip. "Archer," I whisper. "The silk sheets, coffee in the morning… Don't you…um, don't you think you're treating me a bit too well? I don't want to be an inconvenience to you, so please don't think you need to do these kinds of things for me. I'm well aware of what we are and what we aren't."

His expression hardens, something akin to anger crossing his face. "What do you take me for?" he asks, running a hand through his hair as he sits up to face me, the sheet bunching around his waist, his muscular torso and the waistband of his black boxer shorts on display for me. "You can't truly believe I'll happily fuck you but treat you dismissively outside of bed." He reaches for me and gently pushes one of my curls out of my face. "I thought I made it clear that you're mine for the time being, Serenity. I have every intention of treating you as such, so you'll never accept anything less than you deserve."

"You'll ruin me for everyone else," I murmur, hiding my face behind my coffee cup. It's strange to be sitting in bed with him in the morning. It's almost like the time we spend in his bedroom is sacred, like he's an entirely different person between these four walls. Right here, right now, he isn't my brother's best friend nor is he my boss. He's just mine.

Archer grins at me unapologetically, almost like he enjoys the idea of it. "Get ready. I'll drive you to work."

I narrow my eyes at him and shake my head. "No," I tell him as I slip out of his bed, loving the way his breath hitches when he lays his eyes on my bare body. He makes me feel so comfortable in my own skin, and his attention is something I've come to revel in.

"*Darling*," he begins to say, a sexy smirk on his face. "Come on, I'm just giving you a ride. Call it repayment for the way you rode *me* last night."

I gasp, and then I burst out laughing. "That was… Wow."

He chuckles and leans back in bed as I reach for my clothes, finding them all neatly folded on a chair in the corner of his room, along with one of his T-shirts. "I really love hearing you laugh," he says, his voice soft.

My heart skips a beat, and I glance over my shoulder, thrown off by the way he's making me feel. "Ezra is going to wonder where I was last night," I tell him as I reach for his tee and pull it over my head. If he asks, I'll just tell him I spent the night at Theo and Kristen's house, but I never should've stayed over while Ezra is just a few doors down. He's rarely here, but when he is, he's a little overbearing.

My words wipe his smile off his face, and I look down when I see guilt flicker in his eyes. "He's not scheduled to go on another business trip for about two weeks now."

I nod, and Archer stares at me longingly.

"I like having you in my bed at night," he tells me. "Honestly, I hate having to rush, and it just doesn't feel right to have sex and then go our separate ways."

"I like it too," I admit. Something about falling asleep in his arms soothes my aching heart. It makes me feel wanted for more than just my body, and though I'd never have dared ask for it, it's exactly what I needed. "But we have to be careful. Ezra can't find out about us. All of the reasons you initially told me we shouldn't do this still hold true."

He buries a hand in his hair, and I soak in this sight of him leaning back in bed, his muscles on display. "I know," he murmurs. "I know, but I don't particularly like it. I warned you, didn't I? I'm an all-or-nothing kind of guy, and I'm too old to be sneaking around."

I tense, a deep ache settling in my chest. "I get it," I tell him, my voice soft. "If you…if this is all too much, we don't have to continue. I'll still give you the painting. Honestly, I'm already really grateful you made my first time so good, and I understand if—"

"How did you get there when what I was trying to say is that I hate having to hide you, *us*?" He rises from his bed and walks up to me, his gaze unwavering as he cups my face. "You promised me we'd communicate with each other, didn't you? No assumptions, no misinterpreting things. All I'm saying is that I'm not loving that I can't even drive you to work, that I have to pretend you're just another employee at the office, and on top of that, I can't have you while Ezra is around. That's *all* I'm saying."

I nod and step closer to him, my hands sliding around the back of his neck. "I'm sorry," I whisper. "I'm not used to this, Arch."

He grabs my waist, his eyes on mine. "Nor am I," he says, sighing. "In many ways, this is new to me too." He reaches for one of my curls and wraps it around his finger. "I guess the real problem here is that I can't get enough of you."

I grin at him, my heart pounding wildly. "The feeling is entirely mutual." I hesitate, and then I rise to my tiptoes to press a kiss to his cheek. "I'll see you at work, okay? I know you don't want to sneak around—"

"For you I will," he says, looking at me in a new way, like he genuinely cares about me in a way he didn't before.

Twenty-Five

ARCHER

I frown when the intercom on my desk buzzes, announcing a guest I didn't expect. I sit up as Zane walks into my office moments later, a man I don't recognize by his side. His visit completely catches me by surprise, and it takes me a moment to rise from my seat.

"Zane," I murmur.

He smiles tightly, seemingly still somewhat awkward around me. I've gone home a couple of times to check up on Celeste on weekends when Ezra's been here, and Zane and I have gotten a little closer, but we're still miles off from how we used to treat each other.

"Apologies for dropping by unannounced," he says, sounding hesitant, like part of him genuinely thought I'd turn him away. He's been on my list of approved visitors for years, and that'll never change. "I wanted to introduce you to Elijah Kingston, but making it happen was all quite short notice."

I tense as the name rings a bell, my movements stiff as I shake the hand of a man very few have ever met. Elijah Kingston is one of four Kingston brothers, and the most elusive of them. They call him the

King of Spades, and though he supposedly runs the Kingston family's parent company, rumor has it that's just a front. More than once, I've heard substantial rumors claiming Elijah Kingston was behind successful presidential campaigns and the rise and fall of several large companies. The man single-handedly influences the world economy however he sees fit, without anyone realizing. Elijah Kingston is the man you turn to when no one else can help you, but making a deal with him is no different to making a deal with the devil.

I look into his dark eyes, entirely unable to get a read on him. He smiles, seemingly politely, but something about him is unsettling. He strikes me as the kind of man with no conscience, which is likely exactly how he transformed the Kingston family's reputation, almost entirely removing all their visible ties to organized crime, turning one of his brothers into a politician and the others into respectable and generous business owners. You can't do that without getting your hands dirty.

"I didn't know," Zane says, looking down. "I didn't hear about Tyra until Celeste told me a few days ago. I know my words don't mean anything so long after the fact, but had I known, I'd have been there for you, Archer. The moment I found out, I reached out to Silas Sinclair, but he specializes in personal security and wasn't able to help."

He glances at Elijah then. "I asked one of my friends for a personal favor. I can't make any promises, but if anyone can find her, it's Elijah." He runs a hand through his hair and sighs. "I get what it's like to need answers, to need closure. I know this won't make up for all the harm I did in the last few years, but consider it an olive branch."

I nod, surprised by the gesture. I know Zane well enough to hear the words he isn't saying. He's sorry I got caught in the crossfire when Celeste ended things with him years ago, and he's trying to get back to where we used to be. Maybe we'll never be as close as brothers again, but I appreciate his efforts.

"Tell me everything you know," Elijah says, and I do, recounting every detail, every clue I've uncovered that led nowhere. He listens patiently and takes notes, his face completely emotionless. It takes me a moment to realize why his behavior seems so familiar—he's acting the way every law enforcement agent did when they interviewed me about Tyra. It's entirely at odds with the rumors about him, and I'm not sure what to make of it.

"There are police investigative reports," I tell him, concluding my recap, and he nods as he glances at his tablet.

"I'll review those," he says.

I begin to tell him that they're classified, only for him to shut me up with a smile. Right. Nothing is classified to a man like him.

"I'll do what I can," he says, his gaze drifting away. "I know what it's like to live with uncertainty. It's almost like your whole life is on hold, like you need permission to live, even knowing you'll never get it. I don't know if we'll find her, Mr. Harrison, but I'll do everything in my power to make it happen."

I nod and shake his hand, oddly reassured by the look in his eyes. He looks like someone that truly gets it, but I can't tell if it's genuine or not. "Thank you," I tell him, feeling lighter than I have in a while. "Both of you."

Zane nods and steps backs, a hint of discomfort in his expression, like he wishes he could do more when he's already given me more hope than he can imagine.

I sit as the two men walk away, involuntarily reaching for the charm around my neck. *Permission to live.* I didn't even realize that's how I feel until Elijah voiced it. I feel like I'm not allowed to move on until we know what happened to Tyra, and for so long, I didn't even try. In the last couple of days, the guilt has started to turn into resentment, and I suspect it has everything to do with Serenity.

I'm on autopilot as I walk out of my office in search of a glimpse of her. It's become my favorite hobby, and I take a moment to enjoy it, watching her bite on the edge of her pen as she thinks, before scribbling something down on the countless to-do lists she loves to stick to her monitor.

Being with her was supposed to be simple, but somehow, the thought of this thing between us being temporary doesn't sit well with me. "Fuck," I mutter to myself when she leans back in her seat, the sunlight hitting her face beautifully.

She looks up and finds me staring at her, her expression instantly showing that she's flustered. She doesn't know, does she? She makes me want to live again—fully. I'm enthralled as she rises from her seat, her eyes moving around furtively as she walks past me and looks back, our eyes locking before she disappears around the corner. I grin before following her, my heart skipping a beat when I realize she's headed to my office.

Serenity gasps when I pull her against me moments after my door closes behind us, my hand cupping the back of her neck, her eyes on mine. "Archer," she breathes. "I just...I...um... You seemed like you needed—"

"You," I tell her, my head dipping down. "I needed you." *More than I even realized.* I don't know what it is about her. Maybe it's the fact that she knows me like no one else does, the way she's been there through it all and the way she shares my pain. I'm not sure what it is about her that allows me to let her in like I've let no one else—not even Tyra.

She sighs, her hands finding their way to my shoulders as she rises to her tiptoes and meets me halfway, my lips crashing against hers in a needy, all-consuming kind of way. She moans against my mouth, and it drives me fucking wild. I know I only have a few moments with her,

CATHARINA MAURA

but fuck, I wish I could carry her to my desk and make her scream my name for everyone to hear. My need to claim her, to mark her... it's new, not something I've ever felt before. This isn't escapism, like I thought it'd be. It's so much more, and it's everything she doesn't want.

I know exactly why Serenity chose me—because she didn't think I'd ever be serious about her. She thinks I'm emotionally unavailable, forever tied to Tyra, and I'm starting to wonder if that's true.

Twenty-Six

Serenity

"Where are we going?" I ask, my eyes wide as we park right in front of a private jet. Archer hasn't quite been himself in a couple of days now, so when he suddenly suggested going on an overnight trip while Ezra is away, I wasn't sure what to make of it.

Archer grins at me and takes my hand, entwining our fingers as he pulls me along. It's been a while since I've seen him smile so sincerely. I haven't pried, but it's clear something that happened last week upset him, and I suspect it has something to do with the two men I saw walking out his office, both of them clearly rich and powerful. I'm not sure if it's a business problem or something else, and I'm not sure how to help without being intrusive.

"The Netherlands," he says as he leads me onto the plane.

I gasp, pure giddiness rushing through me as I turn to face him, my hands wrapping over his arms. "Are we…are we going to—"

"To Keukenhof to see the one of the world's largest flower gardens?" he asks, smirking. "That's exactly what we're doing, darling. We're going to tick off the highest item on your to-do list. There's only a two-week window to see the flower displays you want to see, so we have to go today."

I stare at him in pure disbelief. A couple of weeks ago I saw him flicking through my endless to-do lists in bed, and he seemed to pay special attention to what I call my *Ultimate To-Do List*, my version of a bucket list. I didn't think much of it then, and never in a million years did I think he'd remember the items on them.

"Wow," I murmur, repeating the word over and over again as he kneels in front of my seat and buckles me in, pure amusement glittering in his eyes.

"God, I love making your dreams come true," he says, cupping my cheek. "There's nothing better in life than being the reason behind your smile. Nothing at all."

I look into his eyes and wrap my hand around the back of his neck without thinking. He chuckles as I pull him closer, my lips finding his. I'm not sure what I was expecting when I put his name on my list, but this is so much more.

"Fuck," he whispers against my mouth, his forehead dropping against mine. "I can't wait till we're airborne so I can carry you to the bedroom in the back. I'm going to make you ride my cock as we fly over the clouds, your moans filling the cabin."

I smirk and take his bottom lip between my teeth teasingly before letting go. "I can't wait."

He groans as he pulls away, his cheeks a little flushed and his erection obvious in those sweats I love. I can't help but giggle as he sits down opposite me and readjusts himself, frustration written all over his face. The way he wants me never gets old.

Archer looks into my eyes the moment the seat belt sign is turned off, and he smirks as he reaches inside his sweats. I stare at him, wide-eyed, as he takes out his cock and wraps his hand around it. "See what you do to me?" he asks, pumping his hand up and down. "I can't even sit opposite you without wanting you."

I glance around furtively, and he chuckles. "Don't worry, darling. I instructed the flight crew not to walk into the cabin unless there's an emergency. They won't disturb us."

"Is that so?" I murmur, unclasping my seat belt.

Archer raises a brow when I rise from my seat, only to drop to my knees in front of him. He seems shell-shocked, and I can't help but laugh. "What did you think I'd do if you teased me like that?" I ask, replacing his hand with mine.

He moans when I squeeze hard as I move my hand down, holding the base of his cock while I lean in, my tongue darting out to caress the tip. "Fuck, Serenity. What are you doing?"

I grin up at him, confidence blending with desire. He does that to me—makes me feel empowered and sexy in a way I didn't before. "Place your hands on the armrests," I tell him.

His eyes flash defiantly, but he does as I asked. Archer has never denied me anything, and I don't think he ever will. I've never felt as spoiled as I do with him, as well taken care of. There's nothing I could ask for that he wouldn't give me, whether that be his time or thousands of dollars of painting supplies that I'll only use a handful of times.

"What is this? Payback for the way I pulled you into my office after that meeting last week?" he asks, squeezing his armrests as I take him into my mouth, my tongue swirling experimentally. My heart begins to race at the memory of him telling me to hold on to the edges of his desk as he laid me out on top of it and buried his face between my legs, instructing me not to come unless he told me to—all because he'd been jealous of the way Mark kept looking at me throughout the meeting. He's pettier than I'd ever thought possible, and I love the way he gets all possessive when he's jealous.

I suck hard and slowly take him in deeper, my entire body reacting to the way he feels against my tongue. Our eyes lock as I begin to move a little, my movements cautious and inexperienced. He smiles at me with eyes heavy with desire, and he sighs happily as he watches me suck him off.

"You're such a good girl," he whispers, caressing me with his gaze. "You're perfect for me, aren't you? Look at the way you take my cock, darling. It was made for you, did you know that?"

I hum, pleased with his praise, and he moans, his hips rocking as I increase my pace. I watch as he slowly loses his composure, his hand moving into my hair as he guides me. "Fucking gorgeous," he murmurs. "How are you mine? How the fuck did I get this lucky?"

I moan, loving that look in his eyes. He does this sometimes. When he's in the throes of passion, he says whatever is on his mind, and over time, his little whispers have become more endearing, more loving. Archer grunts and pulls my head away moments before he comes, catching it with his hands, his breathing erratic.

I let out a disappointed little sound, and he stares at me lazily. "I'd have swallowed," I tell him, and that look in his eyes...I have a feeling it's one I'll always remember.

Twenty-Seven

ARCHER

I'm completely enthralled as we enter Keukenhof—not by the endless flowers, some of them forming either 3D art installations, or 2D ones that can only be viewed from certain angles, but by Serenity and her endless excitement.

I've never met anyone who enjoys things so thoroughly, who lives so fully. She gives everything her all, and it's fucking inspiring to witness. Just being around her reminds me to live more in the moment, to be more present. In just a few months, she's taught me more than she realizes, more than I ever could've anticipated. She's changed me for the better, and I didn't even realize how bad of a state I was in before her.

"Wow, it's so empty," she says, entwining our hands as she pulls me through the park, her eyes glittering as she takes everything in. "This park is only open for a few weeks a year, so I'm surprised it isn't packed."

I fall into step with her as I gently guide her where I want her to go. "That's because I booked out the whole place for you today. You've wanted to come here for so long now, and I wanted to make sure you could see everything you wanted to without having to squeeze past people or queue."

She pauses in the middle of the path we're on and turns to face me, pure disbelief in her eyes. "You did that for me?" she asks, her voice high-pitched, a hint of panic in it. "Archer, that would've cost thousands of dollars."

Just over a million, actually. I smile and step closer to her, my touch gentle as I brush her curls out of her face. "You're worth it."

She looks into my eyes, her gaze soft and filled with an emotion I don't dare name. Things have rapidly changed between us, and I don't think either of us ever saw it coming. We were never meant to fit together so well, but we do, and I'd be a fool not to enjoy every second I get with her.

Serenity rises to her tiptoes, and I sigh when her hand wraps around the back of my neck before she pulls me in for a kiss. Being with her feels magical, and even more so as we're surrounded by flowers everywhere, the sun shining down on us.

I pull back and reach for my phone, and she grins as she instantly brings her face closer for a photo. It's something I've started to do recently—capturing the fun things we do together, the places we see. It's odd because I've never had an interest in capturing moments to keep for years to come, but with her I do. In a matter of weeks, I've accumulated hundreds of photos of us together or just of her—painting, working, sitting on my kitchen island in nothing but my T-shirt as she watches me cook for her.

"Come on," I tell her, resuming our walk. "I have a surprise for you."

I wonder if this moment is as precious to her as it is to me. I can't recall the last time I felt so truly at peace. Being here with her, walking side by side, her hand in mine as the sun shines down on us…it's a relatively simple moment, but fuck if it isn't beautiful. What is it about her that suddenly makes me appreciate the little things when I never did before?

"*Archer,*" she says, her voice trembling as we reach the end of the path and the start of endless rows of pink tulips, her favorite flower. Another path runs in between two of the rows, and on it, there's a full picnic waiting for us. I know that's not what's got her so emotional, though. It's the easel I had set up for her, with all of her favorite painting supplies on a small table next to it.

She turns to look at me, her eyes rapidly filling with tears. It makes me panic instantly, and I grab her face, my heart racing. "Don't cry," I beg, unsure where I went wrong. "This was supposed to make you happy, darling. We don't have to—"

She rises to her tiptoes, her hands balling in my T-shirt as she pulls me close and kisses me. I groan and cup the back of her neck, my heart aching when I feel a tear drop down her cheek and onto mine. "I'm just happy," she says, pulling back. "This is just such a big dream come true, and I'm just really happy to be here with you."

"So they're happy tears?" I murmur, swiping them away with my thumbs.

She nods, and I breathe a sigh of relief as I press a soft kiss to her forehead, my heart overflowing with an unfamiliar emotion. "The happiest of tears," she promises, grinning at me in that way that makes the butterflies in my stomach go wild.

"Go on then," I murmur, noting the building excitement in her expression. "I know you're dying to paint."

She does that little excited jump that I love and turns around, her dress swaying before she runs toward the flower field, leaving me standing here, laughing as I follow her. I watch her and open up the champagne as she sets up, having become familiar with her process.

CATHARINA MAURA

The moment that brush of hers touches her canvas, everything fades way. Everything but me. I'd like to believe that I'm the only one that can draw her attention away from her canvas without earning her ire. I hand her a glass of champagne, and she smiles at me, her expression conveying pure contentment. "To us," I murmur, tapping my glass to hers.

"To us," she repeats, her eyes on mine as she takes a sip. I can tell she's trying to give me her attention when all she wants to do is paint, and something about that is so fucking endearing.

"Let me watch you paint," I tell her. "You're always beautiful, but when you're painting, you're fucking otherworldly."

Her expression shows that she's flustered, and she grins before she turns her back to me and begins to capture the scene around us. I wonder if she realizes that her art has been a little lighter these days, when it used to be far more somber.

I watch her lose herself in her work as I sit back and go over some paperwork, patiently waiting for her attention to wane as the sun slowly begins to lower, hours passing by. Eventually, Serenity lifts her canvas off the easel and places it on the ground, leaning over it to paint from a different angle and giving me one hell of a view of her ass.

I groan and approach her, startling her as I push her white dress up to her waist before pulling down her thong. "Keep painting," I tell her as I lean in for a taste. "Keep losing yourself in your favorite hobby, darling, and in the meantime, I'll lose myself in mine."

Twenty-Eight

SERENITY

"God, I'm so tired," Theo tells me as I pack my bag, glad our workday seems to have flown by for once. I nod absent-mindedly, my mind on Ezra and finding a way to see Archer tonight without making him suspicious. He got back home yesterday and doesn't have a trip scheduled for another two weeks. It makes me feel terrible, but I kind of wish we weren't living together, so I wouldn't have to explain my absence.

I wasn't sure what to expect when Archer and I started seeing each other, but I definitely never expected him to make me feel so cherished and wanted. I didn't think he'd fulfill emotional needs that I didn't even realize I had.

"Serenity?"

"Hmm?" I murmur, snapping out of my thoughts to find Theo staring at me, his chair close to mine.

"Did you even hear a word I said?" Theo asks, frustrated.

"I'm sorry," I tell him, realizing I've been entirely unable to focus on him because I was thinking of Archer. "What were you saying? I just didn't really sleep well last night, and honestly, I'm ready for bed."

I managed to sneak out of the house late last night, surprising Archer in bed. Having to wait till I'm sure Ezra is fast asleep is exhausting, and having to sneak back in early in the morning leaves me with very little time to actually sleep.

Theo stares at me, his gaze conflicted. "You've been like this for a while now, a bit absent-minded. Even when you came over for dinner, you were mostly on your phone." He hesitates, and my stomach drops. I'm not sure I can lie to him if he asks me anything outright. If Kristen hadn't interrupted at dinner, I probably would've admitted who I was texting then.

"Come to think of it, I forgot to thank Kristen that day," I rush to say, eager to change the topic as I rise to my feet. "That pasta she made was incredible, and the wine was too. I had a great time."

He blinks in confusion as he falls into step with me. "You did?" he asks, his voice tinged with disbelief.

I grin at him. "Of course," I lie. "I got to hang out with two of my closest friends and have some of my favorite food. What's not to love?" The lies come easier now, the words feeling lighter. This is exactly what I'd hoped to be able to do someday—at least *pretend* I'm happy for them. If not for Archer, I may never have managed it.

"I see," he says as we pause in front of the elevator, his tone not quite what I expected it to be. He sounds conflicted. Does he realize I'm merely pretending?

"Serenity. Theo."

I look up to find Archer walking up to us, and my heart skips a beat as I take in the pinstripe three-piece suit he's wearing. All day, I expected to catch a glimpse of him, only to be disappointed. I didn't think I'd see him until tonight, if at all, and I can't help but smile despite my fluster.

"Mr. Harrison," I say, loving the way his gaze darkens as it briefly roams over the red dress I'm wearing today. He keeps his face impassive, but I've learned to read his eyes, and I know he likes what he's seeing.

"On your way home?" he asks, his tone polite and friendly, even as he steps between Theo and me.

"We are," Theo says, sounding a little frustrated. "I thought maybe we could go grab that ice cream you said you wanted to try on our way home?"

Archer's fingers brush against mine, and my heart begins to beat a little faster. "Maybe some other time," I tell Theo just as the elevator doors open. Ezra is still in a meeting, so Archer and I only have an hour or so before he gets home, and I'd like to make the most of it.

He leans back in the elevator, still standing between Theo and me, a surprisingly smug smile on his face. "Can I offer you a ride, Serenity?"

My gaze cuts to his, and I bite back a smile as heat rushes to my cheeks, my mind replaying what he texted me an hour ago. *I need you to ride my cock, darling.*

"I'd love that," I tell him, reveling in the way he smirks, the two of us enjoying our little inside joke.

"How about tomorrow?" Theo asks. "Let me buy you some ice cream tomorrow. You used to love getting ice cream together, and I don't want to let that tradition die."

I tense, longing emanating from my chest. He's right. Those were moments I really looked forward to, when it'd just be me and him after class, and we'd talk about anything and everything. "Sounds good," I tell him.

Archer tenses beside me and places his hand on my lower back. "Let's go," he says, his tone a little colder now as he leads me to his car. He holds the door open for me as usual, but he doesn't quite look at me.

"You're mad," I murmur when he still hasn't said a word halfway home.

"No," he says, denying it. "I'm jealous."

I turn my head, my lips parting in surprise. "What? Why would you be jealous?"

He reaches for me and places his hand on my thigh, just under the hem of my dress. "I told you that I don't share, Serenity. I wasn't referring to just your body. I hate the idea of you sitting next to him, having ice cream together and pretending it's a fucking date."

I place my hand over his, unsure what to say. "He's got a girlfriend. I'm not delusional, Archer. I know I can't have him, that it's not a date. The reason I'm trying so hard to get over Theo is so I can preserve my friendship with him. Avoiding him altogether isn't going to help."

He pulls his hand away as he parks the car. "I see," he tells me, throwing me a polite smile before getting out of the car and walking around it.

"Archer," I murmur as we step into the elevator together. "Don't be jealous…" He raises a brow when I push against his chest, until I've got him pressed against the wall. I move to stand between his legs and rise to my tiptoes, our eyes locking before I lean in and kiss him. He groans in approval and cups the back of my head as he deepens our kiss, his movements languid, teasing.

I squirm against him, and he chuckles against my lips. "Darling," he whispers, just as the elevator chimes. I step back, and he reaches for my hand with a smile on his face. I grin at him as he pulls me to his door, letting go of me to unlock it.

We walk in, only to pause when we find Ezra standing in Archer's living room, a beer in his hand. He frowns when he sees me, and my stomach drops.

Twenty-Nine

ARCHER

"What are you doing here?" Ezra asks his sister, looking straight past me, confusion flickering through his eyes.

I hold up my hand and shake my head. "I think the better question here is why the fuck are *you* in my house, drinking my beer?" My heart races as I try to recall what Sera and I must've looked like as we walked in together. I wasn't holding her hand, but had we been smiling a little too widely? Was I looking at her with my desires written all over my face? "You gave me a near heart attack."

Ezra smiles, but it doesn't reach his eyes. "Couldn't help myself. I have no idea how you keep getting your hands on these niche micro-brews, but they're something else." His gaze returns to his sister, and it's clear he expects an answer to his question.

"Archer told me I could use his guest room to paint in since he doesn't use it," Serenity says, walking past me to hug her brother. Her tone is light and calm, but I notice the way her hands tremble just a touch. My girl is as rattled as I am. "More importantly, I thought you had a client meeting?"

He wraps his arm around Serenity, his gaze roaming over her face. "Work wrapped up earlier than expected, so I managed to get home early for once."

I shrug out of my suit jacket, and Serenity's eyes flick to my chest before she drags them away. I try my best not to smile, not wanting to make Ezra even more suspicious than he already is, but it's hard to resist when she looks at me with such regret, like she wishes she could've been the one to undress me.

"So you came over to paint?" Ezra asks, letting go of Serenity to move toward my guest room, like he doesn't believe her. "You never said anything when we spoke about you picking up painting again."

She nods and follows him, wringing her hands nervously. I can pretty much guess what she's thinking. She's wondering if we left any evidence of us anywhere but my bedroom. Since we started sleeping together, I've started to find her hair everywhere, but I don't think it's the kind of thing Ezra would notice.

Ezra opens the door and freezes at the sight of the easel in the corner, his expression changing as he takes in the silhouette Serenity started to paint. He turns to look at me, surprise flickering through his eyes. "What is that?" he asks, almost like he's hoping it isn't what he knows it is.

Serenity steps forward. "It's the price Archer asked me to pay for the favor he granted me," she tells him, clearly trying to stay as close to the truth as possible, and it makes me feel like shit. "It's a replica of The Muse's ballerina piece." It's one of many canvases in the room, and the one she works on least frequently, but it's unmissable.

Ezra's gaze cuts to hers, and he searches her face. For what, I'm not quite sure. His jaw clenches as he turns to look at me. "I'm surprised you're letting Serenity use your guest room when you normally don't tolerate anyone but me invading your space or privacy."

Serenity tenses, and she looks down, hiding her face from me. Something about the way her shoulders droop doesn't sit well with me. The last thing I want is for her to feel unwanted in my home.

I sigh and wrap an arm around her shoulders, causing her to tense. She looks up at me sharply, seemingly having forgotten that me holding her this way isn't anything new. "Honestly, I only barely tolerate you, Ezra. Letting Sera use my guest room in return for an original Serenity Adesina painting, however, is hardly a bad deal."

I squeeze Serenity's shoulder reassuringly, needing her to know that Ezra's words and opinion don't matter. "You're both being weird," she says, stepping away and into the room. Ezra straightens when she throws him an irritated look. "Is there a problem with me coming over to paint?" she asks pointedly.

"No," I reply instantly, before Ezra can. "He's just giving me shit because that's what I did to him when he started spending time with Celeste."

Ezra sighs and runs a hand through his hair. "I'm just surprised," he says, his voice weak. "You never even told me that you'd started painting again, let alone that you have a whole room filled with supplies in Archer's house."

She walks up to her brother, her expression placating. "I'm sorry," she murmurs. "You've been gone so much, and I didn't think much of it. I already took up your guest room, but Archer's was free, so it just made sense to paint here."

He nods and brushes one of her curls out of her face. "I wish you'd told me, but regardless, I'd rather you paint here than—" Serenity's eyes widen, and Ezra snaps his mouth shut for a moment. "Than somewhere Mom would see it," he finishes weakly.

Serenity's expression falls, and she looks down, looking utterly defeated, and it takes all of me not to pull her into my arms.

Ezra mutters something under his breath and raises his hand to his head to squeeze his curly hair. "That was the wrong thing to say," he admits. "I wasn't thinking, Ser. I'm sorry. You can paint wherever you want. Remember what I told you?"

She nods and forces a smile, and all the while, I wonder how I missed it. She didn't stop painting because she wasn't interested in it anymore—she stopped because of her mother.

"Speaking of Mom," Serenity says, her voice weak, "it's her birthday next month and we need to choose a gift." She glances at her easel, and it's clear she wishes she could paint something for her mother. It's unbelievable to me that anyone could look at Serenity's work and not see how fucking priceless it is.

"You're coming home with us, right?" Ezra asks, lifting his beer bottle to his mouth.

I nod and pull my tie loose. "Of course. I'd never hear the end of it if I missed your mom's birthday."

He nods as he begins to run me through gift ideas, and I glance back at Serenity as he walks out of the room. "He clearly has no intention of leaving anytime soon," I murmur.

She looks at the door and nods. "I do actually need to paint for an hour or so today," she says, turning her back to me. "I owe you a painting, after all. Gotta hold up my end of the bargain."

"Serenity."

She looks over her shoulder, but her eyes don't quite meet mine. "You'd better go before Ezra gets even more suspicious than he already is."

I nod, my heart heavy as I walk out of the room. This is not how I thought my evening would go. Fucking hell. I'd planned to make her forget all about Theo and his goddamn ice cream. I wanted her to still feel me between her legs by the time she sees him tomorrow, but I'll be lucky if I even get to steal a single kiss from her now.

Ezra looks up from my sofa, and I sigh as I sink down next to him. I've never minded his penchant for showing up at my place uninvited, especially since he let Celeste live in his home for years while he took my guest room, but today I wish he hadn't.

"You're having her paint Tyra," he says, and I tense, staring ahead. "Fuck, she finally picks up painting again, and that's what you're having her paint? You know how much she loved Tyra, and it'll kill Serenity to paint her for you."

I bury a hand in my hair and look away, unable to refute his words. The worst part is that this isn't about Tyra anymore. It never really was, and it took me a while to realize that. "I'm trying to let her go," I admit.

He looks at me like he doesn't believe me, his gaze filled with pity. "Is that why my sister is currently in your spare room, painting an image that you'll keep forever?"

Thirty

ARCHER

I lean back on the bed in my guest room, my laptop on my lap. I'm supposed to be working, but all I can focus on is Serenity and that look in her eyes as she paints. She's completely consumed by it, and it's such a beautiful fucking sight that I can't tear my eyes off her for more than a few seconds. It doesn't help that she's wearing nothing but a loose T-shirt of mine.

She's working on *The Ballerina*, but seeing it doesn't do anything to me anymore. I didn't even realize that until Ezra seemed distraught at the sight of it. When I look at that painting, all I can think of is Serenity—not Tyra.

I don't know how she's done it, how she's managed to occupy all of my thoughts, but she has. There's no space for anything but her, and as time passes, I feel less guilty about it. It might be wishful thinking, but I'd like to believe that Tyra would've wanted us both to be happy.

"Darling," I murmur, closing my laptop. I don't know why I even bother anymore. I can barely get any work done when I'm in the same room as Serenity. We've fallen into a routine that I'm enjoying more than I should, and we've taken to spending nearly every free second we've got together. I've begun looking forward to weeks that Ezra isn't here, and I know she has too. "Come here."

She glances at me and narrows her eyes in annoyance, but even so, she puts her brush down and joins me, sitting down on the edge of the bed. I love how she always puts me first, even when she'd rather be painting. I wonder if she realizes what that means to me. No one has ever put me first like that. Not even Tyra.

"What is it?" she asks, placing her hand on my thigh.

I smirk at her as I pull my T-shirt over my head, quietly appreciating the way all her irritation melts away as she drinks me in, her eyes roaming over my chest and abs, desire for me rapidly chasing away her desire to paint.

"I have an idea, baby."

She groans, unable to drag her eyes off my abs. "You're playing dirty again, I see," she murmurs, her gaze settling on the charm around my neck for a few seconds.

Trying to distract her while she paints has become one of my favorite hobbies, and I'm not even sure why. Stealing her attention away from something she loves so dearly makes me feel so fucking wanted, it's surreal. "I want you to paint something on my chest."

Her eyes widen. "What?"

I grab her hand and make her fingers trail up my abs, until I've got her palm pressed flat against my chest, my hand over hers. "Right here. You want to paint, and I want to watch every single expression on your face as you do so, so paint something on me."

"That's a terrible idea," she says, her voice weak. "The paint I use isn't good for your skin."

I laugh and shake my head. "Then why have you always got it all over your body? Keeping it on for a few hours won't hurt me. Please?"

Her eyes roam over my body, and my stomach clenches when she nods. "What do you want me to paint?" she asks as she grabs a few brushes and her paint board.

"Your happiest memory of us," I tell her as she straddles me.

Her expression softens, and my hands wrap around her waist. I smirk as I push the T-shirt she's wearing up, and she chuckles as she raises her arms for me, letting me take it off. "I thought you said you wanted me to paint?" she reminds me, her eyes twinkling as I look at her naked body hungrily.

"I do," I groan, pulling her closer so she's sitting on my abs. "But I also told you that I wanted to watch you as you do it. So let me look at you—all of you."

Now she smirks at me as she begins to paint, eliciting a gasp from me. "Is the paint cold?" she asks.

I nod and squeeze her ass. "It's fine. I've got you to keep me warm."

I watch her as she transforms my chest, cataloging all of her expressions—the way she scrunches her brows and purses her lips in the sexiest way as she tries to focus. The way she tenses her abs when she can't figure out which color to use, and the way she smiles when everything blends together the way she imagined it. She's easily the most beautiful woman I've ever met, but right here, right now, she's the prettiest version of herself I've ever seen.

Serenity bites on her lip when I trail my hands up, until I'm cupping her breasts, my thumbs stroking her nipples until they harden for me. Her breathing becomes more shallow, but she doesn't stop painting. I grin as I slide a finger down her ribs and in between her legs, loving the way her breath hitches when I caress the inside of her thighs, taking my time to play with her body, touching every part of her I can reach.

It doesn't take long for her to get wet, and I groan when she shifts a little on my abs, her wetness spreading over my body. It's not enough—I want her dripping for me, but I've got time.

"*Archer*," she warns when I begin to massage her thighs, my thumb just about brushing her clit every once in a while.

"Hmm?" I murmur, loving the way her eyes have become glassy, the way she's struggling to focus on painting. "Am I distracting you?"

"*No*," she retorts, throwing me a sexy little glare before she continues to paint. "Not at all."

I chuckle as I reach for one of her brand-new paintbrushes and begin to caress her nipples with it, earning myself some beautiful moans. She's breathing hard, turned on beyond measure, but she won't stop painting. Her artwork is starting to take shape now, and my heart warms when I realize she's painting the day I took her to the flower field—it's my favorite memory of us too. In the weeks since then, I've taken her on weekends away every time Ezra's been gone, showing her every art gallery she's wanted to see while she accompanies me to try all kinds of food all over the world—but that day in the flower field is still my favorite, and I'm glad it's hers too.

I smirk as I drag the paintbrush down her stomach, and her eyes flutter closed when it disappears between her legs, caressing her clit. "*Archer*," she repeats, her tone pleading now.

"I love the way you moan my name."

Her eyes lock with mine, and she glares at me as she drops her brush on the bed and reaches behind her, roughly pushing my sweats down. My lips part in surprise when she lifts and repositions herself, one hand on my abs as she lowers herself on top of me, taking all of me.

"*Fuck*," I moan, my head falling back as desire rushes through me.

I stare at my girl in disbelief as she picks her brush back up and continues to paint, my cock deep inside her. "Lie still," she demands, even as she begins to rock on top of me, fucking me with shallow thrusts. "Don't even dream of coming until I'm done painting."

"You're kidding me," I tell her, my cock already throbbing.

She raises a brow and turns her paint board. "Do I look like I'm joking?"

I laugh—I can't help it. She's got me so fucking smitten, and I wouldn't have it any other way.

Thirty-One

SERENITY

"Tell me I'm not the only one who feels like we haven't spoken to each other in ages, even though I see you almost every day?" Theo says, falling into step with me as we walk out of the office. "Even just grabbing ice cream together ended up taking nearly two full weeks. It's crazy how things kept coming up."

I bite back a smile as I think back to all of Archer's attempts to keep me from going out with Theo. The things that kept coming up might have seemed coincidental to Theo, but they were anything but. "I know what you mean, but it was to be expected," I tell him. There's no way Archer was going to make things easy for Theo. "Work keeps us both so busy, and you've got Kristen. I saw the photos she's been posting of everything you two are doing on the weekends. Looks like you've nearly made your way through the list I made."

He tenses, his expression becoming apologetic. "You truly make the best to-do lists."

My stomach flutters as I think back to the one I made on which my only to-do was *Archer* "I'm glad you enjoyed it," I murmur, finally at peace with the fact that I didn't get to experience any of the things on my list with him.

We pause in front of the ice cream parlor we'd planned to go to, and I frown. "Under new management. Closed for renovations," I read out, surprised and mildly annoyed. "Ugh. I was really looking forward to trying their Ferrero Rocher flavor."

"It's okay," he tells me, placing his hand on my shoulder. "There's another one a few blocks away."

I nod and follow him, my gaze drifting to the arm he's kept around me. "Don't do that," I tell him, gently removing it.

Theo frowns. "Why not? I've always done that, Ser."

I pause and turn to face him. "I know, but you weren't dating Kristen before." I sigh and tuck one of my curls behind my ear. "Of course she knows that we're just friends and nothing would ever happen between us, but quite frankly, I wouldn't enjoy seeing my boyfriend being so physically close to another woman, no matter how long they've been friends."

I smile at him, and this time, it comes a little easier. Ultimately, I just want the people I love to be happy, and that includes Kristen. Besides, if Theo and I were meant to be, it would've happened far sooner. "I just think it's important to be respectful. I don't ever want to do anything that would hurt her, and I'm sure you feel the same way." Kristen and I aren't as close as we were, but I think with time, maybe we can be again.

His expression hardens. "I don't, actually." He steps closer to me and reaches for one of my curls. "When Kristen told me she wanted us to try dating, there's one thing I made incredibly clear to her. I didn't want anything between me and you to change, and if she didn't like the way you and I treat each other, I wasn't willing to try being with her at all."

"W-What?"

He cups my face, his eyes burning with something I've never seen before. "You've always been the most important woman in my life, Serenity. That didn't change just because I started dating Kristen, so stop avoiding me. Stop ignoring my texts, and stop keeping your distance. Do you have any idea how much I miss you? It's fucking torture to watch you sit so close to me at the office every damn day when I can feel the distance between us increase each time we talk."

I lean in to his touch, my heart racing. When he says things like that, the feelings I thought I'd suppressed come roaring back to life. "I didn't know you felt that way, Theo."

"No," he says, frustration ringing through his voice. "There's a lot you don't know." He sighs and pulls me into his arms, hugging me tightly, not a care for the fact that we're standing in the middle of the sidewalk. I breathe him in and hug him back, my head pressed to his chest.

"Just stop acting like we're no longer friends, okay?" he murmurs into my hair, his grip tight and reassuring. I'd gotten so used to Theo's long hugs, but now they don't feel quite right. His arms aren't quite big enough, and his body isn't quite hard enough.

It hits me then.

He feels off because he isn't Archer.

"I'm sorry," I tell him, pulling away to look at him. "I was just trying to do the right thing, for all three of us."

He places his index finger underneath my chin, and once again, I'm reminded of Archer. It's something he likes to do when I refuse to meet his eyes. "Don't decide what is right or wrong all by yourself. What's right to you feels entirely wrong to me."

I nod, and he smiles, his arm wrapping around me as he pulls me along, only for his smile to drop when we reach the next ice cream parlor and find that closed too. "What the fuck?" Theo says as we both stare at the same sign that was put up at the last place.

"I'll just google one nearby," I murmur, reaching for my phone. I unlock it and instantly turn away from Theo when I find a text message from Archer waiting for me.

> **ARCHER**
> how's your ice cream?

My stomach flutters, and I smile to myself as I text him back.

> **SERENITY**
> two of the places we tried going to were closed, so we're just walking around now.

My heart skips a beat when he texts me back instantly.

> **ARCHER**
> wow, that's so weird. I've got ice cream at home if you want it.

I bite on my lip when he sends me a photo of him on the sofa, gray sweats hanging low enough to expose his Adonis belt and his entire torso bare, a bowl of ice cream balancing on his thigh and the sexiest smirk on his face. Damn. Just the sight of him has me clenching my thighs.

"Found something?" Theo asks, moving closer. I lock my phone immediately, and he frowns. "What's wrong?"

"Oh, nothing," I tell him, trying my best not to act flustered even as I pull my phone to my chest.

He sees right though me, and something unfamiliar flickers through his eyes. "Who—" He shakes his head and buries a hand in his hair. "No, never mind," he says, reaching for his phone, his movements a little frantic. "Let me look up a place we can go to."

I study him, wondering why he didn't just ask me who I was texting. Was he respecting my privacy, or did he just not want to know?

Thirty-Two

ARCHER

"Shotgun!" Serenity yells over her shoulder as she runs past Ezra and places her hands on the front passenger door handle of my car, her eyes brimming with victory. *Fucking adorable.*

"You don't need the front seat," Ezra tells her, lifting her up and moving her out of the way. "Your legs aren't long enough to need the space."

She pushes him and switches places with him. "And we both know you're just going to sleep through most of the drive, so you may as well sit in the back."

Serenity looks at me for support, but I just shake my head and get behind the wheel of the new Windsor Motors car Zane gave me. He told me he gifted it to me so I could test it for his brother, but I know him well enough to realize he was just looking for an excuse to give me something he wanted me to have.

"Ezra!" I hear Serenity shout, but I know better than to get involved in sibling fights, so I simply start the car and turn on the seat heating before selecting a playlist. Sure enough, three minutes later, the doors open, and Serenity gets in next to me, while Ezra takes the back seat.

"I don't know why you even bother," I tell Ezra. "You have never, in your entire life, not given in to your sister."

He throws me an irritated look and yanks on the seat belt, putting it on angrily. Meanwhile, Serenity is beaming. "Oooh, seat heaters," she says, sighing happily.

My heart skips a beat at the sight of her smile, and I look away as I back out of my parking spot.

I try my hardest not to sneak looks at Serenity as I get on the highway, but I can't help myself. I've barely seen her since Ezra has been home all week, and I've missed her.

"I can't believe him," Serenity whispers, looking over her shoulder when Ezra begins to snore lightly not even thirty minutes into our journey to their parents' house. "I knew he was going to fall asleep straightaway."

I chuckle, amused by the level of her outrage when they've had this exact argument at least a hundred times. "You got the front seat, like you wanted," I remind her.

She huffs and reaches for my phone. "Can I change the music?"

I nod, only to hesitate when she points my phone my way. "The code is 0105." Her expression falls when she recognizes Tyra's birthday, and a new kind of guilt hits me. "I need to change it," I murmur, my stomach turning when she looks away.

"No," she says, her voice soft. "It's perfect. I never want her to be forgotten, Arch. I never wanted to take her place, and I know I never could. It's why we work so well together, right? Because I respect the fact that your heart will always be hers. You're just mine for a moment."

I tighten my grip on the steering wheel, wishing I could refute her

CATHARINA MAURA

words without starting an argument. I want more than either of us signed up for, and hell, I'm not sure if that's even an option.

"Let me know if you want me to take over," she tells me eventually, her voice soft and sweet. "I can drive if you'd like."

I smile at her and shake my head. "And make you give up your hard-earned passenger princess privileges? I wouldn't dare."

She chuckles, her head falling back just slightly, and fuck if it isn't a gorgeous sight. "I appreciate that more than you realize."

"Then show me your appreciation," I murmur, my tone flirtatious. Fuck it. If she'll only give me a few moments, I'll make them last.

Her eyes widen, and she looks over her shoulder at Ezra, who's still snoring. "Show you how?"

I reach for her and entwine our fingers before lifting our joined hands to my lips to kiss her knuckles. "I'm sure you can come up with something. We'll be at your parents' house all weekend. We'll find some time to sneak away."

"*Archer*," she says, her tone admonishing.

I smirk and place our joined hands in my lap. It's odd, because I've never enjoyed holding hands with anyone, but I like touching Serenity in any way I can. "Don't pretend you don't want to."

She throws me a shy look and pulls her hand out of mine to mess with my phone, skipping through songs endlessly, unable to make up her mind. If Ezra were awake, he'd already have snapped at her. He hates it when she does that, but personally I couldn't care less. Eventually, she settles on an album she likes, and I grin when she lip-syncs one song after another, making sure not to wake Ezra.

"You never actually told me how your ice cream date with Theo went," I say as I take the exit that leads to her hometown, the journey having flown by thanks to the mostly empty roads. We drive past *The Ballerina*, but this time, I see it in a new light. It's a gorgeous work of art and a true testament to The Muse's skills, but it doesn't evoke the same emotions it used to.

She throws me a glare. "It wasn't a date, and you know it."

"Sure," I murmur, unable to keep from being petty.

"If you must know, we didn't even get any ice cream. Every store we went to was closed, so we just ended up walking around for a bit before heading home."

I smirk, entirely too fucking pleased with myself for buying every single ice cream parlor in a five-mile radius so I could close them all for the day and shut that tradition of theirs down. It's clear having ice cream with him was going to mess with her emotions, and it wasn't going to happen on my watch. "Should've come home to me," I murmur. "I'd have given you all the ice cream you could've possibly wanted."

"I thought about it," she whispers, her gaze heated.

"Then why didn't you come over? I was waiting for you."

She glances at Ezra again. "You know why."

I grumble in dissatisfaction, and she sighs as she places her hand on my thigh. My cock hardens instantly, and her breath hitches when she notices. "Do you have any idea how many times I looked at that photo you sent me?" she whispers.

My gaze cuts to hers, and my mind instantly runs wild with thoughts of her in her bed, her phone in her hand. "Yeah?" I murmur, straightening as I refocus on the road, even as her hand begins to wander.

"Yeah," she says, her index finger caressing my cock over my slacks. "I missed you, Archer. Missed the way you kiss me, the way you refuse to let me go at night, and the way you hold me in your sleep."

I pause at the stoplight and turn to look at her, drinking her in. I know I shouldn't, not with Ezra sitting in the back seat, but fuck, I can't help myself.

Her gaze darkens when I lean in and place my index finger underneath her chin before leaning in to steal a kiss. She makes the softest, sexiest sound in the back of her throat, and it takes all of me to pull away.

"I want you in my bed tonight," I whisper, my heart racing as I follow the familiar road to her house. "I'm losing my mind, Serenity. I'm fucking desperate for you."

She nods as I pull up in front of her house, her breathing erratic. "I'll try," she promises.

We both startle when Ezra yawns just as I've parked the car, and she shoots me a panicked look. I turn to look at Ezra, and he looks back at me, seemingly disoriented. "We're here?"

My shoulders sag in relief, and I nod as I get out of the car, my heart beating wildly. Serenity is worth it, but fuck, I'm not made for sneaking around.

Thirty-Three

ARCHER

"Having all my kids home is the best birthday present I could've asked for," Malti, Ezra and Serenity's mother, says, her arm wrapping around my shoulders.

Ezra pauses in the middle of the kitchen, a stack of plates in his hands. "You might as well just come out and say it, Mom. Archer is your favorite child, and he isn't even yours."

He throws me a withering glare, and I smirk back at him as I lean into Malti, reveling in the love I'm always showered with in this house. "He's just jealous," I tell her, and she squeezes my arm in response.

In the last decade, Ezra's family has truly become my own family too. They were there when my grandfather disowned me, and then again when I ended things with Tyra, only for my life to implode shortly after. They've been there every step of the way as Ezra and I built our company from the ground up, and throughout the years, this is where I'd find myself when I had nowhere else to go.

Guilt eats at me at the thought of how badly we'd all be impacted if Serenity and I don't wrap this thing between us up neatly, but at the same time, I can't find it in me to regret being with her. The reservations I had are all gone, replaced by the way she makes me feel—the way she makes me want to *live*.

"Let her have her favorite," Caleb, Ezra's stepdad, says. He mirrors his wife's stance and wraps his arm around Ezra with a kind smile on his face. "You're *my* favorite child, after all."

Ezra grins, and though they look vastly different, their smiles are the same. I've never once seen Caleb treat Ezra coldly or differently, and their bond is one I've always immensely admired. Caleb has always supported Ezra unconditionally, taking Ezra's side against his wife at times. Most of our investment funds came from him, and he's been refusing our repayments, let alone any interest we've tried to pay him.

"I'm sorry—*what?*"

Malti and Caleb both freeze at the sight of their daughter, who walks into the kitchen holding the party decorations she'd been tasked with finding. From the second we arrived, we've all been put to work, each of us responsible for different parts of tomorrow's party. "You always do this," Serenity says, her beautiful hazel eyes blazing with mock annoyance and her long, curly hair flowing over her chest. "When these two idiots are around, you both just forget I exist!"

"Yeah right," Ezra says, shaking his head. "You know full well you're the favorite child, so don't you dare throw a fit."

Serenity narrows her eyes as she dumps the decorations on the table. "Archer," she snaps, grabbing a handful of balloons. "Stop monopolizing my mom's love and help me blow these up."

Malti just chuckles and throws me a sweet sympathetic look when I push off the counter to join Serenity at the table. "I don't know where she got that temper of hers," she whisper-shouts.

Caleb bursts out laughing and stares at his wife in disbelief, every single one of us aware that Serenity *definitely* got her temper from her mother. I merely shake my head and take the contraption Serenity hands me, using it to blow up the balloons she handed me while she strings them together to create an arch.

Halfway through, I reach for my phone and send her a text, wishing I could've just said the words.

ARCHER

for the record, you're *my* favorite

She raises a brow when her phone buzzes on the table, and I watch her, loving the way she smiles when she reads my text. She raises her head, her gaze roaming over my face before she looks down again.

SERENITY

I think you might be my favorite too

ARCHER

you think so? Sounds like you need some convincing

She and I continue to work on our balloons, stealing glances at each other while her family buzzes in and out of the room, and it's surprisingly thrilling. It's fun to have a secret that's just ours, and it comes with a kind of intimacy I've never experienced before.

SERENITY

what if I do?

ARCHER

> come to my room tonight, and I'll show you
> that you're my favorite over and over again.

She smirks at her phone, desire blending with delight in those pretty eyes of hers, and I can't for the life of me tear my gaze off her.

"Serenity, is Theo coming?" Malti asks, breaking the spell I was under.

She nods, and my smile melts away.

"He is?" I ask without thinking.

"Yeah, he's driving down for it." She smiles at her mom then. "You know he'd never miss your birthday."

Malti looks her daughter over, a hint of concern crossing her face. "Is he bringing Kristen?"

Serenity tenses, and I look away, hating the way she reacts to Kristen's name when it's linked with Theo's. "I'm not sure," she says, her voice tinged with sadness. "He didn't mention he would, and I didn't ask."

I stare at her as her mother leaves the room, leaving us alone. "Are you still in love with him?" I ask without thinking. They have so much history, and how the fuck could anyone compete with that? I can have her in my bed and make her moan my name, but it feels like the second she walks away from me, her thoughts drift back to him.

She looks up, uncertainty written all over her face. "I...I don't know."

I reach for another balloon and watch it inflate. "Do you truly not know, or are you reluctant to admit that you still have feelings for him?"

She takes a deep breath and looks to the side. "Does it matter?"

"What if I tell you it does?"

"Why?"

"It can't be a surprise to you that I don't enjoy sleeping with a woman who'd rather be with someone else."

Her eyes widen, a hint of insecurity flickering through them, and it takes me a moment to realize how what I just said might have come across.

"Fuck," I mutter. "You know I didn't mean it like that, darling. You know what you do to me, how much I want you."

She nods, but I can tell her feelings are hurt. "I know," she murmurs, but I don't think she does. There's no way she could understand how fucking wild she drives me. "I know, Archer. That's not the part that hurts. It's the fact that it isn't me who'd rather have someone else. It's you."

"You know that's not true," I say instantly, denying it.

She glances at my phone, and my heart sinks. My password. *Fuck*. "I don't blame you," she says, her voice trembling. "I understand. Truly, I do. I knew what I was getting into, but so did you."

Thirty-Four

SERENITY

I sigh as I distribute the snacks Mom prepared across the tables in the backyard, my mood sullen. Ezra kept Archer and me up all evening with board games that neither of us wanted to play, but neither he nor I could come up with a good excuse not to when it's what we've always done when we're all home.

In the end, I had to call it a night and head to bed by myself, quietly resenting Ezra for keeping me from Archer on a night I really wanted to be with him. He and I have never argued, and I wouldn't say our conversation yesterday was an argument per se, but something about it didn't sit well with me. I'd been so frustrated that I nearly snuck out with my stash of spray cans that I keep hidden. I haven't felt the urge to do that since Archer showed me what he'd done to his guest room for me. It doesn't help that Mom and Dad put us to work again the moment we woke up this morning, depriving me of a chance to speak to him.

"Serenity!"

I turn around at the sound of Theo's voice, and for the first time in years, my heart doesn't skip a beat. Instead, I look around the rapidly filling backyard, my eyes settling on Archer. He's standing next to Dad and Ezra, the three of them sorting out the barbecue together.

Archer's eyes meet mine just as Theo's arm wraps around me, and I tense. "Hey," Theo says, surprising me when he lifts me off the ground and hugs me tightly.

He smiles as he puts me down, and I smile back at him involuntarily. "What was that for?"

Theo shakes his head and brushes one of my curls out of my face. "Just happy to see you."

"You literally saw me two days ago."

He grins at me. "Exactly. I didn't get to see you yesterday, and it felt like an eternity."

I laugh at his ridiculousness, but my gaze keeps drifting back to Archer, whose expression has hardened. My heart sinks when he turns his back to me, and I step away from Theo.

"Where is Kristen?"

Theo's smile melts away. "We had an argument, and she decided to stay home."

"I'm sorry," I tell him, unsure what else to say to that. "Is there… is there anything I can do?"

He shakes his head. "No, nothing at all." He throws his arm around me. "Except maybe grab a drink with me. Did I see you spiking your mom's lemonade when I walked in?"

I throw him a conspiratorial look as I lead him closer to the drink station, hyperaware of how close it is to where Archer is standing. He looks at us as Theo and I head his way, his gaze settling on the arm Theo still has wrapped around me, and I try my hardest to resist the urge to shrug it off like I did last time, when Theo told me he didn't want anything between us to change.

I pour both of us cups just as Mom walks up to the boys with one of my older cousins by her side.

"Archer," she says, grinning. "I've been meaning to introduce you to Amari. She also works in fintech, and I thought you'd get on great." She all but pushes Amari forward, toward him. "She's single," she adds without even a single hint of subtlety, and my heart drops.

I move closer, a deep and unfamiliar kind of unease unfurling in my stomach when Archer smiles at her. My chest begins to ache when she looks at him appreciatively, and every inch of my body screams *mine*. Why would Mom introduce the two of them like that? We've all been so respectful of his past with Tyra, but it seems she thinks it's time he moves on. I just don't understand: why now, and why Amari?

Archer doesn't even look at me as he asks her what she does and where she works, nor does he notice me as I walk up to them, moving between him and Ezra, so I'm standing on his other side.

Ezra raises a brow, a hint of a smile on his face as he steps aside. "For me?" he asks, taking my drink from me.

"Yeah," I lie, realizing my brother just unknowingly gave me an excuse. Amari places her hand on Archer's arm, and I grit my teeth as I stare up at him. "What about you, Archer? Do you want a drink? You seem thirsty."

He glances at me and shakes his head. "I'm good," he says, before turning back to my cousin, completely ignoring my little dig. "What about you, Amari?" he asks. "Can I grab you a drink?"

She smiles up at him and nods, leaving me standing rooted in place as he leads her back to the drinks table, his hand on her lower back. "They'd make a nice couple," Theo says, and Ezra hums in agreement.

I turn toward them to find both looking at me, and I realize I've been staring at Archer. "Would they?" I ask, my voice coming out a lot more strained than I expected.

"Of course," Ezra says. "They're about the same age, aren't they? If I recall correctly, she's a pretty senior employee in her current company, so I imagine they'd have a lot to talk about."

Theo nods. "Besides, they look pretty good together. Most women look tiny next to Archer, but Amari's height suits his perfectly."

I bite on my lip as their words sink in, and realization soon follows. This thing between Archer and me will end in just a few more months at most, and someday, I'll have to watch him be with someone else. I'll have to live with the knowledge that he'll give everything he gives me to someone else. Someday, he *will* move on, and it won't be with me.

"Right," I whisper, my heart breaking in a way it never has before. I reach for the cup Ezra stole from me, and much to my surprise, he doesn't even bat an eye when I knock it back. He just raises a brow, looking irritatingly amused. "I need a refill."

Theo falls into step with me as I reluctantly walk back to the drinks table, feeling both awkward and miserable. "What's wrong?" he asks, frowning.

I shake my head and try my best to ignore the way Amari laughs at something Archer said, the two of them standing right next to the table, only a few paces away. "Nothing."

"You sure?" he asks as he pours me another drink.

I take it from him and nod. "Yeah, just have a headache," I lie, my voice trembling. "You know what? I think I'll just go lie down for a few minutes."

"Do you want me to come with you?" Theo asks.

I could swear I see Archer tense from my peripheral vision, but when I glance at him, he's smiling at Amari, giving her his undivided attention.

Thirty-Five

ARCHER

I tense when I hear Theo ask Serenity if she wants him to come with her when she just told him she's going to her bedroom. What does he think he's going to do—get into bed with her? Over my dead fucking body.

"So," Amari says, smiling sweetly. "I take it you're seeing Serenity, and Ezra doesn't know?"

My eyes widen, and she chuckles, her eyes twinkling in that way that Sera's do when we share an inside joke.

"It's fine, you don't have to admit it. I can tell by the way you can't keep your eyes off her for more than two seconds—and by the way she lost her composure when her mother introduced us to each other." She grins as Serenity walks past us and into the house. "Tell me you're serious about her, and I'll keep Ezra and her parents distracted for a while."

I hesitate, looking her over. "Theo too," I murmur, tipping my head toward him. "Her best friend."

"Ah, the competition," she says, nodding.

"*Hardly*," I snap.

She laughs, clearly amused by my reaction. "Fine, I'll keep an eye on him too."

"In that case, *yes*. I'm far more serious about her than I have any right to be, and I have no fucking clue how to undo it."

"Then don't," she says, gently pushing me toward the patio doors.

I look back at her in gratitude before walking into the house, my footsteps light as I sneak up the stairs, praying no one stops or sees me. I hesitate in front of Serenity's door, but the sound of the stairs creaking behind me hastens my movements, and I slip into her room as quietly as possible.

She looks up from where she's sitting on her bed, her phone in her hands. Surprise crosses her face, and I bite back a smile as I lean against her door. "Archer," she murmurs, her gaze roaming over my body. There's something provocative in her eyes, blended beautifully with anger.

"Come here, darling."

Her breath hitches, and she looks like she'll refuse, but then she rises to her feet and crosses the room, pausing right in front of me. She grabs my shirt, her eyes finding mine. "What are you doing here?" she asks, her voice soft, hopeful. "I'm surprised you were able to pull yourself away from Amari."

I wrap my hands around her waist, reveling in the feel of her. I've missed touching her like this. She has no idea how fucking frustrated I was last night. It almost seemed like Ezra was *trying* to keep us apart. "Have I ever told you how good jealousy looks on you?"

Her hands slide up and around the back of my neck, her body pressing against mine as she rises to her tiptoes. "Have I ever told you that making me jealous comes at a cost?" she retorts, her lips mere inches from mine.

I smirk as my eager hands settle on her ass, kneading, teasing. "Is that so? In that case, I'm going to have to punish *you* first, darling."

"What for?"

I place my index finger underneath her chin, my eyes narrowing. "You know exactly what for. You looked right at me when you let him hug you like you're *his*."

Guilt blooms in her eyes, and I drop my head against the door, my gaze roaming over her body. "Undress." My voice is soft but firm, and my sweet girl instantly complies, her hands moving to the hem of the red dress she's wearing.

"We have fifteen minutes, at most, before someone comes looking for us," she says, her tone hesitant.

"That's more than enough time to make you come. Don't make me repeat myself."

Her gaze darkens, and I suppress a groan when she pulls her dress off to reveal a sexy set of red-and-black lingerie, her eyes filled with provocation as she steps back and turns slowly, giving me a show.

Goddamn.

I'm fucking spellbound when she reaches for my shirt, our eyes locking as she undoes the buttons. "I'll let you punish me however you please," she says, her palm sliding over my bare chest. "But don't think you'll get away with what you did today."

Her hands settle on the waistband of my trousers, and she looks into my eyes as she frees my cock, her hand wrapping around it eagerly. "Turns out, I'm just as possessive as you are, Archer."

"Yeah?" I murmur, lifting her into my arms. I carry her to her bed, and she pulls me on top of her.

"Yeah," she whispers, before pulling me in for a kiss. I groan when her nails scrape against my scalp, needing her closer. "I wanted to tell her that you're *mine*," she murmurs against my mouth.

My heart skips a beat, and I thread a hand through her hair, pleased beyond words. "The feeling is mutual, darling," I admit, before sucking on her bottom lip. "Every damn time I see you smile at him, I want to pull you close and kiss you for the whole world to see, just like *this*."

She moans as I part her lips and deepen our kiss, tangling her tongue with mine as her body writhes against me. She tugs at my clothes impatiently, our lips barely leaving each other as we undress the other. My beautiful girl moans when I part her legs, and a strangled groan escapes the back of my throat when I find her pussy wet for me.

"Oh God," she says when I push two fingers into her, my thumb on her clit. She pulls on my hair as I tease her. "Please," she begs. "I need you inside me."

Her words instantly make my cock throb, but I shake my head and touch her harder, rougher. "Come for me, and I'll fuck you so good you'll be feeling me for the rest of the day."

Her lips part, and her eyes glitter with desire as I push her to the edge. It's such a fucking riveting sight to watch her come undone for me—always only for me. This sight, this version of her, is only mine. "Archer," she pleads, and I lean in to kiss her, swallowing down all her moans as she comes for me. Knowing that I'm the one that gave her that kind of pleasure makes me feel like I'm on top of the world, and it's surreal how she impacts me.

"More," she begs, panting.

I grin as I drag my cock over her pussy. There's something so intimate about this connection between us. It isn't just lust that compels me to look into her eyes as I sink into her. It's not just desire I feel when her head falls back, and she bares her throat for me. Her legs tighten around my hips when I lean in to kiss her just below her ear, in that spot that makes her shiver.

She tightens her grip on my hair, her hips meeting mine thrust for thrust as I take her hard and fast. "Oh God," she moans, and I pull back to look at her, needing to see her.

"You're *everything*, you know that?" I murmur without thinking, my thoughts hazy, clouded by everything she's making me feel. "You're everything to me."

She moves her legs up, until they're hooked around my waist, letting me take her deeper. I bite down on my lip when she cups my face, her eyes filled with something I've never seen before. Her thumb brushes over the edge of my mouth, and then she balls her hand in my hair, pulling me in for a kiss moments before I come. I groan, and this time she's the one who silences my moans.

She's panting as hard as I am when I collapse on top of her, and the way she hugs me mends something deep inside my soul. No one has ever been able to give me the kind of comfort she gives me, and fuck, I don't know if I'll ever be able to live without it again.

"I don't want to go back down," she whispers, kissing my temple and then my jaw. She has no idea what she's doing to me with her sweet little touches, does she?

"I know, baby," I murmur, pressing a kiss to her forehead. "I don't want to either, but we have to."

She whimpers a little when I pull out, and I glance between us, loving the way she's dripping with my cum. I smirk as I push my fingers into her, pushing it in deeper. Her eyes widen as I curl my fingers, pressing against her G-spot briefly before I pull my hand away and get up to get dressed.

"W-What are you doing?" my darling asks as I swipe her panties off the floor and push them into my trousers' pocket. "I need those!"

I glance at her leisurely as I button up my shirt. "Should've thought about that before you made me jealous."

"Archer!" she scolds as she pulls her dress on, her hair a beautiful, sexy mess. She looks freshly fucked, and I wish I could just keep her in bed for the rest of the day.

"Go on," I tell her. "Go ahead and hug him with my cum dripping out of your pretty pussy, reminding you who you belong to."

She gapes at me, and I chuckle as I tidy her hair for her, curling a couple strands of hair around my fingers like I've seen her do. "You'll pay for this," she promises.

I pinch her chin and steal a kiss. "Can't wait," I whisper against her mouth, before turning and holding her bedroom door open for her.

She breezes past me, trying her best to hide her smile, and I bite on my lip in an attempt to suppress my own grin as I follow her down the stairs.

"There you are," Ezra says the moment we walk out into the backyard. His gaze moves between the two of us, and we both tense. "Where were you?"

I hesitate when Sera shoots me a panicked look. "Serenity didn't feel too well," I tell him. "So I brought her some meds and checked up on her."

He stares at his sister just a little too long for my liking, and my heart begins to race. Can he tell that she looks just a little different? That her hair is messier and her clothes aren't as tidy? That she's still breathing a little harder than usual, and that her lips are just a little swollen?

"I'm glad you feel better," he says, placing his hand on her shoulder before glancing at me. "Thanks for looking after my little sister," he says, but his words are entirely at odds with the cold look in his eyes.

Thirty-Six

SERENITY

"I'll drive," Ezra says as we walk out of the house. Archer frowns, but he throws my brother the keys to his car nonetheless.

"You love sleeping in the car," I remind him. "Why would you want to drive?"

Ezra pauses with his hand on the door and glances over at me. "Just felt like it," he says, his tone oddly frustrated. I roll my eyes as I get in the back seat, only for Ezra to scowl at me through the rearview mirror. "So you'll argue endlessly to have the front seat when it's Archer that's driving, but not when I'm behind the wheel?"

I yank the seat belt and put it on, irritated. I'd been looking forward to sitting next to Archer on the drive back, and not only did Ezra throw a wrench in my plans, he's also being annoying about it. "It's *his* car!"

Archer just shakes his head and sighs as he sits down in *my* seat, adjusting the chair and messing up all my settings. He glances over his shoulder and throws me a sweet smile as Ezra pulls out of Mom and Dad's driveway, but it doesn't stop me from sulking. It's silly, but

I really enjoyed the way he held my hand on the drive here, and there was something so peaceful and intimate about chatting in hushed voices as the scenery passed us by. Instead, I sit back and listen to Ezra and Archer discuss sports scores and work.

"Can I have your phone?" I ask Archer eventually.

Archer nods and grabs it from his dashboard instantly, neither of us realizing the way Ezra looks at me in the mirror.

"It was locked," he says, his tone cold. "You know the code to Archer's phone?"

My gaze shoots up, surprised he's noticed something so small. Sometimes I forget just how detail-oriented Ezra is. "He told me the code on the drive here," I tell him, unsure why that's something that matters at all.

Ezra glances at Archer and nods slowly before refocusing on the road, and I stare at my brother for a moment. He's suspicious of us, and I didn't realize it straightaway.

My mind is working in overdrive as I fiddle with the music, trying to work out what we could've done or said that made him act so odd. Was it the way we holed up in my bedroom at the party? We weren't gone for long, and nothing about it should've been all that suspicious. It's not uncommon for Archer to check in with me and chat for a while.

I bite my lip, my heart beating loudly as I navigate to Archer's contacts and change my name in his phone, just to be sure. If Ezra truly is suspicious, we shouldn't take any risks with the text messages we send each other. There's every chance he'd glance over and read something he should never see, but that won't matter as much if he doesn't know it's me.

I hesitate before replacing my name with the closest thing I can think of, settling on *Sarah*, since Archer often calls me Sera. Our eyes lock when I hand his phone back, and he shoots me a questioning look. I smile back at him, answering his silent question and letting him know everything is fine.

> **SERENITY**
> changed my name in your phone because Ezra is acting a bit weird, and it doesn't sit well with me

I watch him stare at his phone in confusion for a moment, before he smiles. From where I'm sitting, I can just about see his screen, and my eyes widen when he goes into his contact list and replaces the name Sarah with two emojis: a tulip and a heart. Something about it makes my stomach flutter, and I smile as he texts me back.

> **ARCHER**
> okay, darling

> **ARCHER**
> miss you next to me. Missed you in my bed last night too.

> **SERENITY**
> I miss you too. It's hard sitting here and not being able to reach for you.

He sighs, and Ezra turns his head, clearly trying to glance at Archer's screen. Thankfully, Archer locks his phone and puts it away before distracting Ezra with random chatter about the next football game they said they'd watch together.

The journey passes uneventfully, but there's a certain tension in the air that wasn't there before. I can't help but feel like Ezra knows there's something going on between us, and I'm not sure where that leaves us.

This thing between Archer and me is supposed to end in a couple of weeks, and it wasn't meant to affect anyone. If Ezra found out, their friendship would never be the same again, and I can't be the cause of that.

"You okay?" Archer asks as he opens the car door for me, and I look up, surprised. I've been lost in thought for most of the journey, never even realizing we'd made it back home.

"Yeah," I murmur, but he doesn't look convinced. Archer glances me over as he grabs my weekend bag and throws it over his shoulder.

"I'll take that," Ezra says, taking it from him. "Appreciate the help, though."

Archer looks as startled as I feel, something decidedly territorial crossing his face. I shake my head subtly, and he looks down for a moment, fixing his expression before we follow Ezra into the elevator.

We both know my brother well enough to realize he's on edge, but if he knew about us, he'd just have said something. It's likely that he's suspicious but not sure, and we're going to have to tread carefully.

"What the fuck?" Ezra murmurs as we approach his door to find water in front of it. His expression is murderous as he unlocks it, only to find his entire place flooded.

"What happened here?" Archer asks, pulling me out of the way. I place my hand on his back and peek past his arm as Ezra walks in, his shoes squeaking.

Archer turns to look at me, his gaze roaming over my face. "Stay here for a moment, darling," he murmurs, his voice barely above a whisper. "Let me just see what's going on."

I nod, and he follows my brother in, only for the both of them to return mere minutes later, their expressions grim.

"Burst pipe," Ezra says, reaching for his phone. "How the fuck did no one notice?"

Archer grimaces. "If I recall correctly, the unit below you is up for sale. It's probably empty." He glances at me, and then back at Ezra. "Just stay at mine until it's fixed. It'll be okay."

Ezra looks reluctant, but he nods. His expression is grim as he begins to make several calls, and Archer leads me to his home, keying in his code—another variation of Tyra's birthday.

"Take my bedroom," he tells me. "It has its own bathroom. I'll take the guest room, and Ezra can take the sofa. If need be, we can put a bed in my home office for Ezra tomorrow."

"I can't just take your bedroom, Archer. It's fine. I'll—"

"Don't fight me on this," he says, glancing over to the corner of his living room, where Ezra is calling his insurance company. "I want you in my bed, Serenity. You won't sleep anywhere else."

Thirty-Seven

ARCHER

I look up from my position on the sofa when my front door unlocks, my heart beginning to beat just a little faster when Serenity walks in. She has no idea how much I've been enjoying having her live with me. In just a handful of days, I've been treated to countless sights of her all rushed and gorgeous in the morning, only for her to somehow become even more beautiful by the time she walks into the house in the evening. Her hair somehow becomes more unruly, everything about her coming undone in the most captivating way.

She doesn't know it, but I've been taking my work home with me every day lately, so I can make sure I get home before she does and steal a few moments with her. Having Ezra around has been tougher than I expected. He just seems to be everywhere—I haven't even been able to sneak into bed with Serenity at night, because each time I walk out of my guest room, he wakes up.

"Hi, darling," I murmur, drinking her in.

Her whole face lights up when she smiles at me, her gaze darting around the room. "Are we alone?" she asks as she walks up to me, hope blossoming in her beautiful hazel eyes.

I nod as she places her knee on the sofa between my legs, her hands wrapping around my shoulders as she leans in and kisses me. I groan as I grab her waist and all but tackle her onto the sofa, covering her body with mine. "Fuck," I mutter against her mouth. "I missed you."

Her leg hooks around mine, her hand sliding up from the back of my neck and into my hair. "I missed you more," she says in between kisses, her touch as impatient as mine.

She gasps when I move my lips to her neck, kissing her in that spot that makes her shiver. "How was your day, baby?" Her hand slips underneath my shirt, and I smile against her skin. I love that she craves physical connection as much as I do. "I saw Mark giving you some shit today. I'm all for giving you responsibility and opportunities to grow, but that doesn't mean he can offload his work on you. If he does even one single thing that you don't like, let me know, and I'll fire him."

She laughs and pulls back a little, and I push myself up on my forearms so I can look at her. "He hasn't done anything wrong, Archer," she says, her tone placating. "Stop looking for excuses to fire Theo and Mark. I'm pretty sure this is the fourth time in as many weeks that you've mentioned wanting to fire either of them."

My heart skips a beat at the sight of that smile of hers. "Fine, maybe I just don't like the way they're always looking at you. I need to find a way to make leering at my girl a fireable offense."

She cups my face, and the way she looks at me makes my heart overflow with something I can't quite define. It isn't anything I've ever felt before—it's warm and overwhelming and entirely terrifying. "Your girl, huh?" she murmurs.

"Yeah," I whisper instantly, leaning in to brush my lips over hers.

"Mine." She sighs happily in the moments before my mouth descends on hers, and I can't help but smile. This kiss is different. It's slower, more intentional. Her back arches, and she tilts her head as she brings me in closer, parting her lips for me.

By the time I pull away, we're both panting. "This is the best part of my day," she whispers. "These little moments, when it's just the two of us."

Her eyes fall closed when I kiss her cheek and then the tip of her nose, before moving to her forehead. "Mine too," I murmur, wishing she understood just how much peace she brings me. I've never experienced anything quite like this. Simply holding her in my arms roots me in the present, makes everything but her fade away.

"I wanted to ask if there's anything I can do to help you with the international roll-out plan." Her fingers brush over my temple gently. "I feel like you've been working late every night, and I know there probably isn't much I can do, but if I can lighten your load just a little bit, I will. Maybe I could help with admin?"

I shake my head, my heart warming. "Darling," I murmur, leaning in to kiss the edge of her mouth. "I'm only working late because the thought of you all alone in my bed keeps me up at night. I keep having to distract myself from thoughts of what I'd do to you if your brother weren't cockblocking me at every turn."

She laughs, and I just stare at her, mesmerized. "He's the worst. I really miss spending our evenings in bed together," she admits. "I love having your skin against mine and the way you look at me right before you push into me."

My cock instantly begins to throb, and she grins as she rolls her hips underneath me provocatively, her back arching. "Fucking tease," I groan, spreading her legs farther. Serenity's breath hitches when I slowly drag my index finger across her inner thigh, loving the way her gaze darkens.

"Wet," I whisper as I push her panties aside. Her head drops back when I push two fingers into her, curling them in that way she just can't resist. She moans my name beautifully, and it does something, makes me fucking feral. There's nothing that makes me feel better than hearing her say my name like that.

"Please," she whispers, rolling her hips. "It's been so long, Archer. *Please*. I need you inside me."

I bite on my lip as I reach for my slacks, and as if on cue, I hear my door unlock. "*Fuck*," I groan, rolling off her in a rush, involuntarily crashing to the floor in the process.

She sits up in alarm and tidies her clothes, her gaze roaming over me to make sure I'm okay. I throw her a reassuring look as I sit up on the floor, annoyed Ezra came home so early.

"What are you doing on the floor?" he asks as he walks in, and I take a deep breath as I stare up at my ceiling, praying for patience.

I've lived with Ezra for years before this, but somehow, the two weeks he's been here have been completely fucking unbearable. "Thought I saw a stain on the rug," I lie.

"I'm sorry," Serenity says, amusement dancing in her eyes as she rises to her feet and begins to tidy the blanket she bought for the sofa and the countless cushions we bought in Morocco. "If there's a stain, it was probably me. I'm trying to be careful, but I just keep getting paint everywhere."

I bite back a smile and continue to look down in search of a stain we both know doesn't exist, hoping my cock calms the fuck down soon. "It's fine," I murmur eventually. "I think it's just the rug's pattern."

I look up, only to find Ezra staring past both of us, at the painting supplies I moved out of the guest room and into the corner of the living room earlier today. His expression is conflicted, *haunted*, and fresh guilt crashes through me.

Thirty-Eight

ARCHER

"I need to resolve this before this project can move ahead," Ezra tells me as he stares at one of our implementation timelines, his tone filled with frustration. "I'll have to go and figure out where the issue lies myself."

I sigh and run a hand through my hair when he begins to pace in his office. "You can't keep doing this, you know." I tell him. "We run a billion-dollar company, but we're still the ones running around cleaning up messes left and right. You have to learn to trust someone other than me. You're spreading yourself too thin, Ezra. You cannot continue to be the one who travels to client sites."

He sighs and leans back against his desk. "I just can't help but feel like everything will collapse if I take my foot off the gas pedal. You understand where I'm coming from, right? No one works as hard as we do, and no one knows our business as well either."

I nod, feeling conflicted. "Yeah, but we didn't build this business so you could become a slave to it."

"You're not much better," he says, his tone weak. "Until recently, you've hidden behind work as much as I have."

I tense, my head snapping up to meet his gaze. He looks at me like he has something to say, but then he shakes his head and stares out the window instead. "I'll send Emma," he says, resigned. "You're right. I can't keep doing this. Fuck, I haven't even had a chance to take Serenity out for dinner since she moved here, and it's been months. I promised her I'd show her around, and I haven't been there for her at all, even though I knew she was all messed up over Theo." He buries a hand in his hair and sighs. "Thank God you've been there for her."

I nod noncommittally and look down at my feet, guilt coursing through me at the sound of her name. Thankfully, he doesn't seem to notice as he closes his laptop and gathers the documents spread across his desk.

"Come on," I murmur, forcing a smile. "I'll let you raid my fridge to celebrate your decision to *not* work yourself to the bone anymore."

He walks past me and grins. "There's not much left to raid. You should probably restock."

"Two weeks," I mutter. "You've been living at my house for two weeks and you drank all my damn beer?"

He shrugs as he walks to the elevator. "Let's go pick up Serenity," he says, a faint smile on his face.

I shake my head as I press the down button. "She's at home, and she hates it when I do that. She's still pretty damn intent on pretending she doesn't know either of us at work."

"How do you know?" he asks, staring at the moving numbers on the elevator's display. "That she's home."

I tense imperceptibly. "Got a notification that my alarm system was disabled an hour ago," I tell him without skipping a beat, when truthfully, I know she's home because she texted me. It's the only way we manage to properly talk with Ezra around.

I thought he might question me further, but he doesn't say much of anything on the way home. It doesn't sit well with me that I'm so on edge around him these days. Serenity and I promised each other that us being together wouldn't affect anyone around us, but it has, and even so, I can't bring myself to regret a single thing. Fuck, we could implode, and I still wouldn't want to go back to a time before her.

"You're home!" she says, her whole face lighting up as she rises from the sofa, dressed in one of my old college T-shirts, one of the mugs we bought in Italy in her hands. It's her favorite one—a hand-blown one from Murano, with pink hearts on it.

"Hey, little thief," I tell her, loving the way she's swimming in my clothes. She looks far better in my tee than I ever did, and it's so fucking sexy to see it on her. I can't even explain why—it just makes me happy.

"Serenity," Ezra says, his tone chastising. "You can't just go through Archer's closet like that. We're invading his privacy enough as it is."

"It's fine," I tell him as she walks over and grabs her brother's arm. "I don't actually care. It's just a T-shirt."

She throws me a sweet smile before she drags Ezra to the kitchen. "You heard him," she says. "Besides, this T-shirt is only a small repayment for the pizza I made you guys."

"You made us pizza?" I ask, just as my stomach grumbles.

"Fuck yes," Ezra says, diving in instantly.

Serenity looks at me and smiles. "You mentioned you were craving some pizza," she whispers. "I'm not as good of a cook as you are, but this recipe seemed simple enough."

I look into her eyes, my pinky hooking over hers. "Thank you," I whisper back, the word *darling* nearly slipping out. Having Ezra around is fucking nerve racking. It's driving me completely wild to have her so close when I can't touch her. It's even worse to know she sleeps in my bed every night.

I sigh when Ezra grabs my last microbrew and a slice of pizza, his expression completely delighted as he carries both back to the living room. I've never minded his presence before, but for the first time in a decade, I really wish he'd just get the fuck out so I can be alone with my girl.

I stare up at the ceiling, reconsidering my decision to tell him he should stop pushing himself so hard. I'd fucking die for some alone time with Serenity, and I'd have it if he went on the trip he's sending Emma on.

Serenity chuckles when she reads my exasperated expression, and I groan when she turns to join her brother on the sofa. My mood is sullen as I grab the pizza Serenity made and follow her, not wanting to share it with Ezra.

She looks up at me when I sink down right next to her, my thigh pressing against hers. There's more than enough space on the sofa, but I don't give a fuck. I want her near.

Thankfully, Ezra doesn't bat an eye as he tries to choose a TV channel, his attention entirely on his food and the movie he eventually selects. He doesn't notice when I lift a slice to my mouth, only for Serenity to grab my wrist and steal a bite. Nor does he realize when I smirk at the tomato stains around her lips and reach to swipe it away with my thumb, before bringing it to my mouth and licking it clean.

She smiles at me, and pure contentment courses through me as I wrap my free arm around the back of the sofa, just about brushing against her shoulder. I lean in a little closer than I should, smiling when I notice the paint stains in her hair, only for that smile to fade when I recall what she's painting and what it'll mean for us when that painting is finished.

Thirty-Nine

SERENITY

"Let's try that bistro around the corner for lunch," Theo says as we finally walk out of our design meeting. I hesitate, not sure I want to take a lunch break at all when there's so much work left to do.

"I just want to quickly tweak my CAD based on the feedback we just received," I tell him. Throughout the last couple of weeks, both Archer and Mark have given me an increasing amount of autonomy and responsibility, and I don't want to let either of them down.

"Don't even think about not eating," he replies, his brows furrowed. "Besides, there's something I've been meaning to talk to you about, and you've canceled on me at least half a dozen times now. If you won't let me take you out for dinner, at least have lunch with me."

I purse my lips, my eyes roaming over his face. Ever since my mother's birthday a few weeks ago, he's been trying to get me to have dinner with him, but something continuously comes up. Usually, it's work, and a few times it's been because Ezra needed help with things related to the apartment flooding.

"Sure, let's go out for lunch," I murmur, my tone conveying a hint of reluctance. It hits me then—in the past I'd have gone out of my way to make time for him, but I don't feel that urge to accommodate him anymore.

"Bit late for lunch, isn't it?"

My head snaps up at the sound of Archer's voice, and my face instantly heats. He just looks between Theo and me, his expression conveying what I've come to recognize as jealousy.

"Mr. Harrison," Theo says, smiling politely.

"*Serenity*," Archer says, his tone curt. "I need a word about the design plans you submitted. Follow me."

"Oh, mind if I join?" Theo asks, his eyes on me.

"Yes," Archer snaps. "I mind."

My eyes widen, and I look down as I bite back a smile, not wanting to overstep at work when what I really want to do is throw Archer a warning look. "I'll fill you in later," I tell Theo before rushing to catch up to Archer.

He doesn't say a word all the way to his office, and I begin to worry something truly is wrong. "Everything okay?" I ask as soon as we step into Archer's office.

He closes the door and reaches for me, his hands wrapping around my waist as he pushes me against the wall in one smooth move. "Do I look like I'm okay?" he asks, his forehead dropping to mine. "You know I get jealous when he looks at you with those damn puppy-dog eyes. I hate it." A thrill runs down my spine when he tilts his head and leans in, his lips brushing against mine. "It just makes me want to remind you that you're mine."

I groan and slide my hands up his shoulders and around the back of his neck. "We're at work," I remind him in the seconds before our lips meet, my touch as eager as his. "Ezra is just a few doors down." At work, too, he has a penchant for walking in whenever he pleases.

He kisses me like he's desperate for me, like the distance between us has been killing him too. "I don't care," he groans, capturing my bottom lip between his teeth as he lifts me into his arms. My legs hook around his hips as he carries me to his desk, swiping everything off it before placing me down on top. "I need you," he growls, his hands settling on my hips just as I push his jacket off his shoulders, breaking my own rules. Archer grins at me when I move to his slacks next, his gaze dark. "Not even going to bother with my waistcoat? You just want my cock, don't you, darling?"

"Shut up," I murmur as my hand wraps around it, my heart thumping wildly. "Just shut up and give it to me. It's been so long, Archer."

He chuckles as he spreads my legs, his eyes on mine as he shoves my panties aside, his eyes falling closed when he realizes I'm already wet and ready for him. "Missed this pussy," he tells me as he slips a finger into me.

I shake my head and pull him closer, desperate and impatient. We haven't managed to sleep together at all since Ezra and I moved in with Archer, and I'm at my breaking point. Each time we think we've got a few moments alone, we're interrupted. The endless edging is driving me up the wall.

"Please," I whimper when his thumb circles my clit, his eyes cataloging my every expression.

"Please what, darling? Tell me what you want."

I tighten my grip on his cock and pump up and down the way he likes. "I want you to fuck me, Archer."

He inhales sharply and pulls his fingers away, grabbing my hips instead as he pulls me forward so I'm perched on the edge of his desk. Our eyes lock as he lines up his cock, his grip on my hips tightening as he pushes in slowly.

"Oh God," I moan, loving the way he stretches me out, the way he feels inside me. "*More*. Please, I can take it. Just give me all of it."

He looks into my eyes, his expression a mixture of lust and adoration. "You have all of me," he whispers right before he thrusts all the way into me, pushing into me hard and fast, his movements a little less controlled than usual.

I moan his name, and his eyes light up, his desire blazing a little brighter. There's something about the way he looks at me that makes me weak. He looks at me like I'm his whole world, like I'm all he needs.

My head falls back when he pushes his thumb against my clit, his free hand cupping the back of my neck as his lips find mine. He kisses me like he can't get enough of me, and I bury my hands in his hair, needing him closer.

Archer swallows down every single one of my moans, his fingers as rough as his thrusts, bringing me to the edge rapidly.

"Serenity," he groans, pulling his mouth off mine. "I need to see you come for me. Need to hear you moan my name." He watches me intently, his movements slower now, more intentional. "Come for me, darling."

I give him what he wants, and he bites down on his lip as he watches me unravel, his name on my tongue. Moments later, his forehead drops against mine, the sexiest groan leaving his mouth as he comes right along with me, the two of us lost in each other, in this stolen moment.

My arms wrap around his neck, and he kisses my forehead and then my nose. "You have no idea how much I needed you," he whispers before kissing the edge of my mouth. "Needed *this*."

I cup his cheek and lean in, kissing him softly. "I do," I whisper back, my lips moving against his with every word. "I needed it too."

He pulls back a little and shakes his head, a hint of frustration crossing his face. "No, you don't understand. I think I'm addicted to you," he tells me, his gaze roaming over my face. "I'm counting down the seconds until Ezra leaves to finalize the handover of his project to Emma."

My heart begins to beat a little faster, and I nod before I lean in to kiss his neck, quietly reveling in his words. "Three more days," I whisper, inadvertently admitting I'm counting down the seconds until we get some alone time too.

My feelings for him have evolved into something new, something I've never felt before, and I'm starting to hope I'm not the only one who feels this way.

Forty

SERENITY

"God, it's been so long since I got to wake up with you in my arms," Archer says, pulling me closer. "Your damn brother has really been getting on my nerves lately. Fucking cockblock. I'm so tempted to just acquire more foreign business purely so Ezra will leave us alone more frequently as he goes to implement our systems overseas. If it's a new acquisition, he can't leave it to Emma, he'll have to go himself."

I giggle as I press my lips to his neck. "We can't do that," I tell him, my voice weak. Archer kisses my forehead as his hands roam over my body eagerly, and I laugh and push off him, looking at him through narrowed eyes. "Arch," I warn. "Didn't you tell me that you had a cooking class with your mom soon?"

He groans as he sits up, the sheets bunching around his waist and revealing his body. "Would you like to join me for it?"

I stare at him wide-eyed, surprised by the offer. I know how important this time with his family is to him, so I've always made sure I wasn't around during his weekly call with his mother and sister. I never wanted to intrude, and he has no idea how much it means to me that he'd want me there. "Maybe next time," I tell him, looking down at the big T-shirt I'm wearing, one of his. "It starts in like ten minutes, right? I wouldn't want…I mean, I know you'd just introduce me as Ezra's little sister, but I still wouldn't want to look like trash."

He looks at me, his gaze searching. "What if I introduced you differently?"

My breath hitches, and he stares at me, a glimmer of hope in his eyes. "I…um…"

He runs a hand through his hair as he slips out of bed. "Think about it," he tells me, his voice soft. "I think you'd really like them, you know? And it'd be fun to have you in the kitchen with me on Sundays."

I nod and watch him walk into the bathroom, my heart hammering in my chest. Did he mean what I think he did? I'm no longer sure if we're on the same page, and it scares me to think that my feelings for him are unrequited.

I'm lost in thought as I walk into the kitchen, loving the feel of his large T-shirt on my body. There's something about being enveloped in his scent that makes me oddly happy. It's soothing in a way almost nothing else is.

My heart begins to race when I find cute heart-shaped donuts waiting for me on the kitchen island, and I lift one to my lips carefully, the butterflies in my stomach going wild. Recently, Archer has taken to cooking me all kinds of adorable foods on the weekends we stay in, and I'm not quite sure why. It feels like he's trying harder, atoning for something, though I'm not sure what for.

I sigh as I take a sip of my coffee, my thoughts beginning to roam where I don't want them to go. Does he feel guilty because of Tyra? Things between us aren't exactly what we'd initially agreed on, and we both know it. Besides, I'd be lying if I said I haven't been struggling with the same guilt.

Each time I work on *The Ballerina*, I'm reminded that this thing between us wasn't meant to last forever, that we're supposed to be using each other to get over other people. Falling for each other was never part of the plan.

I'm snapped out of my thoughts by the sound of Archer's doorbell, and I frown in confusion. Did he order something? "Archer?" I shout, before realizing that he can't hear me from the shower.

I glance down at my clothes and hesitate before heading to the front door. I pull it open to find a beautiful woman with long, dark hair standing in front of me, and she looks just as surprised to see me as I am to see her. For a few moments, we just stare at each other, jealousy slowly building deep in my tummy as I take her in. She looks like some kind of supermodel—exactly the kind that Archer was frequently photographed with before me.

"Hi," I tell her, my tone conveying my uncertainty. "Can I help you?"

She pushes her hair behind her ear as she takes in my T-shirt, and I tense. "Um, is Archer home?"

Something that feels a lot like defeat rushes through me as I nod. "Yes," I tell her, stepping back to let her in. It had never occurred to me that I'm not the only woman he's been with in this way. I probably wasn't his first attempt to forget Tyra, and I likely won't be the last. It won't take him long to realize that we've just gotten a bit too caught up in the moment, in this bubble that we exist in, and that we won't work outside of it. "He's…well, Archer is in the shower. He should be out shortly."

"Right," she murmurs as she walks into the foyer, clearly familiar with Archer's home. It makes me deeply uncomfortable to know she's been here before, and I try my best to push the feeling aside. "You look familiar," she tells me. "Have we met before?"

She frowns as I sigh and walk into the kitchen to pour myself a glass of water. "No," I tell her, crossing my arms. "I'd remember if we'd met."

She raises a brow, and I just stare at her for a moment, surprised by her beauty. It seems ridiculous for Archer to even want me when almost every woman he's ever been photographed with is as beautiful as the woman in front of me. She's as beautiful as Tyra was.

"How so?"

I smile humorlessly, my jealousy cutting deep. "I remember every girl Archer has ever introduced me to, and you aren't one of them." I look away then. "Not yet, anyway."

"How about I just introduce myself, then?" she says as I take a sip of my water. "I'm Celeste Windsor, and I'm incredibly curious who you are and why you're wearing a limited-edition T-shirt I bought for my brother years ago."

My eyes snap to hers, and shock rushes through me when I realize who she is. I glance down at my clothes, my cheeks heating in embarrassment. "You're Archer's younger sister," I say, my voice trembling ever so slightly. Jealousy clouded my mind so much that it didn't even occur to me that that's who she must be. In recent years she's been quite reclusive, so I've never met her before, but I should've known when I saw the color of her eyes. They're exactly the same as Archer's.

"I'm Serenity," I tell her. "I'm Archer's business partner's younger sister. My brother just moved in next door a few months ago, but we're just staying here for a little while because a pipe burst in his apartment, and I'm, well, I'm doing an internship at their firm, so I'm staying here too."

I immediately feel like an idiot. Of course she knows Ezra only moved back in next door a year ago, even though he owns the place. *She's* the one who'd been living in his home before then. Celeste smiles at me like she knows I'm not telling her the whole truth, but thankfully, she doesn't pry. I'm so nervous that I'd tell her everything if she asks.

"*Celeste?*" Archer says as he walks into the kitchen wearing gray sweats and a white tee, a towel pressed to his hair. He freezes as he takes in his sister's expression, and I watch as she forces a smile for him. "What happened?"

He sighs and holds his arms open for her, and her eyes fill with tears as she walks up to him. His arms wrap around her as a sob tears through her throat. He doesn't say a thing as he holds her tightly with one arm, patting her back soothingly with the other. "What did he do?" Archer asks, his voice dripping with violence.

Celeste merely shakes her head and buries her face in his chest, soft sobs racking her body.

Our eyes lock, and I throw him an understanding smile as I walk away, giving the two of them privacy. I'm not sure what happened, but it's clear she needs him, and the last thing I want to do is be intrusive when this is clearly a family moment.

Forty-One

SERENITY

My heart wrenches as I stare at my replica of *The Ballerina* in the corner of Archer's home office. I'm satisfied with the way each stroke of paint came together to capture the ballerina's pure elegance and grace, and objectively speaking, it's a piece of art I'm incredibly proud of. Yet I can't look at it without resentment threatening to overwhelm me. Even in this form, a culmination of brushstrokes of my own creation, Tyra is captivating. It's no wonder Archer can't get over her. She isn't the kind of woman you forget. I can't, so how could I ever expect it of him?

My heart aches as I put the finishing touches on the painting, my movements carrying a heavy finality to it. Archer and I promised each other that we'd only sleep together until the painting was done, and I'm not sure how much longer I can keep tweaking it, pretending it still needs something when it's been done for weeks. I need to let him go, but I don't want to. I did exactly what I promised myself I never would—I got attached to someone who'll never be mine. Not truly. Not for more than a few moments.

I sigh and step back to look at it, taking in the inherent beauty in her posture. As time passed, I tried to make her look a little less like Tyra, but no matter how hard I tried, she ended up embodying her fully. It's strange to look at a woman I've always loved and feel even a single hint of resentment when the one in the wrong is me. Archer has always been hers, and I've always known it.

"It's probably your best work yet, Ser."

I turn at the sound of Ezra's voice and find him leaning against the wall. I'd been so immersed in my work that I didn't hear him enter the room.

"Thank you," I tell him, trying my best to smile as I look back at it.

"It looks just like her."

A chill runs down my spine, and I tense. Archer never specified that it's Tyra he wanted me to capture, but I knew that's what he was after when he asked me to replicate my most famous Muse piece. After all, the original piece depicts her too. Maybe not quite as closely as this, but it was always meant to resemble her.

"Did Archer give you a photo for reference? I can tell from the expression you captured that it must've been a very specific kind of ask."

I shake my head, part of me wanting to cut the conversation short here. "He just told me that he wanted me to replicate a specific piece, and I guess I subconsciously drew inspiration from the only ballerina I've ever known." Lately I've only been working on it when Archer is visiting his parents, almost like I'm subconsciously trying not to remind him of her, while keeping her in the back of my own mind.

Ezra searches my face, his gaze conflicted. "You perfectly portrayed Tyra's beauty and grace, and even a hint of that volatile temperament of hers that Archer always loved."

Hearing her name out loud hurts. It suddenly makes her more

real, brings her back into our lives when I've done my best to pretend she isn't standing between Archer and me. With each passing day, it's becoming harder to hold on to her memory, and I've begun to wish I could just forget her. It's unfair to her, and it makes me feel like a horrible person, but I can't help but want what's hers. I want Archer's love, his future, and I know I'll never have that.

"It's not surprising that he's still holding on to her the way he is," Ezra tells me. "She supported him through one of the toughest periods of his life, and he loves her fiercely for it. He always will. Archer hasn't been the same since he lost her."

"No," I agree. "He hasn't." He's thrown himself into his work, becoming a shell of the person he used to be, almost like he didn't know how to live without her. I'd like to think that he's changed in the last couple of months, that he's enjoying spending time with me. But then I look at this painting, and I'm reminded that everything always leads back to her. His world will always revolve around her.

Ezra studies my canvas for a moment. "She wasn't perfect, you know? Far from it. Archer can't move on, but I think it's only because no one can compete with an idealized memory warped by regret. No one will ever hold a candle to her in his eyes, but it isn't because she was the love of his life."

I raise a brow, intrigued and hopeful but scared to pry.

"They fought a lot, and despite being together for years, Archer had no intention of marrying her. I think that deep down, he didn't see a future with her. She held on to him desperately, and he let her because he knew she needed him, and he felt he owed her for being there in his darkest hour. She was there for him when his grandfather disowned him, and she loved him when he and I struggled to make ends meet, reinvesting everything we earned into our company even if it meant sacrificing the groceries we needed."

He runs a hand through his hair and rocks back on his heels, his expression conflicted. "I thought he'd finally started to move on, you know. Until I saw that painting." He shakes his head and stares down at his feet. "He's been smiling a little more, and more than once, he's left work early when he normally never would. I thought he'd finally learned how to be happy again. Was I wrong?"

I tense and brush my hair out of my face nervously. "I...um... How would I know?"

Something akin to disappointment crosses his face, and he sighs, looking over my shoulder for a moment. "You've spent a decent amount of time with him while painting, so I thought you might have noticed some changes in him. He seems different, and I know him well enough to realize a woman is involved. Except...I've never seen him act quite the way he does these days."

"How does he act?" My voice is soft, and the slight tremble to it nearly gives me away.

"*Smitten.* Haven't you noticed the way he's constantly smiling at his phone? All of a sudden, his life doesn't revolve solely around work, and he's started doing things he never did before. Watching movies on the sofa, taking his time to cook all kinds of dishes, traveling on his days off and posting pictures of random scenery on social media when I was pretty sure he'd forgotten his phone even had a camera. He's doing all kinds of things that might seem normal to most people, but that he stopped doing long ago. He's living again, Serenity."

I stare at my brother, hope surging from my chest. He smiles, that same hope flickering in his eyes too. "So you think that this supposed girl is making him happy?"

My stomach twists as I wait for his answer. "Happier than he's ever been before, and I don't think he even realizes it. My concern is that he'll sabotage whatever he's got the moment he realizes he's falling in love because he seems to have convinced himself that he doesn't deserve to be happy."

He looks over my shoulder, at my canvas, and this time, his expression turns into pure despair. "More than that, I'm worried about the girl he's seeing and what it'll do to her to realize she'll never have all of him. Unless he lets Tyra go, he can't be the man she deserves."

My heart stutters when he smiles at me with pure sorrow in his eyes.

He knows.

Forty-Two

SERENITY

I tap my pen against my desk absent-mindedly as I think back to the conversation I had with Ezra, my mind replaying what he said about Tyra over and over again, each echo cutting deeper than the one before it.

He loves her fiercely, and he always will.

I knew it going in, so why does it hurt as much as it does? It's not like I ever thought we could have something real. It was never meant to be more than sex, and what we have isn't built to last. I know that, but it still kills me to know he'll never love me the way he loved her. I'll always be someone that filled a void but never closed it, and I knew it going in.

It's what I wanted, isn't it? I wanted us to move on from each other easily, so we could still be around each other once we part ways, entirely unaffected. Except…I don't think that's what I want anymore. I don't want to go back to a time when we didn't talk every day, where I wouldn't look up at him to find him already staring at me, his eyes shimmering with hidden secrets that only I know. I promised myself I'd never try to replace Tyra, yet now it's her place in his heart I want.

I'm snapped out of my thoughts when the company's internal messaging system chimes, and my heart begins to beat a little faster when I see Archer's name.

ARCHER HARRISON

are you free for coffee?

I raise a brow, surprised by his message. We're trying our best to keep things professional at work, but truthfully, I missed him so much last weekend that I've been thinking about sneaking into his office just so I could kiss him and reassure my aching heart.

SERENITY ADESINA

I'm free now!

ARCHER HARRISON

meet me at that little coffee shop you like, a few blocks down.

I smile to myself as I grab my purse and head out as stealthily as I can, scared someone will want to join me if I tell them I'm headed out for coffee. Theo, especially, has taken to accompanying me for lunch and coffee breaks lately, and it's made it that much harder to even have a private conversation with Archer.

My stomach flutters as I walk into the near-empty coffee shop, finding Archer sitting in the back. He smiles up at me as he rises from his seat, and my heart overflows with happiness.

"Hey," he murmurs, reaching for me.

I gasp when he pulls me into his arms, one hand wrapping around the back of my neck, the other cupping my face. I know I should remind him that we're in a public place very close to work and that we shouldn't be doing this, but instead, I rise to my tiptoes, my lips brushing against his.

He groans, his hand sliding into my hair as he kisses me softly, slowly, his tongue brushing along the seam of my lips, silently demanding I open up for him. I lose myself in him, in this moment that feels so heartbreakingly real.

"I missed you," he whispers against my mouth the moment I pull away, both of us breathing hard. Archer looks at me like he can't get enough of me, and I drink him in, my heart aching for reasons I can't quite fathom.

"I missed you too," I admit, my voice soft, vulnerability shining through. He has no idea how badly I needed to see him today, how desperately I wanted his lips on mine, showing me it's *me* he wants.

Archer pulls out a chair for me, and I glance around, relieved the place is still empty. "It's never this quiet around this time," I tell him as I take a seat. "We're lucky."

He smiles in a somewhat secretive way as he sits down next to me, his arm wrapping around me, and I raise a brow, instantly deciphering that expression of his. "Oh God," I whisper. "It's not a coincidence that it's empty in here, is it?"

He pinches my chin between his thumb and index finger. "My answer will depend entirely on whether or not you'll be mad at me if I tell you that I bought this place because you like the coffee here."

I love you.

The thought comes suddenly, the words sitting on the tip of my tongue, begging to leave my lips. I swallow them down, hiding the feelings I shouldn't have. "I could never be mad at you," I say instead.

God, I've never felt this way before. I thought I knew what it was like to be in love, but I didn't. I had no idea how raw it felt, how real, how *painful*.

"Good," he whispers. "Because the last thing I want to do is make you mad, darling." He leans in, his kiss featherlight this time, like he too feels this moment between us is breakable.

"How is your sister?" I ask, my eyes roaming over his face. "I know you were worried about her."

He smiles, his eyes twinkling. "She's fine. There's a lot standing between Zane and Celeste, but they love each other fiercely, so I have no doubt they'll be okay. It won't be easy, but they'll make it through. They're…honestly, I think they're meant to be."

He grabs my hand and entwines our fingers, and I squeeze tightly, loving the feel of his skin against mine. Archer raises our joined hands to his lips and kisses my knuckles softly. "You know what I kept thinking about last weekend?"

I shake my head, lost in his amber eyes.

"What it'd be like to have you at home with me."

My heart skips a beat, and he smiles, a hint of vulnerability crossing his face. "Celeste very blatantly cheated at a card game we love to play a couple of weeks ago, and I thought it was kind of cute how Zane backed up his wife when I called her out on it. Ever since, I've just been thinking that it'd be nice to have you there with me." He looks away, a hint of rosiness along his cheekbones. "I need backup against those two cheaters. I'll never win a game otherwise."

The thought of going home with him, as his *girlfriend*, makes the butterflies in my stomach go wild. "I'd love that," I murmur, my chest rising and falling rapidly. "Archer…"

He reaches for me and wraps one of my curls around his finger. "Hmm?"

"What would you say if I told you the painting is done?"

He freezes, his eyes finding mine. "I'd tell you that I think I want the backdrop to change."

I study his expression, uncertain what to make of it. Is he trying to postpone the end of this thing between us too—or is he truly just not ready to let her go?

Forty-Three

ARCHER

"You look gorgeous," I murmur, my eyes roaming over Serenity standing in front of my penthouse, wearing a pretty blue dress. Her expression instantly conveys shyness, and I grin as I take her hand.

"What are you doing?" she asks, her eyes widening as she tries to pull her hand away. It took some convincing before she agreed to let me take her out on a date after work today, and I'm not sure what I'd have done if she'd said no. I desperately need a dose of my Serenity, and given what she said about her painting being done, we really need to talk—in private, where we'll be neither rushed nor interrupted.

I catch her hand and entwine our fingers, holding on tightly. "Holding your hand," I tell her as I pull her into the elevator. "Ezra is still at work, darling. Just let me have this moment with you. I'm tired of sneaking around and not being able to touch you. I miss those nights when we'd just have dinner at my house and we'd lie in bed and watch TV at night. I miss holding you in my arms and watching you traipse through my kitchen in nothing but my T-shirts."

CATHARINA MAURA

She squeezes my hand, pure longing in her gaze. "I've missed it too," she says, her voice soft. "It's crazy how much I miss you when you're right here. I love spending more time with Ezra, but I hate that it means having to sacrifice time with you."

I raise our joined hands to my lips and kiss her knuckles, earning myself a pretty little smile that just makes my whole day. "Come on," I tell her as I lead her to my car. "There's somewhere I want to take you."

"Where are we going?" Serenity asks, her hand in mine as I drive down a long, winding road.

"Somewhere special," I murmur. "I think you'll like it."

She sits up as we approach our destination, a soft gasp leaving her lips when I park the car at one of the best hidden spots in the city. "It's beautiful," she murmurs, taking in the skyline.

I smile at her, marveling at all of her little expressions. This is what I love most about her—how much she enjoys the simple things in life. Good ice cream and a beautiful view will make her whole day, more than anything money can buy.

"Come on, the sun will begin to set soon," I tell her as I step out of the car to walk around it. She takes my hand as I help her out of the car, and the way she looks at me...*fuck*. She makes my heart feel raw, exposed. It's both thrilling and terrifying.

"What are we doing?" she asks when I grab a freezer bag from the trunk and open one of the back doors. She follows my lead and gets in, but her expression conveys her confusion.

"I just want to sit next to you and feed you ice cream as we watch the sunset."

Her lips part, an excited little sound on her lips. *"Ice cream?"*

I laugh as I unpack it for her. "That Ferrero Rocher flavor you wanted to try from that place you like."

210

"No way," she says, her eyes wide. "That store doesn't do take-aways, and the last few times I went, they were closed."

I freeze and blink as I try to come up with an excuse, only to realize that I don't want to lie to her, not even over something so little. "They do takeaways...but only for their owner. I bought the chain."

"You *what?*"

I scoop some onto a spoon and hold it out for her, and she stares at me for a moment before her lips close around it. Her eyes briefly fall closed, and she hums in satisfaction.

"Best investment ever," I whisper without thinking.

Serenity's eyes flutter open, and her gaze roams over my face. "Tell me why. You don't even like ice cream, Archer. Why would you buy my favorite ice cream chain and the coffee shop too?"

My heart begins to race, a hint of panic running down my spine. *Because I want to make sure you always have access to anything you want, whenever you want. Because I need to know that any time of the day, I can get you your favorite ice cream and make you smile.*

"I told you that I've always liked the food and beverage industry," I end up saying instead. "These just fit into my existing portfolio really well." It's not a lie, per se—it just isn't the full truth.

Serenity smiles and pushes against my shoulders as she moves on top of me, straddling me. Her eyes twinkle knowingly, and my heart begins to pound wildly. "It's just very coincidental that all these ice cream stores you bought are all closed every single time *Theo* tries to take me to one, but they're open pretty much any other time. Weird, right?"

I clear my throat and place her ice cream in one of my cupholders. "Weird, indeed. I'll be sure to look into that."

"Yeah," she murmurs, her hand sliding around the back of my neck. "You do that, babe."

My eyes widen when I realize what she just called me, and I grin, pleased to have earned myself a nickname. She leans in, her lips brushing against mine softly, once, twice, before I cup the back of her head and pull her in, taking what's mine.

She groans, and I grab her waist, sliding my hands down to her ass, squeezing, teasing as she parts her lips for me, deepening our kiss. I don't think I'll ever get enough of her. Each touch just feeds my addiction.

Her hands roam over my shoulders, and she pushes my jacket off, both of us impatient as we try to undress each other, losing ourselves in the moment. Every moment with her is different to anything else I've ever felt before—it's filled with passion in a way I didn't know existed. It's a fulfilling kind of passion, not one born of disagreement but one that's fueled entirely by our mutual desire to just be together. No facades, no ulterior motives.

She smiles against my mouth when I pull her dress up, and she lifts her arms for me, the two of us trying our best to maneuver in the small amount of space the back seat provides. I grunt when she involuntarily elbows me in the ribs, and she gasps.

"I'm so sorry!" she says as her dress joins my jacket on the floor, leaving her sitting in my lap in her sexy black lingerie.

I chuckle and shake my head as I cradle her face, my heart overflowing with tenderness. "I fucking told you, didn't I? Damn back seats."

She stills in my lap, her smile melting away. "You did this for me," she whispers, her brows furrowing.

I frown in confusion. "Who else would I do this for?" I ask, my voice soft.

She smiles shakily. "No, you...you remembered what I said about wanting to go on coffee dates and making out in the back seat of a car. You remembered, and you made it happen."

"Of course I remembered," I whisper, my heart oddly heavy.

She stares at me with dozens of unspoken questions in her eyes. "Archer...what are we doing?"

My stomach tightens when I read her expression and the finality in it. "That's kind of why I brought you here, Serenity. To talk about us." I gently brush her hair out of her face. "What if...Darling, what if I want to be the man you make all of your memories with? What if I don't want to be the one who you'll compare others to? What if I just want to be your one and only?"

She tightens her grip on my shoulders, her eyes widening just a touch. "Archer, what are you saying?"

"I'm saying that I want more, and I'm hoping that you do too."

She looks away, and my heart sinks. Did I misread her? I was so certain she'd gotten over Theo, but was I wrong? "Is it worth the risk?" she asks, her voice trembling. "You'd be risking your friendship with Ezra and the business you share. Then there's your relationship with my parents, too. Our lives are so entwined, and if we don't work out, we wouldn't be the only ones left hurt."

"You're worth *everything*, Serenity. There's nothing I wouldn't risk for a chance at a real future with you." I take a steadying breath and gently slide my hands down from her waist to her hips. "If that's not... if that's not what you want, I completely understand, and we can forget I ever even brought it—"

She leans in and kisses me, and I groan as I bury a hand in her hair, trying my best to be careful with her curls. "Is that a yes?" I whisper against her mouth in between kisses.

She pulls away, her whole face lit up in the most beautiful way. She smiles and leans back in my lap a little, her body on display for me. "That kind of depends on what the question was."

My eyes widen a fraction when I realize I didn't actually ask her much of anything. She laughs, and my heart warms. "Serenity, will you date me officially? Will you be mine?"

She nods, the back of her fingers brushing over my cheek. "Yes. I've been yours for far longer than you might realize, and I don't think that'll ever change."

Forty-Four

SERENITY

The butterflies in my stomach go wild as Archer and I step into the elevator, our hands entwined and identical smiles on our faces. "We need to find a way to tell Ezra," he says, squeezing my hand.

I look up at him, hesitating for a moment. "I think we should take some time to ease him into it, and I honestly don't want anyone to know at work. I worked so hard to earn a spot on the team and prove myself, and finding out that I'm your girlfriend will just undo so much of my hard work. It'll be even worse when people eventually realize that I'm Ezra's sister on top of that."

Archer pulls me closer, his free hand cupping my face. "Say that again," he whispers.

I grin, instantly knowing what he's referring to. "Your girlfriend," I murmur, my heart racing as pure giddiness rushes through me.

He dips his head and kisses me, stepping forward until he's got me pressed against the elevator wall, his knee pushing between my legs to part them.

I groan and wrap my arms around his neck, loving the feel of his body against mine.

"Fuck," he whispers against my mouth, his forehead dropping to mine. "I can't believe you're mine." He pulls away a little to look at me, his gaze roaming over my face like he can't quite believe this is real and we're officially together now. "Sera," he whispers. "I'll respect your decision with regard to your family and your career, but I need you to answer this one question for me." I nod, and a hint of discomfort crosses his face. "Are you going to tell Theo about us?"

My heart skips a beat when realization sinks in, and I recognize the uncertainty in his eyes. "I will," I tell him instantly. "I'll tell him this week."

Archer's shoulders relax, and I smile as I rise to my tiptoes to press a quick kiss to his lips. "I have no intention of hiding my boyfriend away unnecessarily. All I'm saying is that we need to be cautious and think things through. We should control how and when people find out about us."

His hands wrap around my waist, and he pulls me flush against him. "I need to tell Zane I have a girlfriend now," he says, his eyes twinkling. My heart skips a beat at the sound of it, and we just grin at each other like two lovesick fools. "I never told you, but he made me a bet."

I raise a brow. "What did you bet?"

He parts his lips, only to shake his head, his expression shuttering. "It's nothing, really. I'll tell you all about it someday. As it stands, I suspect he'll win that bet, but honestly, if and when he does, the real winner will be me."

My heart begins to beat a little faster as I try to figure out what he's talking about, but just as I want to start questioning him about it further, the elevator doors open. We step out together, only to be met by a police officer standing in front of the door.

"Mr. Harrison?"

Archer steps in front of me and nods. The police officer shakes his hand, her expression grave. "I'm Officer Stelter. Mind if we step inside? My partner is already in there with Mr. Sterling."

Archer looks back at me as he opens the door and holds it open for the police officer. My heart tightens painfully when he turns away from me to walk in, every instinct in me telling me to be cautious, that something is wrong. I watch as Archer freezes halfway into the living room, his breath hitching.

"Tyra?"

I follow his gaze, pure shock coursing through me when I find her sitting on the sofa, Ezra and another female police officer by her side. It's almost like she stepped right out of my painting, and for a few moments, I just stare at her in disbelief. She's thinner now, her skin an unnatural pale shade that only accentuates the dark circles under her eyes and the bruises on her skin. But even so, her natural beauty shines through—it's unmistakably her.

"Ty," I whisper, my heart breaking at the sight of her. Seeing a woman I've mourned the loss of is jarring to say the least. I didn't think we'd ever see her again, didn't think she truly could still be alive given everything the police told us, and happiness slowly begins to overtake my shock as I stand there, realizing that this is really happening, and she's really here with us, safe and sound.

I take a step forward, only to pause in my tracks when she rises to her feet, tears filling her eyes as she walks up to Archer. Her arms wrap around his waist, and he freezes for a moment before he hugs her back, his hand holding the back of her head, pure agony lighting up his eyes before he closes them, resting his chin on top of her head as he holds her tightly, the way he used to.

My stomach turns, a new kind of despair overtaking me as I watch the two of them together, relief at seeing her only just about outweighing my jealousy. Tyra bursts into tears, harsh sobs wracking her small body, and Archer buries one hand in her hair, the other roaming over her back. "Don't cry, darling," he says, his voice breaking. "I've got you. Everything is okay now. You're home, baby."

My chest begins to ache as he holds her, calling her every term of endearment I thought was mine. I don't even notice when Ezra wraps his arm around my shoulders, nor do I notice the conversations going around me. All I can focus on is Archer and the way everything and everyone else ceased to exist to him the moment he saw her.

"I w-was held captive," she tells him, before her breathing becomes choppy and panic clouds her beautiful blue eyes. She tries her hardest to inhale, only to choke on her sobs, her anxiety building with each attempt to breathe.

Guilt instantly settles deep in my stomach, making me feel like a horrible person for being even remotely jealous when I should be grateful that she's home, though clearly not unharmed.

"Look at me," Archer says, his tone calm and placating. "I'm here with you, Tyra. You're home with me, and you're safe now, darling." He grabs her hand and places it on his chest, the paintbrush charm I'd been playing with in the car grazing her fingers. "Breathe with me," he tells her, his voice so soft and kind that it hurts. "Can you do that for me, sweetheart?"

She nods and follows his instructions, letting him guide her breathing, until she calms down enough to speak. Her attempts to explain what happened just make her sob all over again, and Archer pulls her back into his arms as both officers step forward, explaining that she was taken and held captive by a stalker for nearly two years. I begin to feel sick as they tell us everything Tyra can't manage to say, and all the while, guilt unlike anything I've ever felt before builds deep in my chest until it overflows and turns to shame. While Tyra was held captive and tried her best to survive, Archer and I betrayed her in the worst way. She'd been holding on to hope and memories of us, and we'd been trying to forget her.

Archer looks up, our eyes locking, and I stare at my boyfriend, his ex in his arms and silent apologies written all over his face. He doesn't need to say the words for me to know we're over.

Forty-Five

ARCHER

"Please don't leave me," Tyra murmurs as she sits down on t[...]
the guest room I've been sleeping in.

I kneel in front of her and gently grab her hands, making [...]
to startle her. She hasn't stopped shaking from the moment [...]
and it kills me to see her look so broken when she was alwa[...]
of life. "I won't," I promise her. "I'm just going to grab som[...]
from my bedroom."

"Can't I come with you?"

I hesitate, unsure how to explain that I want to go che[...]
Serenity. She hasn't said a word since we found Tyra sittin[...]
sofa, and the quietly reassuring looks she's sent me just aren't [...]
for me.

"I'll be quick," I murmur, my voice filled with regret as I [...]
feet, feeling conflicted. I don't want to leave Tyra, but all I [...]
about is what must be going through Serenity's mind right [...]

"Please," she whispers when I turn my back to her, her h[...]
ping around mine to stop me. "Don't leave me again."

My eyes fall closed, my heart wrenching as guilt hits me hard, keeping me frozen in place. "Okay, I won't," I hear myself say, knowing it's the right thing to do despite how wrong it feels.

I hear my sheets rustle as she rises to her feet, and my entire body tenses when she hugs me from behind, her arms wrapping around my waist, her forehead pressed between my shoulder blades. "The man who found me…he told me you sent him."

I reach for her hands and hold them, my heart bleeding. For over two years, I imagined having her arms around me just like right now. I pleaded with a god I'm not even sure exists, begging him to return her to me. I should be more grateful, shouldn't be thinking of anything but her and her needs.

"No matter how bad things got, I always knew you'd stop at nothing to find me, that you'd be waiting for me to come back home."

I turn to face her, drinking her in. "I never gave up on you," I tell her honestly. "I knew you were out there somewhere, Tyra. It sounds crazy, but I could feel it."

She places her palm on my chest, over my heart, her eyes on mine. "You're the only reason I survived, you know? The memory of you kept me going when all I wanted to do was fade away."

I smile shakily, my heart heavy. "Not a single day went by without me thinking of you," I tell her. "It was torture to wonder where you were, and if you were okay. It tore me to pieces, Tyra."

She looks up at me, only to startle at the sound of soft knocking on the door I left ajar. Serenity pauses in the doorway, her gorgeous eyes filled with torment. She doesn't even look at me, keeping her focus solely on Tyra.

"Serenity?" Tyra says, her hand still on my chest. I exhale in relief when she steps away from me, taking a cautious step toward Serenity instead.

"Hi," Sera says carefully, her eyes glistening with tears. "I just wanted to see if there's anything you needed. I could make you some tea, if you'd like? We've got some of that green tea you love. Please let me know if you need any clothes or cosmetics or things like that."

I fucking love her heart. Serenity is one of a kind, and she doesn't even seem to realize it. I know her well enough to realize she's hurting right now, that insecurity is threatening to overwhelm her, and even so, she's putting Tyra first.

"God, I missed you," Tyra says, her voice breaking. Serenity sniffles as Tyra takes another step toward her, and then another, until her arms wrap around Sera.

My heart fucking breaks when Serenity begins to cry as she squeezes Tyra, holding onto her tightly. "I m-missed you t-too," she says, her cries turning into sobs. "S-so much."

It fucking kills me to watch the two of them together, knowing that in part, Tyra's disappearance was what brought Serenity and me together. Being with Serenity was freeing because she understood my pain and never tried to replace Tyra, nor did she ever ask me to forget. She loved Tyra as much as I did, and it's clear she still does.

"I'm so happy you're home safe and sound," Serenity says, her voice trembling. It doesn't escape my notice that she still hasn't looked at me, and I hate that everything we have suddenly feels so sordid. "I was so worried, Tyra."

Tyra holds Serenity's face, their dynamics still the same as they've always been. My heart wrenches again when Tyra gently swipes away Serenity's tears in the same sisterly way she used to. "I was worried about you too," she replies. "I was scared that you'd give up on your dreams without me here to push you, and it killed me to know I wasn't here to keep my promises to you. I thought of you every day, Ser."

I look down at the floor, hating the guilt I saw written all over

Serenity's face. She regrets me, and I can't stand here knowing I'm losing her when there isn't a thing I can do to stop it from happening.

"Can I...can I do anything to help?" Serenity asks. "I feel so useless, Ty. I've felt so helpless for so long, and I just...now that you're finally home, I want to be there for you."

Tyra turns, and I look up. "Archer, you, um...you still have all of my things, right?" she asks, her voice barely above a whisper. Something akin to fear blooms in her eyes, her insecurities shining through.

"Of course," I tell her, trying my hardest not to notice the way Serenity's body tenses in my peripheral vision. "It's all in this room, actually. I...after a year of you being gone, I boxed all your things up, but I could never..."

"Thank you," she whispers, her voice breaking. "For not letting me down. It was my biggest fear, you know? That I'd come back, and you wouldn't want me anymore."

I fight my instinct to look at Serenity, trying my hardest to remember that Tyra needs me right now when all I want to do is remind her that we broke up before she went missing. She's vulnerable and traumatized beyond my comprehension, and the very least I can do is bite my tongue and support her as best as I can. I owe her that at least. After all, she'd never have gone on that trip all by herself if I hadn't ended things with her. "You know this is your home too," I tell her as I step away to take some of her boxes out of the closet I stored them in.

"I...I'll go make you some tea," Serenity says, stumbling back. I stare after her as she walks away, her long, curly hair swaying, and I instantly feel the loss. Just a few hours ago, I had her in my lap, her lips against mine, and my name on her lips.

"Why don't you get ready for bed?" I murmur as I place the boxes down. "Give me a shout when you're done, okay?"

She hesitates, but I walk away before she can stop me, the door falling closed as I do. I know I shouldn't have left her, but fuck, I can't leave Serenity alone either, not like this, not when I know she's hurting too.

I find my girlfriend standing in the kitchen, staring blankly ahead as she tries to breathe evenly, clearly on the verge of tears. "Serenity."

She looks up, her eyes widening when she sees me. "Archer," she says, straightening. "Is everything okay?"

I stop in front of her and reach for her, my heart breaking when she flinches and moves away just a touch. "I was just about to ask you the same thing."

"Of course," she murmurs, looking away. "I'm just...I'm just relieved that Tyra seems okay, and that she's home safe and sound. I can't imagine how happy you are to have her back."

"Darling," I murmur.

Her eyes snap up, her pain shining through. "Look, I understand this changes everything. We don't need to talk about it, Archer."

I reach for her and cup her face, my thumb brushing over her lips. "It changes *nothing*," I tell her, my voice rough.

She places her hand over mine and draws a shaky breath, her eyes overflowing with heartache. "How could it not? We got her back when we didn't think we ever would. Besides, you were only with me to get over her, and now you don't need to anymore. This is everything you wanted, Archer. I won't stand in the way of that. I'd never do that to you, or to her. Besides, she needs you. Didn't you hear her? Her biggest fear was coming home to find you no longer wanted her. We can't do that to her. *I can't.*"

I sigh and let my hand fall away. "No, Serenity. I didn't know what I needed until I kissed you, until I woke up with you in my arms for the very first time, your wild, unruly hair fucking everywhere." I tuck one of her curls behind her ear, and her eyes flutter closed briefly, hiding the hint of hope I could've sworn I saw. "It took me a while to acknowledge it, but it was guilt that kept me from moving on, not love. I'm happy to have her back, but this changes nothing between us, Serenity. You're still the only one I want."

"You say that," she whispers. "But we both know you're about to walk back into that room, and the woman you'll hold in your arms tonight won't be me."

SERENITY

"You can finish that tomorrow, Ser. You've been working late four days in a row now."

I look up at Theo, a dull ache keeping me from smiling when all I want to do is put up a front and pretend I'm not breaking. "I know. I just need to write a report on the changes I've made to our design, and then I'll go home."

He leans against my desk, his eyes roaming over my face. "What's wrong?"

My lips part, but I can't find the right words to describe what the last few days have been like. Watching Archer cater to Tyra has slowly broken my heart, each kind action toward her creating another chasm, each smile wounding me further. I'm trying my best not to be jealous, to be understanding of her circumstances and needs, but I can't help it. Each time she reaches for him, her arms wrapping around his waist, I fight the urge to stake my claim, to pull him away and tell him to look only at me. Every night, I lie in his bed, knowing he's lying next to her in my makeshift art studio. It's tearing me apart, and there isn't a single thing I can do about it.

"I'm fine," I tell him, unable to meet his eyes. Work seems to be the only part of my life that hasn't changed, and I've thrown myself into it. I'm craving some normalcy, and the office is the only place I can find it—and only because Archer hasn't been coming in for more than an hour or so a day. He's barely left Tyra's side, and I've done my best not to think about it too much.

Theo places his finger underneath my chin and tips my face up, forcing me to look at him. "You're not fine," he says, a deep ache shining in his eyes. "Not even remotely."

I watch as he reaches for my mouse and turns my computer off, before grabbing my purse.

"Come on," he tells me. "Let's go for a walk and get some ice cream. There's something I've been meaning to tell you anyway."

He offers me his hand, and I stare at it for a moment before placing my palm in his. Theo grins at me and pulls me out of my chair, his arm wrapping around my shoulders as we walk to the exit.

"Serenity?"

My entire body tenses when we find Archer and Ezra standing in front of the elevators, my heart overflowing with longing at the sight of Archer dressed in my favorite navy three-piece suit. His expression hardens when Theo pulls me closer, pure possessiveness flickering through his eyes. My stomach tightens when his jaw locks, something passing between us. This is what I miss most—the intimacy, that look in his eyes reminding me that I'm *his*.

"Where are you guys headed?" Ezra asks, his expression one I'm not familiar with. Intrigue, perhaps?

Theo turns his head to look at me, and all of a sudden, I realize how close his face is to mine. It's something I'd gotten used to before he started dating Kristen, but for months now, we've kept our distance. "Taking Ser out for ice cream," he says, grinning at me. "One way or another, I'm going to put a real smile on her face today because I have yet to see one." He turns back to look at Ezra. "Don't expect her home until I've accomplished my mission."

Archer tenses and begins to tap his foot the moment we enter the elevator, but he doesn't look at me. Instead, he just stares at the floor, his expression unreadable. There are no silent pleas not to go, no attempts to keep me from Theo.

Ezra glances at Archer and throws me a sweet smile. "All right. Have fun, then," he says as the doors open.

I take one final look at Archer, unsure what exactly I'm looking for, and then I follow Theo out, my heart uneasy. He told me nothing would change between us, but everything has. How could it not?

"So what has it been like, living with Archer?" I look up in surprise, and Theo smiles ruefully. "Ezra told me. I can't believe you didn't tell me. It hurts how much we've grown apart in a matter of months, Ser."

"I'm sorry," I murmur as we walk into one of my favorite ice cream shops, the one Archer bought for me. I almost expected it to be closed, like it is every time Theo and I try to visit, but it's open today. "I've just had a lot going on, and we haven't really had a chance to properly catch up." The burst pipe and us moving in with Archer barely registers in light of everything that's going on with Tyra. There's so much he doesn't know, and I'm not sure where I'd even begin to explain.

He sighs and lets go of me as we sit down. "I can hardly blame you since I haven't even told you that Kristen and I broke up three weeks ago. She moved out and went back home."

I freeze and look up. *"What?"*

Theo nods, his gaze roaming over my face. "I've been meaning to tell you, but each time I tried to take you out to dinner, something came up and you canceled."

I reach for him, my hands wrapping around his arms. "I'm so sorry, Theo. Are you okay?"

He looks into my eyes, and that expression…it's one I've seen in Archer's eyes often. It's *longing*. "It wasn't at all what it seemed. I tried, but she and I…we just weren't meant to be."

The server takes our order, and we both fall silent when she walks away. I'm not quite sure what to do or say. I don't want to pry, and I'm not sure how to console him. "I'm really sorry it didn't work out," I tell him, my voice soft. "Is there anything I can do to make you feel better?"

"Yes," he says, reaching for my hand. "There's something I need to ask you, and I need you to answer me honestly."

I nod, nerves buzzing through me. "What is it?"

"There's something she said when we ended things, and it just got me thinking. Kristen told me she realized that what she wanted was a version of me that wouldn't ever belong to anyone but *you*. She told me she fell for a part of me I'd never give her because she isn't you, and it became clear to her that no one could ever take your place in my heart. She was tired of coming second to you when you weren't even in the room."

The words hit me hard, and my heart begins to ache when I realize I made Kristen feel the way Tyra is making me feel. The parallels feel like some kind of bad karma, and I smile humorlessly. I couldn't maintain my friendship with Kristen after I found out she went after Theo despite knowing how I feel about him, so what does that mean for Tyra and me? If she finds out, I won't just hurt her. I'll lose her.

Theo squeezes my hand and sighs. "Before she left, there's one thing she asked…Kristen asked me to really think about why I never fully gave her a chance and why you distanced yourself the moment we started dating, why it seemed like you didn't want to be around us, almost like you didn't want to see us together."

My heart begins to beat a little faster, my stomach tightening nervously. "I…I distanced myself because I didn't want to stand between you two, Theo. I didn't want our friendship to affect your relationship."

He places his free hand over our joined hands, pulling them to his chest, his eyes on mine. "Is that all it was, Serenity? Or were we both just too scared to face our feelings?"

Forty-Seven

ARCHER

I glance at Tyra's sleeping face and carefully slip out of bed, my heart heavy. She can't sleep if I'm not right there with her, reminding her that I'll be there to protect her, and fuck, I want to be there for her, but at what cost?

I didn't even feel like I had the right to beg my own girlfriend not to go out with the one man who could take her from me, couldn't grab her hand and ask her to choose me. All I could do was stand there as he wrapped his arm around her, smiling at her in a way he never did before—like he finally realized how fucking special she is.

I try my best to be quiet as I slip out of my guest room, glancing over at Ezra on the sofa as I pad over to my own bedroom, the one Serenity has been sleeping in. He stirs, and for a moment I'm sure he'll sit up like he usually does, but then he turns, seemingly falling back asleep.

My heart sinks when I walk into my bedroom and find it empty. It's nearly midnight, and she still isn't home. My thoughts begin to spiral as I imagine where she might be, what she might be doing with him.

I slip into bed, my eyes falling closed when her sweet scent fills my senses, and I inhale deeply, reveling in the remnants of her presence. She has no fucking idea how much I miss her, how miserable I've been without her. My days aren't complete without our conversations, and the distance between us is fucking unbearable. She won't reply to my text messages, won't look at me at work, and when she is home, she barely leaves her room. I'm losing her, and I don't know if I have the right to hold on the way I want to.

Time seems to move slowly as my mind tortures me with thoughts of her with Theo, of her showing him everything I taught her, kissing him the way she knows I like. My heart is in fucking tatters by the time the door opens, and I drink her in, taking in that flustered expression I didn't put there, the twinkle in her eyes.

She gasps when she spots me, and I sit up, letting the sheet fall away as I lean back on my palms. "Archer," she says, her voice betraying her surprise. "W-What are you doing here?"

My gaze roams over her body, and the tight black dress that envelops it. I don't have to guess to know she's wearing sexy stockings held up at her thighs, the very same ones that drive me completely wild. Did she show him something only I'd ever seen before?

"This is *my* bedroom, is it not?" I ask, my tone harsher than I'd intended.

She nods slowly and walks farther into the room, placing her handbag on my dresser before slipping out of her heels, her eyes moving over every part of the room but me.

Her body tenses almost imperceptibly when I slip out of bed and walk over to her, and it fucking destroys me to have her respond to me that way. She inhales shakily when I slide my hand around the back of her neck, my thumb resting along her jaw. "Look at me." She keeps her eyes downcast, and pure sorrow settles in my gut. "Please look at me, darling."

Serenity lifts her face, the same ache I'm feeling reflected in her eyes. "Don't call me that," she says, her voice breaking. "Do you have any idea what it does to me to hear you call *her* darling, when I thought that name was just mine?"

My eyes fall closed. "I'm sorry," I whisper, my forehead falling to hers. "I'm so sorry, Serenity."

"Don't be," she says, her tone carrying a tinge of bitterness. She pushes against my chest, and I reluctantly let go of her.

I watch her as she moves through the room, plugging her phone in to charge and placing her trusty notebook on my nightstand. Normally, I'd have loved how at home she feels in my room—how much it seems like *ours*. Tonight, it just makes me feel like an unwelcome stranger in what has always been one of my favorite spaces, even though I'm standing here with my favorite person.

"Were you with him all night?"

Her spine goes rigid, and defiance crosses her face as she looks at me. "Yes."

I raise my fist to my mouth and bite down on it, despair spreading from my fucking heart. "Did anything happen that you think I should know about?"

She leans back against the wall, her gaze roaming over my face. Her expression softens, her anger dulled by the fear and jealousy I can't hide. "He broke up with Kristen and told me he has feelings for me. We talked, and he asked me if he stood a chance or if it was too late."

I clench my jaw and look away, surprise rendering me speechless. I noticed the way he started to look at her when he no longer had her full attention, but I foolishly thought I had nothing to worry about. "What did you say to that?" I ask, scared of what her response might be.

She smiles humorlessly. "I told him I needed time to think."

I bite down on my lip as she turns and walks into my en suite bathroom, and I hesitate for a split second before following her in. Our eyes meet in the mirror, and something in her gaze makes me wrap one hand around her waist.

"Tell me you're still mine, Serenity," I beg, my voice soft, pleading.

She leans back, pressing herself against my chest. My arms wrap around her, one palm flat to her stomach while the other moves to cup her jaw as I tilt her head and make her face me, needing her to look me in the eye if she's going to break my heart.

"I'm yours, Archer Harrison, whether I like it or not."

I exhale in relief, my hand slipping into her hair as I lean in to kiss her, craving her with every fucking fiber of my being. She moans, and I turn her around, needing her closer.

Serenity rises to her tiptoes as I caress every inch of her I can reach, undoing the zipper on the back of her dress impatiently, needing to feel her soft skin. My heart rests a little easier when she slips her hand underneath my T-shirt, letting it trail over my abs in that way she likes.

I groan when she pushes the fabric up and I help her lift it over my head. It falls to the floor, and desire glitters in her eyes. *This*. This is exactly what I needed. I needed her to look at me like I'm the only one she wants, the only one that can give her what she needs.

"Archer," she whispers, her eyes locking on the charm around my neck. "We can't. You know we can't."

I look her in the eye as I reach over and turn the shower on. "No one will know."

Forty-Eight

SERENITY

Archer's eyes are filled with hunger as we undress each other, his hands trembling ever so slightly, like this moment feels precious to him too. "Fuck," he groans when I stand in front of him in nothing but my hold up tights.

He caresses the top of my thighs, where the edge of my stockings meets my skin, and all the while, he stares at me like I'm a mirage, like I'm his every dream come true. Knowing he still wants me heals a little part of me he doesn't even realize is broken.

"I need you to keep these on for me," he murmurs, just before he pulls me into the shower and against the wall. I gasp and place my hands on his chest, warm water spraying down on us as he holds my face, his eyes blazing. "This pretty little mouth is mine," he growls before leaning in to kiss me.

I rise to my tiptoes, my arms wrapping around his neck as I kiss him back, returning every bit of passion and desperation tenfold. He swallows my moans as one hand moves down to my breast, kneading and pinching, his touch punishing as he caresses my body the way only he can.

"*Oh God,*" I moan when he pushes my legs apart with his knee, his fingers teasing without entering.

"Look at me," he demands when my eyes flutter closed. I obey, my heart racing when I find him staring at me like he's enchanted. "This pussy," he growls, pushing two fingers into me while pressing his thumb against my clit. "Is *mine.*" He begins to swirl his thumb, his movements harsh and swiftly bringing me to the edge. "Do you understand?"

I nod, my hips moving involuntarily. The heat in the shower and the way he's touching me has rapidly made me lightheaded, heightening every sensation. He curls his fingers, and I arch my back, riding his hand eagerly. It's been so long since I felt so close to him, since I had his undivided attention.

"You're so beautiful," he groans, his fingers moving faster. "There's nothing like watching you come for me, you know that? Nothing makes me feel more powerful."

He watches me as I slowly unravel, until my muscles begin to contract around his fingers. I can't recall the last time I saw him smile so widely, pure satisfaction shining though his eyes as I bite down on my lip, trying my best to keep my moans in.

I gasp as he grabs my hips, lifting me up and against the wall in one smooth move. I instantly wrap my legs around his waist, my hands sliding into his hair as he looks into my eyes. "I've never wanted anyone the way I want you," he tells me. "Never wanted to belong to anyone the way I belong to you, Serenity."

His breath hitches when I reach between us and line his cock up. "Then show me," I whisper. "Show me that you're mine."

He tightens his grip on my hips as he pushes into me slowly, intentionally, his eyes never leaving mine. The way he moans when he bottoms out inside me has my head falling back against the wall, and I smile when he kisses me just below my ear, his soft pants tickling my skin. "You have no idea how much I needed this," he whispers, before grazing my neck with his teeth. "I think of you every second of every day, Serenity."

I can't suppress a moan when he pulls back, only to thrust into me harshly, our eyes locked. "You want me to show you I'm yours?" he asks, doing it all over again. "Just look at me, baby. Look at what you've done to me."

His fingers dig into my skin as he holds me up, and my nails scrape across his scalp in that way he likes.

"I've never been so desperate for anyone. Never *ever* have I felt like my heart is no longer mine, like it's entirely at your mercy to do with as you please."

He draws a long, pleased groan from my throat when he tilts my hips just right, hitting that spot inside me that drives me wild. The way he smiles at me, looking entirely too satisfied with himself, tells me he knows exactly what he's doing to me.

I tighten my grip on his hair and pull his mouth to mine, losing myself in him in this moment. He groans, his tongue parting my lips eagerly. "I'm close," he whispers against my mouth, his movements becoming a little more erratic. "I can't...fuck, *Serenity*."

The way he moves his hips, rotating them just right, his movements strong and intentional, tip me over the edge.

"Oh *fuck*," he moans when my pussy contracts around him, his voice far too loud, though he doesn't seem to care. "Yes," he groans. "*Yes.*"

I tighten my legs around his hips as he comes deep inside me, the sounds leaving his lips driving me wild. There's something so incredibly sexy about Archer losing control like that because of *me*.

He smiles at me when his body relaxes, and I gently trail a finger between his brows and down his nose. He chuckles as he bites me softly, and I pull my hand away, giggling back at him.

The same words I keep trying to hide rise back to the surface, but I can't voice them. Not now. Not when it'd seem like emotional blackmail to tell him how I feel, guilt-tripping him into saying it back.

He groans as he slips out of me and gently lowers me to the floor, his forehead dropping to mine. I whimper when he cups the back of my neck and leans in to kiss me. My lips trail to his neck, and he moans in the sexiest way when I kiss him in the same spot that always makes a shiver run down my spine. He inhales sharply when I suck down on his skin right where his neck meets his shoulder. I pull back when I realize it'll leave a mark, and all of a sudden, something dark and unpleasant rushes through me—something that makes me hate myself.

"No," Archer says, grabbing my hair and guiding me to his chest. "Mark me, darling. Right here, over my heart. It's yours. *I* am yours, Serenity."

He pulls me closer, until my lips are pressed against his chest. His eyes are filled with a different kind of desire as I do just that and mark him as mine, satisfaction coursing through my body.

He smiles at the dark red mark when I pull away, his eyes glittering with something I've never seen before. "Good girl," he murmurs, before pulling my face to his, kissing me slowly.

Forty-Nine

SERENITY

I stare at Archer through the mirror in his bedroom as he gently combs my detangling leave-in treatment through my hair with a wide-tooth comb, his movements patient and diligent. I've never seen him focus on a task quite as much as this one, and something about it makes me smile.

"What?" he asks.

I love you. "Nothing."

His gaze darkens, and he smiles back at me, his gaze briefly roaming over the T-shirt I'm wearing. It's the same one he walked in wearing, and though he hasn't said anything, I know he loves seeing me in it. Almost as much as I love seeing him in nothing but the pair of black boxers he's wearing.

"Let me dry your hair for you with that diffuser thing you like. Where is it?"

I shake my head and turn to face him, my heart heavy. "No. It'll make far too much noise. I'll just wrap my hair up and let it dry naturally." I hesitate, my fingers brushing over the mark I left on his skin. It darkened, standing out against his light skin.

Seeing it brings me a sick kind of satisfaction, and I wonder if he knew it'd put me at ease to know he either wouldn't take his shirt off in front of Tyra or that he simply didn't care if she saw. It's reassuring in a primal way that should embarrass me, but instead, I embrace it, reveling in the feeling.

"Archer…you should go," I say nonetheless, unable to suppress the tinge of guilt that took root the moment Tyra came back home.

He freezes, his gaze cutting to mine. "What? Why?"

I let my hand fall away, my possessiveness at war with my desire to do the right thing. "What if Tyra wakes up? I know she's been having nightmares." I look away, my heart aching. "I can hear her at night." I don't have the heart to tell him that I can also hear the way he consoles her softly, the way she repeats his name over and over again, like he's her lifeline.

Archer reaches for me, and I gasp when he lifts me into his arms in one smooth move, his eyes on mine as he carries me to his bed. "Don't think about anyone but me," he says as he lays me down, not caring about the way my damp hair messes up his sheets. He settles on top of me and holds himself up on his forearms. "Not tonight, Serenity." He lowers himself on top of me, placing his head just below my shoulder.

"It's hard not to," I admit as I wrap my arms around him, enjoying the feel of his weight on top of me.

"I know," he whispers. "I'm trying to be there for her, but I just… *fuck*. I can't help but feel like I can't win." He tightens his grip on my waist, his breathing becoming uneven. "It feels like I'm losing you, Sera. Am I?"

I play with his hair, my touch soothing. "I don't know," I reply, my voice breaking.

He pushes himself back up on his forearms to look at me. "Is it because of him?" he asks, his expression mirroring the insecurity I've been feeling. "You were only seeing me to get over him, and now you don't need to anymore," he says, throwing my own venom-laced words back at me. "When you told me something along those lines, who were you really talking about?"

I push against his chest, sitting up as anger ignites deep in my chest. "I'm not the one sleeping next to Theo every night, holding him in my arms and consoling him. I don't make you watch as he hugs me, looking up at me like I'm his whole world."

"Don't you?" he snaps, sitting up too. "You aren't clueless, Serenity. You knew it'd fucking kill me to watch him wrap his arm around you like that, at my own fucking office."

"You think it doesn't hurt to watch Tyra touch you like you're still hers? Every time I see you with her, I'm just reminded that everything that I thought was mine was merely borrowed. What do you think that does to me, Archer?"

I try my best to blink back my tears, but they fall nonetheless. Archer instantly cradles my face, the fight leaving his eyes. "I never meant to hurt you, darling," he whispers, his forehead falling to mine. "What do you want me to do?" he asks, his voice breaking. "I can't turn her away when she needs me, Serenity. There's nothing romantic about it—not to me. You know that, don't you?"

I pull back to look into his eyes, unsure if I believe him. "I told you once that I never wanted to take her place, and I still don't. I love her too, Archer. More than you could possibly understand. You have no idea how torn up I am about this whole situation, how sick it makes me feel to want you when she needs you in a way I can't even comprehend. I don't know how to deal with the jealousy I feel when I don't think I'm even entitled to it. I…"

"You are," he says, his voice breaking. "You *are* entitled to me. I love you, Serenity. With all I am. All I have."

CATHARINA MAURA

I stare at him speechlessly, not even aware of the tears that have begun to stream down my face until he catches them with his thumbs.

"I love your heart, your soul. I love you for who you are, every single aspect of you. I'm yours, Serenity Adesina, whether you'll have me or not."

"I love you too," I tell him, only to fully burst into tears at the admission. "Oh God, I love you so much, and I shouldn't. Archer, we shouldn't. We can't. We both love her, and we can't do this to her. You know we can't."

He takes me into his arms and holds me tightly, his silence speaking volumes. He knows as well as I do that us being together would inflict more harm on the one person that can't take any more of it. "We'll figure it out," he says, his hand moving over my back soothingly. "I'm at as much of a loss as you are, but there's one thing I'm absolutely certain of: I won't let you go, Serenity. I don't ever want to go back to a life in which you aren't mine."

Fifty

SERENITY

I look up when Theo places a cup of coffee on my desk, a sweet smile on his face. "Don't do that," he murmurs, his gaze roaming over me. "Don't avoid me because of what I said."

"I'm not," I reply weakly. Truthfully, I haven't even thought about him. All I've been able to think about all day is my conversation with Archer last night and how it felt to fall asleep next to him, only to wake up alone. I'd felt a bit more at ease until I saw him coming out of the room he now shares with Tyra, and I realized he'd left me at night to join her in bed.

Theo sighs and drags his chair over. "I know you well enough to know you're avoiding me. I can handle rejection, Serenity. What I can't handle is losing you altogether. If friendship is all you're able to give me, then I'll happily take that."

I nod, unsure what to say. I loved him for years, but what I felt for him pales in comparison to my feelings for Archer, and I can't tell what's real anymore. I waited so long for one single chance with Theo, and it feels like I'm wasting this opportunity, like I owe it to myself to at least think about it…when I truly don't even remotely want to.

"I know, Theo. I'm sorry. I wasn't trying to avoid you, but I guess I subconsciously did just that."

He smiles, but it doesn't reach his eyes. "I don't want you to apologize for doing what's right for you, even if it hurts me," he tells me, looking away.

His words startle me, but I nod nonetheless. He takes one more look at me, and then he rolls his chair back to his own desk, leaving me staring at him. It isn't hard to remember why I fell for him in the first place. If he'd never started dating Kristen, would we have found our way to each other by now? It's all I can think about all the way home—all the what-ifs. What if Tyra had never gone missing? What if I'd had the courage to confess my feelings for Theo sooner? What if I'd followed my dreams instead of turning to street art, and I'd never ended up at Serenity Solutions? Would Archer and I, despite all of that, still have found our way to each other?

I'm absent-minded when I walk in, only to find Tyra standing in the living room, her hands held up in defense and her eyes wide. It takes me a moment to realize that I accidentally slammed the door closed—loud sounds trigger her. Tears fill her eyes, and her breathing becomes ragged as I take a step forward, panic taking hold of her and consuming her whole.

"Tyra," I murmur, my voice soft and placating. "It's me. Serenity. It's just me."

Recognition flashes through her eyes, taking the edge off her panic, but she's too far gone to regulate her breathing.

"I'm sorry, Ty," I tell her, taking a step closer. "I'm so sorry. I really didn't mean to startle you."

Her shoulders relax, and I take another cautious step forward, carefully watching her to make sure she doesn't recoil. She tries her best to breathe but only manages to choke in the process, tears streaming down her face as she sinks to the floor, burying her face in her hands.

"It's okay," I whisper as I kneel in front of her, my stomach twisting as guilt takes root. "Can I hold your hand?"

I hold mine out to her, letting her make the call. She's been trying to hide it, but I noticed she doesn't like to be touched if she isn't the one taking initiative. Tyra looks into my eyes, her breathing slowly returning to normal as she takes my hand and squeezes tightly.

I sit with her like that, our hands joined, my thumb drawing soothing circles on her skin. It hurts to witness her fragility when I'd always admired her strength. She was someone I looked up to, the first one to protect me and stand up for me, even against my mother when need be. To know someone took that strength from her and broke her...it destroys me. She's lost so much, and I can't be the reason she loses anything else.

"I really need Archer," she tells me, her expression pleading. "I don't feel safe when he isn't there, Serenity. I can't...I can't be without him. It's so hard for me when he leaves for work, and lately he's been staying gone for longer than before. I just keep thinking that someone is going to walk in and take me, and I'll be trapped all over again, and this time, I won't make it out alive."

"You're safe here," I promise her. "No one but Archer, Ezra, or me can enter. There are multiple layers of security, and Archer hired extra security personnel that he's stationed in the lobby and in the hallway. No one can get to you here, Tyra. I'm sure of it."

She nods, and I hold my arms out for her. She tries her best to blink back her tears, only for a sob to tear through her throat when she hugs me, her head on my shoulder. I hold her tightly, gently rubbing her back, and all the while, my own heart shatters into a thousand pieces. It'd destroy her if she found out about Archer and me, and I don't think I could live with myself if I did that to her. I don't think Archer could either, so where does that leave us?

"He doesn't love me anymore," she sobs. "I can tell, Serenity. He's trying so hard, and he's so good to me, but I can see it in his eyes. I was so certain that I'd come home, and every argument we've ever had would be forgotten, and we'd get back together. The memory of him is the only reason I survived, and now...I don't have anything left. I don't dare leave this house, and I can't dance anymore, and even Archer...I don't even have him anymore. I just...maybe I just should've..."

"Come with me," I whisper. "There's something I'd like to show you."

She takes my hand and follows me to Archer's home office, where we moved most of my bulkier art supplies to when Ezra moved in. Her eyes widen in surprise when she sees the canvas propped up in the corner. Her body shakes as she approaches it carefully, disbelief written all over her face.

"Archer asked me to paint that for him," I tell her, my voice breaking. "I've been working on it for nearly six months now, and it's finally done. He wouldn't have asked me to paint you living your biggest dreams if he didn't love you."

It kills me to say it, but I know it's true. Each brushstroke hurt more than the last, but nothing compares to the pain of watching her look at Archer's quiet proclamation of love for her...crafted by *my* hands.

"You haven't left the house yet, but the passcode to enter his home is your birthday backwards. The code to his phone is too but the right way around. You're an inextricable part of him, Tyra. You always will be. He never let you go, and he never will."

She turns to look at me, and for the first time since she returned, there's a touch of hope in her eyes. I don't have it in me to extinguish it when her love for Archer is what gives her the will to live, to fight.

Fifty-One

SERENITY

I sit up in bed at the sound of Tyra's agonized cries, and Archer's soothing voice soon follows. "Tyra," I hear him say. "I'm right here with you. You're safe in my arms, Ty."

Her cries start to sound muffled, and my eyes flutter closed when I realize he must be hugging her, the two of them cuddled up in bed.

I sniffle softly, fresh tears escaping my own eyes. I've never felt such intense self-loathing, nor have I ever felt this kind of twisted jealousy blended with shame. He tells me he loves me, but it's clear he still loves her too. Maybe not in the way he used to, but he does, and if I didn't love her just as much, I'd resent him for it.

I slip out of bed as she begins to cry in earnest, repeating his name over and over again, almost like she's stuck in a memory. The mere thought of her having prayed his name like that while she was held hostage tears me to pieces, and I can't listen to this. Not without hating myself for every touch, every stolen moment that should've been hers.

I pause in surprise when I walk into the hallway to find Ezra standing in front of their door, his gaze cutting to mine. He doesn't say anything as I walk past him and into the living room, his footsteps quiet behind me. "Let's have some tea," he says, his voice hoarse. "I can't sleep either."

I hesitate, my fingers itching with the need to paint. It's the only way I know to process my emotions, to ease the pain. My eyes flutter closed when I remember that some of my supplies are still in Archer's spare room—*Tyra's room*. It's irrational and it's unfair, but for one single moment, bitterness rushes through me.

"Here," Ezra says, taking a seat at the kitchen island. I join him reluctantly, wishing I could just walk out of here and escape for a few hours. Instead, I sit down opposite my brother and warm my hands on the mug he hands me, my favorite one, the one Archer and I bought when he took me to Italy.

"You look like you haven't slept in weeks," I tell him, knowing full well that I probably look the same.

He grimaces and takes a sip of his tea. "How could I?" he asks, his voice breaking. "It hurts to hear her fall apart like that every damn night and being unable to take away her pain." He pushes a hand into his hair and takes a shaky breath. "Hell, even if I could, it isn't me she wants."

Ezra looks away, almost like he realizes what he just said, and I stare at him in disbelief, unsure what to say. That look in his eyes…it isn't just concern. His feelings for her extend beyond friendship, and I can't believe I missed it. How long has he felt that way? "I'm sorry, Ezra," I murmur, my heart aching. "Give her some time. He's just… Archer is just the person she's most comfortable with right now, but that doesn't mean that—"

"It's fine," he says, cutting me off, forcing a smile. "It's just that she's been my best friend my whole life, and it's killing me that I can't be there for her when she needs me most. I get why it's Archer she needs, but fuck, I wish she'd rely a little on me too." He knocks his tea back and rises from his seat. "I'm just going to try to get some sleep," he tells me. "I'd tell you that you should too, but I know you won't. Just be careful, okay? Wear a thick coat when you go out, and don't get caught."

My eyes widen a fraction, and my brother smiles at me knowingly. I part my lips to ask him how he knows what I'd been planning to do, but he just gently pushes a strand of my hair out of my face. "The charm you lost on the night Archer caught you? The one that he now wears around his neck like a damn trophy? Did you forget I had that handmade for you? It's one of a kind." He smiles ruefully. "You also seem to have forgotten that we can track each other's locations."

My breath hitches. "You knew," I murmur, and I think we both know it's not just my art we're talking about now. He knows about all of my trips with Archer, the fact that I was always with him while Ezra was gone.

He nods. "I wish you'd told me, and honestly, I wish you hadn't ever felt the need to resort to it at all. Your work belongs on canvases, not on abandoned buildings. I should've stood up for you when I noticed Mom pressuring you to give up painting. I should've realized that you'd stopped painting when you went to college, and I should've asked why. Tyra would have."

I look away, unable to refute his words. If not for her, I'd have given up so much sooner. Even when I first tried out street art, it was because of her. I owe her so much, and all I've given her in return is betrayal of the worst kind.

"She needs him," Ezra says, his tone pleading. "You know that, don't you?"

My head snaps up, my stomach dropping. That look in his eyes renders me speechless for a moment. "I…yes, of course I know that."

Ezra studies my face, and then he looks down at his feet. "I'm sorry, Serenity."

I almost ask him what he's sorry for, but I don't want to talk to him about Archer. Not when it's clear that he doesn't think Archer would ever choose me. I'd been hopeful when he told me that Archer seemed happier after we'd been together awhile, but I should've heeded his warning.

I'm worried about the girl he's seeing and what it'll do to her to realize she'll never have all of him.

I'd dismissed it then, quietly confident in what we were building together, only to realize we set our foundations on quicksand. Now here I am, watching everything we had collapse and disappear, and I'll have to do it with a smile on my face because this is exactly what I signed up for.

I'm still thinking about Ezra's words as I stand in the same spot where Archer asked me to date him officially, a beautiful city skyline behind me. My mind tortures me with images of Tyra wrapping her arms around his waist and him placing his chin on top of her head, his warm body pressed against hers and his cologne enveloping her.

The worst part is that it isn't even my imagination; it's my own memories that are killing me as I paint a piece depicting a man holding a woman's hand—except he looks past her with an expression conveying longing, at the woman standing in the background, a red thread connecting him to her. I hesitate for a moment before filling in the details, giving the woman by his side wild, curly hair, just like mine, before adding a pair of pink pointe shoes dangling from the hands of the woman in the background, her long, blond hair illuminating her features, making her look near angelic.

I choke back a sob as I stand back to look at it, my heart shattering in a thousand pieces. For the first time ever, painting didn't ease my soul. It didn't take away my tormenting thoughts. I don't think anything ever will. Archer will forever be the man I won't get over—the one that got away.

Fifty-Two

ARCHER

"How are you holding up?" Ezra asks as he drives us home. I sigh and lock my phone, uneasy. I thought we were doing a little better after that night we spent together, but Serenity has barely been texting me back lately, and we haven't had a real conversation in days.

She comes home late and leaves early, and when she *is* home, she spends all her time with Ezra, not giving me the slightest chance to have a private conversation with her, let alone kiss her or hold her in my arms.

"I'm fine."

"No," Ezra says, running a hand through his hair. "You're not even remotely fine. Somehow, you're worse than when Tyra disappeared, and I don't understand why. You don't seem happy to have her back. Relieved, *yes*. But somehow, you seem far less happy than you were just a few weeks ago." He glances at me. "I'm worried about you, man. You realize I've witnessed you survive some of the worst things that have ever happened to you, and none of those times were you as intensely unhappy as you are right now. Tell me how to help, Archer."

I lean back and stare out the window. "You can't," I admit. "There is no solution, nothing either you or I can do that'll make things better."

I'm starting to wonder if I can make Serenity happy at all, and the more I think about it, the more I begin to doubt myself. I was never her first choice, and I can't help but wonder if she'll take Tyra returning home as an excuse to give Theo a chance. I couldn't even blame her if she did, nor do I have any right to stop her, to beg her to stay with me, when all I've brought her lately is misery.

I see the way she averts her face each time Tyra reaches for my hand. Tyra is so fragile that I can't tell her about Serenity, and Sera doesn't want me to, but fuck, *I* want to. I need the truth out in the open, but I can't be selfish. Not now. Serenity would never forgive me if I hurt Tyra.

He looks me over as we walk into the elevator. "Well, our renovations are nearly done, so Serenity and I will be out of your hair in a couple of days at most. Hopefully that'll help."

"What?" I ask, panic seizing me.

Ezra studies my face, and I try my best to regain my composure when truthfully, I don't want Serenity to leave. I already see so little of her. If she leaves, the distance between us will only increase, and I'm not sure I can take it. It's fucking killing me to lose my girl slowly, while I try my best to hold on.

"I'm moving back in *next door*, Archer," he tells me as we enter the elevator.

I nod and run a hand through my hair, trying my best to hide my unease. "Right," I murmur as we walk into my house. It's odd how it doesn't feel like home anymore, and I suspect it has everything to do with Serenity and the way we turned this place into our safe haven. It doesn't feel like ours anymore.

Tyra rises from the sofa when I walk in, her eyes lighting up, and I force a smile as I seek out Serenity. She turns around, and I just stare at her for a moment, taking in that messy bun and the loose, large T-shirt she's wearing. It takes me a moment to realize it isn't mine, and something dark and possessive settles in my stomach. I don't recognize it, so whose is it?

She thinks I don't realize it, but I've heard her slipping out of the house late at night, and I've tried my best not to wonder where she's been going, who she's been spending her nights with. I've seen the way Theo smiles at her at work, the way they've grown closer again. I noticed the little touches that weren't there before, the way she'll rest her head on his shoulder occasionally and the way he places his hand on her back as he takes her out for lunch. I don't dare ask questions that might come with answers that'll destroy what's left of my sanity, and what right do I have when it's Tyra that I fall asleep next to at night?

"You're home much later than usual," Tyra says, lowering the volume of the movie she was watching.

I nod and try my best to tear my eyes off Serenity. "Yeah, Ezra and I had a meeting that ran late," I explain as I take off my suit jacket, my gaze drifting back to Serenity.

Sure enough, she's staring at me in that way I like—like I'm hers. Her gaze follows my hands as I undo my waistcoat, and my mind tortures me with memories of the way her eyes glitter each time she does it for me, and the way she'll glance at the charm around my neck, her finger trailing over it appreciatively before she runs her hand down my abs.

I expect her to keep watching me as I tug on my tie, but instead, she turns around and walks away in the direction of my study. I freeze imperceptibly and hesitate before following her, too tired to care about how it looks or the questions it may raise.

Her head snaps up when I walk in, and I tense when I realize she's standing in front of her replica of *The Ballerina*. "Serenity," I murmur, my voice breaking. She tenses when I walk up to her, and my heart begins to ache when she turns her back to me, her fingers gently gliding over the surface of her painting.

I pause behind her, before I lean in to drop my forehead to her shoulder. "Whose is this?" I ask, sliding a trembling hand underneath her T-shirt, until I'm holding her waist. It feels so good to have her skin against mine, and fuck, I've missed it more than I realized. "Whose T-shirt are you wearing, darling?"

Her head falls back, and I turn my face to kiss her neck, needing her with an intensity I've never experienced. This isn't lust—it's desperation, a desire to feel complete again in a way only she's ever made me feel. "It's Ezra's," she tells me as I slide my hand to her stomach, splaying my fingers possessively.

"Why aren't you wearing one of mine?" I ask, my hand sliding up until the tips of my fingers caress the underside of her breast, my lips pressed just below her ear. She has no idea how much I need this proximity, how much I need *her*. Just a few of these moments are sufficient to refuel me for days on end.

Serenity sighs, her back straightening a little. Normally, she'd place her hand over mine and guide me to where she wants me to touch her, but today she turns around and steps back, putting distance between us. When her eyes meet mine, they're filled with resignation.

"Archer," she says, her tone conveying regret. Something about the way she looks at me puts me on edge, makes me brace myself. "The painting is done, and so are we."

I freeze, my heart squeezing painfully. "Don't do this," I beg. "Serenity, please don't do this."

She reaches for my tie and loosens it, the way she has countless times, but this time, there's a deep sadness in her eyes that makes me wonder if this is the last time I'll get to experience her hands on me like this.

"She needs you more than I do, Archer. The sneaking around, the guilt, I can't take it. I feel like I'm your mistress, and I'm hurting her by coveting what never would've been mine if not for that stupid list I made. You waited for her for so long, and all that time, she was waiting for you too, *praying* for you. I just can't…I can't do this to her. I couldn't live with myself if I did."

"No, Serenity. I waited for her because I felt *guilty*, because she disappeared during a trip I should've accompanied her on. If you're going to end things with me, then let's at least be honest about the facts. I don't love her, nor do I want to be with her. She's a friend I care about deeply, but that's all she is to me. You walking away from our relationship won't change that."

I place my index finger underneath her chin and force her to face me, my eyes on hers. "So tell me the truth, Sera. Are you leaving me for him? Tell me what's going on in that beautiful mind of yours. Explain it to me because there's no way in hell I'll let you go without a fight."

"I'm ending things between us for all the reasons we initially decided we'd never be together. There was already so much at stake for us, but the stakes are even higher now. We only just got Tyra back, and I can't lose her again. If she ever found out about us, it'd destroy her. There's no future for us. There's no outcome where you and I get to be happy without hurting anyone else. You see that, don't you? Us being together *hurts* others. Could you really live with yourself knowing how selfish we've been and how much pain we've caused? I can't, Archer. I can't do it. I won't be the reason one of the women I love most doesn't overcome the greatest tragedy she's ever experienced."

I stare at her, taking in her resolute expression despite the tears in her eyes. There's no changing her mind, and it fucking kills me to know she's right. Walking away is the right thing to do, but nothing has ever felt more wrong.

Fifty-Three

ARCHER

"Are you okay?" Tyra asks as I put on my shoes, feeling numb. I've barely slept, my mind replaying Serenity's words over and over again, torturing me endlessly. "You were twisting and turning all night. Is it…is it uncomfortable to sleep next to me? I'm sorry, Archer. I just…I just feel so safe when you're with me. That night they brought me here was the first time I slept through the night since—"

She's trembling, almost as though she's scared to speak up, to voice her worries. My heart squeezes painfully as I straighten, throwing her the sweetest smile I can muster. "I'm fine, I promise. Just a bit tired."

She steps closer, and I freeze when she straightens my tie for me. "I know you better than I know myself," she says, her voice breaking. "I notice the way you tense just slightly every time I touch you, almost like you're trying not to recoil. I know something happened yesterday and that you're upset, and I really hate that you're trying to hide it from me. I just…I just want to forget, and I want things to be the way they used to be. I want to be the person you talk to when you're worried, the one you instinctively reach for, but I…"

Guilt twists its knife in my heart, and I hesitate before wrapping my hands around her arms. "I just don't want to add to your mental load," I tell her when, deep down, I wish I could remind her that we broke up before she went missing, and going back to what we used to have is just going to make both of us unhappy. I'd never say it, but the words are constantly on the tip of my tongue. I keep them under lock and key, reminding myself over and over again that it'd hurt her unnecessarily, all for a tiny reprieve of the guilt I'm feeling, and it isn't worth it. She deserves my support in whatever way she needs it, and I need to do better.

"I'll heal," she tells me. "My mind isn't broken, I swear. I'll probably never dance again, and maybe I won't ever be the girl I was before, but with you by my side, I can overcome my fears, and I can learn to live again. The only reason I'm still here is because I've fought to survive that hellhole, and I'll continue fighting, for myself, for us. So please…don't give up on me, Arch, and don't coddle me either. Don't treat me like I'm breakable."

"I'm not trying to coddle you," I murmur, gently tucking her hair behind her ear. "If anything, I'm in awe of your strength, Tyra. I'm proud of you, and I'm just trying to support you in the best way I can. Tell me, sweetheart. What do you need?"

She places her hand against my chest, right over my heart, and it instantly reminds me of Serenity. Just like that, pure agony rushes through me, and I do my best to school my features, to focus on Tyra instead of the memory of Serenity ending things with me. It's near impossible for me not to recoil at her touch when deep down, I know that she's the only reason Serenity walked away. Ultimately, Serenity chose Tyra over me, and I can't even blame her for it.

"I just need you," she says, her voice soft, hopeful. "I need you to treat me like you used to."

I nod hesitantly, unsure I can give her what she's asking for yet entirely unable to deny her when it's clear it took courage for her to even voice her needs. "I'll do my best," I whisper.

She nods and steps back, and I force a smile before walking out the door, hating myself for my own selfishness. I should follow Serenity's wishes and example by putting Tyra first, but all I want to do is beg my girlfriend not to leave me, the whole world be damned. I'm not the man Serenity thinks I am, but fuck, I have to try to be. It's all I can think about on the way to work. I need to do the right thing and be there for Tyra. She was there for me during one of the hardest parts of my life, and I have to be there for her in the same way. I owe it to her.

"Archer?"

My heart soars at the sound of Serenity's voice, and I pause half-way to my office, hope blossoming in my chest. "Hi," I murmur, drinking her in. She's fucking gorgeous today, in that cream blouse and black pencil skirt, and it hurts to look at her knowing she's no longer mine.

"Mr. Harrison," she corrects herself, shaking her head. "Could I have a word, please?"

I tense, forcing myself into the professional role she expects me to play as I lead her to my office, my heart hammering in my chest. Did she change her mind? Did she toss and turn all night like I did, realizing that being together secretly is better than not being together at all?

She walks into my office and pauses halfway into the room when I close the door behind me. Serenity turns to face me, and for the first time in a very long time, I can't read her expression. She doesn't smile the way she normally does when we're alone, and she doesn't look at me that way I like, like she knows I belong to her.

"I'm resigning."

My stomach drops, and I take a step toward her. "No." I can't lose her entirely. I need these little glimpses of her. I need our conversations and little excuses to drive her home so I get her to myself for just a few moments.

"I've already put in my two-week notice, and I'm moving out too. I know Ezra is moving back into his own place soon, but I'm not moving with him. I'm leaving, and I wanted you to hear it from me."

"Serenity," I murmur, helplessness rushing through me as I lift my hand to her face. "Don't leave me. Please, don't do this."

Her expression cracks, and I take a step closer to her, thankful that she's letting me. "I can't be here and watch you with her. I know it's exactly what I'm asking you to do, but my heart can't take it, Archer. I can't be around to watch you get over me and rekindle what you lost."

I pull her against me, reveling in the feel of her body against mine. "I'll never get over you, Serenity. This thing between us is what I've always been searching for, what was missing in every relationship before you. You leaving won't change that."

She looks at me like she doesn't believe me, and I don't know how to make her understand that she is it for me, despite everything. "I'll give it all up for you," I tell her. "The company. Ezra. Everything. I don't need any of it as much as I need you, Sera."

Her arms slide around my neck, and she looks up, tears in her eyes. "You know it's not that simple. It's not just the company or Ezra, and you know it."

I drop my forehead to hers, wishing I could make her stay and knowing she won't. "Please," I whisper, dipping my head until my lips brush against hers. *"Please."*

Her fingers slide up my neck and into my hair, and then she rises to her tiptoes, her lips meeting mine. I groan as I tighten my grip on her, my hands roaming over her body as I part her lips with my tongue.

She moans, and my heart begins to race as desire rushes through my body. Serenity gasps when I lift her up, taking a moment to move her skirt enough so her legs can wrap around my hips as I carry her to my desk, my movements filled with desperation, almost like every fiber in my body knows this'll be the last time I get to have her.

My breath hitches when I slide my hands underneath her skirt to find her wearing those stockings I love, and I pull back to look at them, my breathing erratic. "*Fuck*," I moan as she reaches for my slacks and undoes them, that same desperation in her eyes. She looks at me like she thinks she'll never see me again, and it fucking kills me.

My eyes flutter closed when her soft fingers wrap around my cock, and I push her panties aside impatiently as she lines me up. "I love you," I whisper as I push into her, my thumb pressed against her clit. "I love you so fucking much, Serenity. I always will."

Her head falls back when I thrust into her, making her take all of me. I'm near delirious with the need to mark her, to make her remember me no matter where she goes. My touch is rough as I push her to the edge of an orgasm, enjoying every pant, every moan. I commit it all to memory, terrified this is the last time I'll witness her lose control for me like that. "I can't," she pleads, her hips rocking.

"You will," I tell her. "Come for me, darling. Show me my favorite sight. Make me the happiest man alive, even if it's only for a moment."

She obeys my command, her pussy contracting around me in that way I just can't resist. I moan, not giving a damn about the sounds we're making as I come right along with her, my forehead dropping to hers. How am I supposed to live without this connection between us? How am I supposed to live without her?

"Stay," I whisper. "Please stay."

She pulls back to look at me, her breathing uneven. "I love you," she whispers. "I love you, and I'm sorry."

"You love me," I repeat, bitterness bleeding into my voice as I pull out of her. "But you love her more."

My heart fucking shatters when she doesn't refute my words, regret written all over her face.

Fifty-Four

SERENITY

"Excellent job," Mark says, his eyes roaming over my face, a hint of pride in his eyes. "You've grown so much in the time you've been working here. Truly, I don't know of any other design intern that's so rapidly become invaluable. It's a shame you're leaving."

I force a smile, glad my misery isn't obvious. I get it now—why Archer was so obsessed with work for so long. It's an endless loop of adding things and crossing them off to-do lists, and I love that, always have. It keeps my mind off the things I don't want to think about, and it keeps me from walking into Archer's office and telling him that I miss him.

The last couple of days have been tough as I started to pack my bags, neither of us sure how to act around each other anymore, and all the while, we're both trying to be there for Tyra in our own ways. It's hard to smile through the pain, and I'm glad I won't have to do it for much longer anymore.

"Serenity?"

I look up to find Theo walking back in from lunch with a huge, beautiful bouquet of tulips in one hand, a vase in the other. He spent all morning trying to convince me to have lunch with him, but I've been too listless to even pretend, and the thought of having to make conversation was just too much for me.

"For you," he says, handing me the bouquet.

I stare at it, taking in the gorgeous tulips with wide eyes. "For me?" I repeat dumbly.

He chuckles and places it in the vase for me. "Yeah, Ser. For you." He glances back at me, a sweet smile on his face. "I thought it'd make you smile." He leans against my desk and reaches for me, his touch gentle as he cups my face. "I'm not sure what's going on, but the way you've been focusing on work isn't normal, and I'm worried about you."

I lean into his touch, needing the comfort he's offering me. Truth be told, I missed him. I missed our friendship and knowing that there was one person in the world who understands, even when I can't find the right words to explain what I'm feeling, what's bothering me.

"I'm sorry," he says, his voice filled with regret.

"For what?"

His hand moves to my hair, and he gently wraps one of my curls around his finger, the movement so reminiscent of Archer's usual tenderness that it nearly brings tears to my eyes. "For allowing this distance to form between us. It's why I never even tried dating anyone, you know? Because the thought of anything changing between us wasn't worth it. It never has been. If not for the way..." He shakes his head. "Never mind. All I'm trying to say is that I'm sorry things changed between us when I promised myself they never would. I'm going to do everything in my power to get us back to where we were, and if I'm lucky...maybe somewhere even better."

I see the hope in his eyes, and just a few months ago, it'd have been everything I'd ever wanted. I'd be lying if I said that no part of me wants to see the dreams I've had for years materialize, but somehow the dreams I had before pale in comparison to the reality of Archer.

"Hey," Theo says, his voice soft, snapping me out of my thoughts.

"I'm sorry," I tell him. "What did you say?"

His expression falls, and he sighs. "You know, not long ago, I'd have known exactly what you were thinking without even having to ask. Now I don't even know where to begin wondering. The worst part is that I did this to myself by not prioritizing our friendship when I told both myself and you that I would."

"No," I tell him, reaching for him. "No, Theo. I…I've just…" I look into his eyes, unable to explain myself when there's so much he doesn't know. He doesn't know about Archer and me, nor does he know about Tyra. I wouldn't even have told him about the burst pipe and Ezra and me moving in with Archer if he hadn't mentioned it. "God, you're right," I murmur, a deep kind of loneliness settling deep in my chest. He was always the first person I turned to when anything happened, even if it was only to talk.

He grabs my hand and holds it tightly. "Let me be there for you now," he says, his tone pleading. "Let me make up for my absence."

I smile at him. "Don't be ridiculous," I reply. "There's nothing you have to make up for. Friendships are a two-way street, you know? I'm as much to blame as you are."

He draws circles across the back of my hand with his thumb, his gaze searching. "Let me take you out for dinner," he says, his voice soft. "You don't have to answer the question I asked you if you aren't ready, but let's just spend some time together. It's been so long since it felt like we were just *us*."

"I can't," I tell him gently. "I'm sorry. Maybe some other time?"

He squeezes my hand, his expression pleading. "I thought it might be nice to go to that little Italian place you put on your list of places to visit here." My heart wrenches at the thought of everything on my list I know he's done with Kristen. "I've never been before," he adds, almost like he just read my expression.

I smile at him ruefully, silently lamenting the loss of everything I thought we'd experience together. There are so many places he probably can't go to without thinking of Kristen, and similarly, there are so many things I'll never be able to do without thinking of Archer. I should've known, even back when I made that stupid list. Archer Harrison isn't the kind of man you forget. He isn't someone you can walk away from without leaving part of yourself behind.

"A dinner date, huh?"

My head snaps up at the sound of Archer's voice and I find him standing a few paces away, his face moving from my face to the hand Theo is holding. My heart clenches painfully when I see the pain in his eyes, the silent accusations.

"Mr. Harrison," Theo says, his tone polite.

Archer doesn't even acknowledge him; he just stares at me, his broken heart on display for me.

"Serenity," he says, my name a quiet plea on his lips. Archer looks at me like I hold his heart in my hands, and I'm squeezing a little too tightly, slowly killing him. He looks at me like he loves me more than anything. Will that look fade in time? Will I come back here someday and find him looking at Tyra like that, like he always used to?

Archer lowers his gaze and forces a smile. "I'd meant to ask you if you were available to work overtime tonight, but never mind. You two enjoy your date."

He turns and walks away before I can refute his words, and it leaves me feeling empty. "I can't do dinner," I tell Theo, my eyes on Archer's retreating back. "Ezra told me I don't have to complete my notice period, so I'm leaving tonight."

"I missed my chance, didn't I?" Theo says, drawing my gaze back to him.

I hesitate and look away, not wanting to hurt him. "I'm sorry, Theo."

He sighs and runs a hand through his hair. "I'll wait," he tells me, his voice soft. "I'll wait for you to get over him, no matter how long it takes."

I stare at him wide-eyed, and he throws me a shaky smile.

"You look at him the way you used to look at me," he says. "I tried to ignore it, pretended not to notice…but how could I not? I've always known you better than anyone else. I'll be there, Serenity. In a few months, or even years down the line. Maybe the time just isn't right for us now, but maybe someday it will be. I'll wait forever for a chance to be with you."

"Don't," I tell him, gently rejecting him the best way I can. "Don't wait for me, Theo. Forever isn't long enough for me to forget about Archer."

Fifty-Five

ARCHER

I pause by my front door and take a deep breath, trying my best to improve my shitty mood before walking in. This entire week has been a fucking clusterfuck, and I miss my girl. Serenity is my safe haven, and I miss the way her hair smells when I hold her in my arms. I miss her smiles, and the way she'll listen to me talk endlessly about work matters she doesn't give a fuck about.

I miss the way she steals bites of my food, and the way she laughs at my stupid jokes. I miss the way she shivers when I run my finger down her spine, and the way her breath hitches when I kiss her neck.

I sigh and rest my forehead against the door, my heart aching as I remember Theo asking her out while I just stood there, wishing it could've been me saying those words to her. Is she sitting opposite him right now, smiling at him in that intimate way I'd come to consider mine? Will he walk her back to my own fucking home and kiss her good night?

I clench my jaws and steel myself before unlocking my door, my heart stuttering when I realize I never changed the code. I expected Serenity to believe in me, in us, when I hadn't truly let go of my past. I made her key in a code that reminded her of Tyra every damn day, and I didn't even realize it.

"You're home," Tyra says when I walk in, and I pause, looking around my home and finding it looking different. It takes me a moment to realize that a couple of little things are gone—the little dish Serenity bought for my car keys, her polka dot umbrella. My heart begins to race, dread washing over me as I walk farther into the living room and find the blanket she loves missing from the sofa, along with the cushions we spent an hour choosing at a small market stall in Morocco.

"Archer?" Tyra says. "What's wrong?"

I run a hand through my hair, my breathing uneven as I walk into the kitchen and pull one of my cupboards open. "Where is that stupidly huge mug with the pink hearts?" I ask, my voice hoarse. I bite down on my lip as I walk to my bedroom, scared of what I'll find. "Where the fuck is everything?" Panic seizes me when I find my room devoid of Serenity's things. "Who changed my silk bedding? Where is the jewelry box that was on my nightstand?"

My thoughts begin to spiral as I step into my walk-in wardrobe and find all of Serenity's things gone, her favorite T-shirts of mine folded neatly, a handwritten note on top of them.

Thank you for letting me borrow everything I wanted, even if it was only for a moment. I'm returning it all to you now, as promised.

All my love,
Serenity

"Archer, you're worrying me," Tyra says, gently placing her hand on my bicep. I step away instinctively and turn to face her, trying my best to remain calm despite the pure chaos in my mind.

"Where is she?" I ask, my voice breaking on the last word.

Tyra searches my face before taking the note I'm holding out of my hands, her expression stoic as she reads Sera's message. "She left," she explains.

"What do you mean, *she left*? She still has a week of her notice period left, and why the fuck would she leave without a word? What happened?"

Tyra looks back at me, something shifting in her expression. "Ezra took her to the airport, Arch. He told her she didn't need to stay for her notice period if she didn't want to, so she left. I helped both Ezra and her pack earlier today. He's moving out today too. I thought you knew."

I bury a hand in my hair and sink down on my bed, hating that clean laundry smell. It doesn't feel right at all. My bedroom is supposed to smell of the millions of hair products Serenity uses, blended together with that damn bodywash that leaves glitter all over my skin when our bodies melt together. I don't even have a moment to feel relieved that she isn't on a date with Theo—her absence steals away every thought, leaving nothing but misery.

My hands tremble as I reach for my phone and navigate through my contacts, my heart aching as I stare at the heart and tulip emojis for a second before I click the dial button. It goes to voicemail instantly, but that doesn't stop me from dialing her number again.

Tyra sits down next to me, her eyes roaming over my face, something akin to concern in her eyes. "She's on a flight," Ty says, her voice soft.

I nod and put my phone away, my wits just enough about me to realize I shouldn't let her see how I've got Serenity saved in my phone.

"Right," I murmur. "Did she tell you where she's going?" We haven't spoken about her leaving at all, neither of us wanting to acknowledge it, but we should have. If we had, I would've known where she's going, where to find her.

"She said she wanted to travel for a while, see if she gets inspired to paint. She loved working for Ezra and you, but painting has always been her real passion. Serenity has always dreamt of being showcased in galleries, and I think taking some time off to explore that option is exactly what she needs. Don't you?"

Tyra places her hand on my thigh when I remain silent, and I tense. "It felt like there was more to it, though. Serenity didn't explicitly say it, but from what I understand, she had her heart broken and needed a fresh start. I was being a little nosy, and Ezra eventually told me that Theo is dating someone else. We always thought that they'd end up together eventually, and I'm honestly surprised they haven't."

"Yet," I murmur, my voice laced with venom. "They haven't gotten together *yet*, but they probably will. She wanted him once. With time, those feelings will probably return, and next time, he'll be there to reciprocate." My mind begins to torture me with thoughts of a future where she'll have gotten over me, and I grit my teeth as I think of her in his arms, his hands roaming over her body, discovering every sensitive spot I thought was mine.

She'll giggle when he touches her feet, only to moan when he spreads her legs and runs his finger up her thigh. He'll find out that she loves wearing those sexy stockings and that a single kiss can make her wet. He'll hold her in his embrace after, feeling the way her hair tickles his face, the way her breathing slowly deepens as she falls asleep on his chest. He'll accompany her to her mother's birthday, holding her hand as she smiles up at him, and I'll have to stand there and watch the love of my life love someone else.

Fifty-Six

ARCHER

I stare at the notifications on my phone, alerting me to a new painting from The Muse. My fingers instinctively graze the silver pendant around my neck, and my heart begins to thunder when I recognize the location.

I'm on autopilot as I get into my car and drive to the last place I took Serenity before we began to fall apart. All the while, my chest aches with longing for her. She hasn't replied to any of my text messages, nor is she taking my calls. She's distancing herself, and I don't know how to let her go.

I sigh when I notice how busy this usually deserted place is, people swarming one of the walls. I'm numb as I push through them, only to freeze at the sight of the painting that confirms all of my suspicions. My lungs struggle to fill with air as I stare at my sweet girl's fears and pain on display for the whole world to see.

All around me, people discuss the significance of the painting, but I don't need to guess. It's me and her, our hands entwined even as a red thread of fate connects me to Tyra. She's holding on with all her might, but I'm longingly looking back at Tyra, at my past. It takes me a moment to realize that the red thread is frayed, and Serenity is holding a pair of scissors behind her back, nearly entirely out of view.

I'd been wondering what she'd been thinking before she called things off, and part of me felt like she did it, in part, because of Theo. I thought she'd taken Tyra's return as an opportunity to end things with me so she could explore her feelings for Theo.

I was wrong.

She left because she wanted to set me free, so I could be with the person she thinks I'm destined to be with. I have no doubt her love for Tyra was one of the reasons she left, but maybe I was wrong to say she loves Tyra more than she loves me. I was missing a crucial part of the puzzle and let my own fears fill in the blanks when I should've tried harder to understand her. She's just trying to do the right thing—when neither of us knows what's right or wrong anymore.

My heart squeezes painfully as I analyze every little detail, every expression she painted, every color she chose. She left because she didn't think I'd choose her in the end, and I failed her if I didn't instill enough faith in our relationship. I failed her by not changing my phone or door code, by asking her to paint *The Ballerina*, and then again by standing back as Theo asked her out, making her feel like I didn't care. I failed her, and I lost her.

My mind is whirling as I drive home, my fingers caressing the charm around my neck as I replay every conversation in my head, wondering if I could've made her stay. If she had stayed, would our circumstances have torn us apart? Her heart broke each time Tyra reached for me, both for herself and for Tyra. How much of that could she have withstood before it broke us?

I try my best to think of every scenario, every outcome, uncertain how she and I could've made it through this intact. How could I ask her to come back to me when I can't see a future in which she's truly happy with me? I know her, and I know her heart. She could never live with herself if she caused Tyra any harm, and fuck, I don't see how we could be together without hurting her. Tyra tore us apart, but not in the way Serenity thought she would.

I'm shaking as I walk through my front door, desperate for a glimpse of her and knowing I won't find it. She removed every trace of her, of us, and I finally understand why. She was giving me a blank canvas, not realizing I don't want it. I want her, and her kaleidoscope of colors.

"Archer," Tyra says as I walk into the living room, her voice trembling. I find her sitting on the floor wearing her old pointe shoes, pain written all over her face. Guilt grips me hard and fast, and I kneel beside her, trying my hardest to set aside my own feelings, so I can be the man Serenity believes I am. It's harder than ever before, and even as I stare at the tears in Tyra's eyes, I fight the urge to tell her all about Serenity, and how much I fucking love her.

"Hey," I gently murmur instead, taking in the way she's cupping her ankles, unsure what to do or say. I've learned that often she just needs me to sit with her, so that's what I do, breaking my own heart in the process. I try my hardest to clear my mind, giving her the support she deserves. "I see you're trying on your old shoes. These were your favorites, weren't they?"

She raises her face to look at me, tears in her eyes. "There were only two things I thought of every time I needed my mind to take me elsewhere—you and dancing again." She sniffs, her breathing uneven. "Whenever I could, I'd practice in secret...until one day I got caught."

She buries her face in her hands, a sob tearing through her throat. "He broke my legs, telling me not to even dream of dancing in front of an audience again, showing off my body onstage when it should only be for his eyes."

Fuck. Tyra's therapist has been visiting every day, but Ty hasn't said much about what happened beyond telling us that she was taken by a stalker and held in his basement all that time. I had an idea of what she must've gone through, but hearing it makes me feel like the biggest fucking asshole for ever even dreaming of leaving her to find Serenity. Before anything else, Tyra was one of my closest friends, and I need to remember that.

I carefully take her into my arms, and she throws her arms around my neck as I try my best to console her. "I'll kill him myself the second he's found," I whisper, fury rushing through me.

"You don't need to," she whispers. "I pulled the trigger myself. The man you sent…Elijah…he offered me his gun, and I took it. They'll never find him."

Shock courses through me, and I tighten my grip on her as she cries her heart out for everything she lost, everything she's endured, everything she had to do. All the while, I can't believe she's here with me. I can't believe her strength and her courage, and fuck, I can't believe my own goddamn selfishness.

"I can't dance anymore," she cries. "My legs didn't heal right, and it hurts too much. I lost one of the two things I loved most, Arch. You're all I have left."

"Ty," I whisper, my heart aching. "I…" My eyes flutter closed, and I sigh as I hug her tightly. "Yeah," I tell her, swallowing down every other response. "You've got me, Ty. For as long as you need me."

Fifty-Seven

SERENITY

The edges of my lips turn up as I place my easel on the balcony of my room in an adorable bed-and-breakfast in Rome. It isn't quite a smile, but my heart feels a little less heavy today. It's been weeks, and still, I haven't stopped thinking about Archer for more than a few moments. Everything I do reminds me of him, and little pieces of him are in every painting I've created. He's become my muse, and he doesn't even know it.

My heartache eases just a touch as a familiar scene begins to take form on my canvas. The memory makes my stomach flutter, and I sigh as I paint yet another piece for my popular Lovers collection. I started creating videos of my painting process, and they've gone so viral that all my work sold out quicker than I could've imagined, and the demand is higher than I ever thought would be possible.

This time, I'm painting silk sheets, red tulips, and messy hair, laughter and playfulness meeting bold provocation and sensuality. It's us. The very best parts of us.

My hand slips when my phone begins to buzz, and I take a

steadying breath as I reach for it, bracing myself for what I know I'll find. *Tyra.* I paste on a smile before accepting the video call and placing my phone on the windowsill, so she can see me easily.

"Hi, sweetheart," she says, smiling across my screen. "How is my favorite girl doing?" she asks, positioning her phone on the edge of Archer's sofa. I've gotten a bit more used to it, but her familiarity with his home still hurts every single time. "Tell me all about Rome."

It's odd how I'm filled with both joy and sorrow at the sight of her. Seeing how well she's doing now makes it all worth it, but I'm trying my best not to think too hard of the implications of it all and what Archer is doing to make her look like that. "Rome is wonderful," I tell her, genuine delight in my voice. "Truly the best ice cream I've ever had. Honestly, I might just stay here for the ice cream alone."

She laughs, and I stare at her in disbelief. It took weeks for her to even start smiling, and I wasn't sure I'd ever hear her laughter again, yet here she is, the same honorary older sister I thought I'd lost forever. I knew leaving was the right thing to do, but it hurts to wonder how Archer put that smile back on her face.

"You can't stay," she says, grinning. "I already miss you too much as it is, and I think both Ezra and Archer might actually cry if you so much as joked about it. They miss you too."

My smile slips a fraction at the sound of his name, and I look down. I don't miss the possessive tone, and it hurts more than she'll ever know. When I first left, Archer tried calling me every day, but gradually, those calls and texts started to come every few days, until eventually, they stopped. I knew they would, and I knew it was for the best, but even so, I find myself startling a little each time my phone buzzes, in hopes that it's him.

"Anyway, tell me about your paintings. I want to hear everything!"

I glance back at my canvas, debilitating shame coursing through me when I realize that I was painting someone that never should've been mine, not even for a moment. I have no doubt that it's all in the past for him, a sordid affair he'd rather forget about. Yet here I am, painting our secrets for the world to see. What is it I'm trying to accomplish? Is it truly just a form of therapy, or was I looking for a reaction I'll never get?

"I sold every single one of them," I tell her, my voice trembling. "For far higher prices than I ever thought possible and far quicker than I expected."

She gasps excitedly, and I take in the pure pride and joy on her face. Her love for me is clear as day, and it'd kill me if she ever looked at me with disappointment and betrayal. I never should've done what I did.

"Did you tell your mom about that?" she asks carefully.

I smile ruefully. "No," I murmur, unable to hide my disappointment. "She still won't speak to me. I just…I just don't get it. I'm making more now than I would have as a junior at any firm. It's not like I'm a starving artist, like she thought I'd be, so why can't she—"

"Give it time," Tyra says, her tone reassuring. "Sometimes it's hard, you know? To admit that you were wrong without your pride getting hurt. Maybe that's all it is, Ser."

I nod and pick up my brush, suddenly unable to paint. The same scene that soothed my aching heart just moments ago now sickens me. What was I thinking, painting Archer and me together like that? No one would know it's us, but he would. He'd know, and he'd hate it. He wouldn't want any reminders of us to exist, and that's exactly what this is.

"Anyway, I found out something super interesting," she says.

I raise a brow as I begin to clean my brushes. "What's that?"

"Apparently, there's this artist called The Muse."

My heart stops, and my gaze cuts to hers. "Oh yeah?"

She smiles knowingly, adoration in her eyes. "Yeah. Ezra told me about The Muse when I asked about the ballerina painting in Archer's living room, so I looked into them. I joined a couple of Muse fan groups, and I started to notice something very interesting. The Muse seems to have been traveling through Europe, painting on the walls of small mom-and-pop stores that need support. Each of those paintings then draw a ton of new customers into small towns and the stores surrounding it, and dozens of businesses that would've closed manage to survive. All because of The Muse. The interesting part is that they've been in all the same cities you've been in."

I stare at her wide-eyed, unsure what to say. "That's…that's very interesting indeed."

There's something in her eyes I can't quite decipher, and it makes my heart beat a little faster, adrenaline rushing through me. "Well, if I were The Muse, I'd start putting some of my work up for auction anonymously. Muse is clearly trying to do some good in the world, and just imagine how much money one of *those* paintings could raise. Muse would pretty much instantly be financially independent, proving everyone who never believed in them wrong, while being able to donate as much as they'd like."

I nod, my heart thundering in my chest. "That would never even have occurred to me," I murmur. She's always motivated me this way, helping me think of ways to someday turn this into a career, all the while supporting me and encouraging me not to give up. She's always been my biggest supporter, and she was the one who gave me my first few high-quality paintbrushes. She bought them for me with her first paycheck. "Tell me. What else would you do if you were The Muse?"

She looks away for a moment, her expression unreadable. "God, I'd give the world to be The Muse," she says, her voice soft. When she turns to face me again, her sweet smile is back in place, but it doesn't quite reach her eyes. "I'd follow my dreams, Serenity. All of them. I'd chase my own happiness, regardless of the consequences."

I can't decipher what she's trying to say, but I know Tyra well enough to know there's a hidden meaning in her words. "What—" I begin to ask, only to be interrupted by the sound of Archer's voice.

"Oh, yay, you're home early!" she says, looking up.

My heart begins to race, and my hands instantly become clammy as I stare at my screen, my entire body reacting to him, even though I can't see him. From what I can tell, he's standing in front of her, the back of her phone to him.

"You said you weren't having a good day, so I brought you that lemon tart you always loved," he tells her, and the tiny sliver of hope I'd been holding on to shatters.

"From that little bakery on the other side of town?" she asks, her whole face lighting up as she seems to reach for it, pulling a small cardboard box to her chest. "You went all the way there for me?"

"Of course," he says, his voice soft, filled with the same affection I'd grown used to. "Do you think you're up for a walk today? The weather is really nice, and if we're lucky, some random strangers might let you pet their dog at the park."

I swallow hard and wring my hands, unsure what to do or say. She always calls me while he's at work, so I've never found myself in this situation before. "Hey, um, I need to go," I say, my voice breaking. It's clear Tyra forgot all about me the second he walked in. He's still her whole world, like he always has been.

She looks at me and reaches for her phone. "Oh, say hi to Archer before you go!" she says, before pulling him closer and into the frame.

I watch as he realizes that I overheard their conversation, and the guilt in his eyes wrecks me. "Hi," he says, and I inhale shakily, taking him in. He's wearing the navy suit I love, and he looks like he'd rather sink through the floor than talk to me.

"Hi," I murmur, each shard of my broken heart cutting deeper as he stares at me, clearly at a loss for words. We used to talk for hours even before we ever got together, and now there's nothing left for us to say.

"Um, well, have fun at the park," I tell him, trying my hardest to force a smile. "And enjoy the lemon tart."

His eyes flutter closed, but not before I see the regret in them. "*Serenity,*" he says, in that same way he used to, like my name is a prayer, a vow. I take one more look at him and end the call, only to be faced with the contours of his face on my canvas.

He's moved on, but here I am, clinging to every precious memory we made. How do I forget, like he has?

Fifty-Eight

ARCHER

I sit down on the floor of the gallery I purchased for Serenity, every artwork I anonymously bought from her lining the walls. I managed to buy all of them except for one. This gallery is my personal sanctuary, my escape. It's where I go when I need to feel closer to her, when I need to surround myself with our memories.

I raise my wine bottle to my lips as I stare at her latest pieces, a collection she's named The Lovers. It's undoubtedly us, and it brings me a small amount of consolation to know she still thinks of me. I can find myself in the silhouettes she painted, in the tulips and the silk sheets, in the still life of a forgotten breakfast in bed that includes the same heart-shaped donuts she loves so much, the entwined hands of two lovers visible at the edge of the painting, his on top of hers.

I see us in the flower fields she's painted, eating crepes on the streets of Paris, and my arm wrapped around her in a gondola on the Grand Canal in Venice. She's painted all of our best memories, and I'm scared she did it so she could finally get them out of her head forever.

I know my girl, and if she's painting us with those somber colors, despite the happiness attached to each of those memories...it's because she's trying to move on. With each finished painting, she's probably getting closer to forgetting me, until one day, her paintings will no longer feature me.

I took her to all of those places to help her tick things off her to-do list, but if I'm truly honest with myself, I also did it because I knew it was Theo she wanted to make all those memories with—and I wanted it to be me.

Except, in the end, it's still him she chose.

My heart wrenches as I reach for my phone and scroll through the same photos on social media that have been torturing me for days now—photos of her with Theo, at the same crepe place I took her to in Paris. She's creating new memories with him to replace ours, and it's fucking killing me to sit here so helplessly as she builds a future that doesn't include me.

I can't help but wonder whether it was a coincidence that he met her in Paris less than a week after I saw her so unexpectedly over video. Did she misunderstand what she heard? Did I push her into his arms with my careless words?

I know for a fact that Theo is only with her for a few days, since he only asked for leave until Monday, but a lot could happen in that time. I inhale shakily and lie back on the floor, my eyes trained on the ceiling. I try my best to control my thoughts, but they insist on torturing me with images of her dancing in the rain with him, of him pulling her closer, their eyes locking the way ours used to just before he dips his head and takes what's mine.

He'll discover things that only I knew—the way she likes to be kissed, and every part of her body that's sensitive, right down to that small patch on her inner thigh that I love to mark with little love bites. He'll find out how fucking magnificent she is when he lays her down in bed, her gorgeous bare skin complemented by the light sheets as her wild hair surrounds her like a dark fucking halo.

He'll hold her in his arms and experience the pure peace only she can bring and the way the warmth of her body just seeps into your heart too, making you feel like you're on top of the world. Someday, I'll see them together, and he'll hold her hand and kiss her knuckles like I used to, and she'll grin at him, her eyes twinkling like they used to for me. I'll stand there and pretend it doesn't fucking destroy me to watch her love someone that isn't me, and she'll look at me like I'm nothing but her brother's best friend, like everything we had was just a passing memory, a fling not worth mentioning.

I draw a shaky breath when my phone begins to ring, snapping me out of my downward spiral. I sigh as I stare at Tyra's name, my eyes falling closed as I pick up.

"Arch?" she says, her voice filled with clear worry. "Ezra and I were just wondering where you are. He came over for dinner, but he needs to leave soon."

"I'm still at work," I lie, my voice hoarse. "I'll be home soon, okay?"

I hear some shuffling and the slamming of a door, followed by Ezra's voice. "I know you're not at work," he says, his voice hushed. "Where are you, Archer? Where the fuck have you been disappearing to lately?"

I sigh as I sit up and look around at the countless paintings surrounding me, fragments of happier times. I just know that ten years from now, I'll still walk in here when I need a reminder of what it was like to be happy. Serenity isn't someone I'll ever forget.

"Nowhere," I tell him. "It doesn't matter. I'll be home soon."

I sigh as I end the call and jump to my feet, forcing myself back into the role I'm expected to play. I've never felt so conflicted before. I genuinely want to be there for Tyra, and I'm trying my best to be a good friend to her, but it's killing me inside to know I can't give her what she wants, and in turn, I can't have what I want. I've tried to tell her that there's someone multiple times now, but every time I try, she changes the subject, almost like deep down she *knows*, but she doesn't want to hear it. Every attempt to tell her that things between us will never go back to what they were results in a panic attack, and it hurts to see her that way.

What is the right thing to do? I can't do or say anything that'll harm her, but I also can't give her false hope. I run a hand through my hair and sigh, my heart aching. I know she's trying her best, and she's come so far in a matter of weeks, but will she ever get to a point where she can handle the knowledge that she can't ever regain what she lost?

Fifty-Nine

ARCHER

I sigh as I lift my towel to my hair absent-mindedly, feeling entirely numb. Each day seems worse than the last, and I'm just not sure I know how to be happy without Serenity. I don't think I ever really was before her. I never felt as alive as I did with her, and now that she's gone, I'm once again just going through the same old motions, day in and day out.

I startle when my bedroom door opens and turn to find Tyra walking in. "Sorry. I should've knocked," she says, her gaze roaming over my half-naked body. She pauses halfway through as her eyes zero in on the tattoo on my chest.

"It's fine," I tell her, forcing a smile. It took a couple of weeks, but I was eventually able to move back into my own bedroom while she stayed in my guest room. I still wake up and join her at night when she needs me, but she's starting to stand on her own two feet now. She never even questioned it when I started to move to my own bed once she'd fallen asleep, and I'm glad she hasn't. I'm not sure what I'd say, how I'd even begin to explain.

Tyra pauses in front of me, her eyes roaming over the painting I had tattooed on my chest, reminding me of one of the best days of my life every time I look into the mirror. It's the same scene Serenity once painted on me—the sun setting over a field filled with red tulips.

Tyra raises her hand, and I flinch when she grazes my chest with the tips of her fingers. "It's beautiful," she whispers. "How long have you had it?"

I step back and reach for one my shirts, my heart heavy. "A couple of weeks."

She nods slowly and stands back as I get dressed, her expression conflicted. "You're in love with someone else, aren't you?"

I freeze, my gaze cutting to hers. Her voice no longer trembles when she speaks, and she's able to hold my gaze for longer than she used to, but she's still fragile. Nightmares still torment her, and she still has several panic attacks every day, not to mention her near inability to leave the house.

"Arch," she says, her voice soft. "You haven't touched me in any way that could be deemed anything but appropriate, and you distance yourself from me every chance you get. You may not have said it, but your body language did. I thought that if I ignored it, maybe it'd go away and with time you'd warm up to me…but then you started sleeping in your own bed again and I knew I didn't stand a chance."

"I'm sorry," I tell her, unable to refute her words. "I can't be with you that way, Tyra. But I'll be there for you as best as I can, for as long as you need me. You'll always be important to me, Ty, but I…I can't be more than a friend to you."

"Who is she?" she asks, her voice breaking. Tears start to gather in her eyes, and I look down, my chest aching. The thought of me loving someone else clearly hurts her, but the pain she feels now would be nothing compared to what it'd do to her to find out it's Serenity. I've watched the two of them grow closer, and I know Tyra wouldn't be able to take it.

"It doesn't matter, Ty. The woman I'm in love with is someone I can't ever have, but even so, I don't want to be with anyone else, not ever again. She is it for me. I've…I've been wanting to tell you, but I didn't know how."

She looks up, a lone tear running down her cheek. "Does she give you what I never could? Does she make you laugh, Arch? Does she make you happy?"

I look into her eyes, forcing myself to face her. "She did," I whisper, pure longing threatening to overwhelm me.

She looks at me with that same expression Serenity had on her face when she ended things with me, heartbreak mixed with resignation. "I've tried so hard to exist in this safe little bubble you created for me, never realizing that you were suffocating in it. Or maybe I did realize, and I just didn't want to acknowledge it for fear of what it'd mean, but that's not the kind of person I want to be, Arch."

"Tyra," I murmur, taking her hand. "I see you fighting every single day, and you're easily the bravest person I've ever met. I didn't tell you this to make you feel guilty for relying on me. Being there for you was a choice she and I made together, and it's not one I regret." I gently catch one of her tears with my thumb, my heart aching for her. "Day after day, I watch you take little steps forward, slowly regaining your independence, no matter how hard you have to fight for it. I'm honored to be holding your hand on your journey to recovery, Tyra." *Even if it hurts. Even if it cost me everything.*

"I've already gotten a bit more used to leaving the house, but please give me a little longer," she pleads, her voice breaking. Her panic attacks mean she can't drive, but in the last couple of weeks, she's gone out a handful of times without me, taking my security team with her instead. We've both actively been trying to ensure she learns to stand on her own two feet again, instead of becoming overly reliant on me. She's fighting as hard as she can, never asking for more than she truly needs. "Let me lean on you a little longer, Archer. I can't...I can't let you go yet."

I nod and pull her closer, hugging her tightly as she bursts into tears. "I'm here," I promise her, ignoring the numbness that I can't cast away. "I'll always be there for you."

Sixty

SERENITY

I stare at the beautiful sunset across the Grand Canal in Venice, my heart aching as I think back to that long weekend with Archer, when he took me on one of the gondolas and made one of my biggest dreams come true. I thought time would dull the pain, but it hasn't.

I still miss him with every heartbeat, and every single one of my paintings still contains pieces of him, of us. I can't let him go, no matter how hard I try. The mere thought of going back home and facing him fills me with dread. I'm not ready to see him treat Tyra with so much care, no matter how much I love her. It'd destroy me, but I can't stay away much longer either. My dad has started to worry, and Theo has begun calling me multiple times a day to check in with me. I can't keep running forever, but God, I wish I could.

"Serenity?"

I turn around at the sound of a familiar voice, my eyes widening when I find Tyra standing behind me, her eyes lit up with affection as I stare at her in disbelief. "Ty?" I mutter, dazed.

"Surprise!" she says, sounding positively giddy as she grabs my hand before briefly looking over her shoulder at Ezra, who's standing a few paces away, his phone in his hands.

I instantly begin to search for Archer, disappointment washing over me when I don't find him anywhere. "Ezra agreed to accompany me," she tells me, squeezing my hand. "I'm here to bring you home."

She looks so much more full of life now. I'd noticed it over video, but seeing it in person is surreal. It's odd how bittersweet it is to see her doing so well. It proves that walking away was the right thing to do, and a small part of me was hoping that I'd been wrong when I made that decision.

"You came all the way here just to take me home?" I ask, shell-shocked.

She laughs and entwines our fingers before pulling me along. "I told you over the phone, didn't I? I told you that if you didn't come home, I'd come get you myself."

"I thought you were joking," I tell her, my voice trembling. I can hardly believe that she's really here and that she's leading me to a car that's waiting for us.

"You should've known better," Ezra says, smiling at me sweetly. "If you'd just listened to her, she wouldn't have dragged me all the way here."

His expression is entirely at odds with his words, and he looks at her like he'd go to the ends of the world for her simply because she asked. I watch them as he helps her with her seat belt, dozens of questions on the tip of my tongue that I don't dare ask.

Does Archer know they're here? Does he want me to come back at all, or would he prefer not to face me? I can't stand the idea of going back home and seeing him look at me with regret when he's the best thing that ever happened to me.

"We already collected your luggage from the hotel. We're flying straight home," Tyra says, her tone resolute.

I begin to protest, but she shuts me up with a look. "You've stayed away long enough, Serenity."

"Tyra," I begin to say, but she shakes her head.

"There's somewhere I want to take you, something I want to show you, and if after that, you still want to be here, I won't say a word. I won't stop you. But please, just do this one thing for me, Ser."

I look into her eyes, wishing I could tell her how much I've already done for her and knowing that I can't. What I did was make amends for my sins. I never should've fallen for the man she loves, never should've even added his name to my list, and I'm paying for it now.

"Come on," she says as she leads me onto the private jet that Ezra and Archer share, her familiarity with it making me uncomfortable. This is why I didn't want to go home—because I'll have to watch her retake her rightful place in Archer's life, and it'll destroy me to know she's got everything I've ever wanted. I'm scared I'll end up resenting her or that I'll slip up and say the wrong thing, causing her pain she absolutely doesn't deserve.

It's all I can think about the entire flight home, and I can't see a way out. I can't be the person she needs me to be. Not yet. Not while I'm still in love with the one man I can't be with.

My thoughts are still on Archer as I'm led into another car upon arrival, dread coursing through my body. I'm scared that seeing Archer will push me into another downward spiral, just like when I left. For the first few weeks, I barely ate or slept, spending every second painting in an attempt to dull the pain. I can't go through that again, not now that I've finally managed to pull myself out of it.

"We're here," Tyra says, snapping me out of my thoughts. I'd been so absent-minded that I didn't pay any attention to where we were going, and the moment I realize where she took me, my entire body tenses.

"Tyra," I murmur, my voice trembling, pure trepidation coursing through me. Why here? Why now?

"Please," she murmurs, reaching for my hand. "Give me ten minutes of your time. I know I've already asked for a lot, but please, Ser... please just hear me out."

I'm sick to my stomach as she leads me to the same vantage point where Archer and I decided to start dating officially, and my heart begins to hammer in my chest when my painting comes into view, a man standing in front of it.

I'd recognize him anywhere—the contours of his shoulders, the way his suit fits, and the way his hair is just a little wavy. He turns, and I stop in my tracks, unable to school my features. Similarly, he looks at me the way he used to, like he can't quite believe what he's seeing. He drinks me in, pure longing in his eyes.

"Thanks for coming," Ezra says, sounding apologetic.

"You said it was an emergency," Archer says, unable to tear his eyes off me, his tone conveying his confusion. "You said we needed to talk. What's going on here?"

I watch as Ezra moves to stand by Tyra's side, his arm wrapping around her shoulders as they look at each other, something passing between them. Tyra takes a deep breath, and Ezra tightens his grip on her, pulling her a little closer.

"I told you there's something I needed to show you, didn't I?" she says, addressing me.

I nod, and she gestures at my painting. I take a step closer, my eyes widening when I realize that it's been amended. It's been done masterfully, and the changes are minuscule, but they're there.

The red thread I painted no longer connects Archer to her, and tears begin to fill my eyes when I realize it now connects him to me. The scissors are gone, replaced by a bunch of red tulips, and most notably, Archer's expression isn't what I painted. Instead of longing, he now looks back with friendly fondness.

She pushes away from Ezra and walks up to Archer, grabbing his hand before leading him to me and reaching for mine. Tyra looks up at Archer with so much love that I can't stand to look at her without guilt tearing me up. "You ended things with me before everything happened because you knew we weren't right for each other, but I wasn't ready to admit it. I wasn't ready to let go of the idea of us, even if holding on hurt you more than I ever intended. I clung to you stubbornly and refused to acknowledge how much my actions were hurting you, and I…"

She turns to look at me then. "I'm not proud of the way I've behaved, Ser. I've known about you two for a few weeks now, but I pretended not to because I couldn't deal with the thought of not having Archer by my side when I needed him more than anything. I stood back and watched you two put me first, sacrificing your own happiness for mine. I stayed silent as guilt and heartache tore you apart because I couldn't cope with the idea of things changing and I desperately wanted normalcy and the life I left behind. He wasn't mine, Serenity. You didn't take anything from me, and there's nothing for you to feel guilty about. If anyone is to blame here, it's me." She glances at Ezra, their eyes locking for a moment before she turns back to me. "It took me a while to acknowledge that I can't regain what I've lost and that if I tried to, I'd just lose more in the progress. If not for Ezra…"

She bites down on her lip as she places my hand in Archer's, a tear running down her face. Her eyes fall closed for a moment, and then she looks at me, a shaky smile on her face. "Please do what I never could and make him happy. Please bring back his smile and let him return yours. Please don't let anyone deprive you of your happiness— not even me. And please…please forgive me."

Sixty-One

ARCHER

Serenity is quiet as we walk into my home together, neither of us quite sure what to say but aware that we need to talk—in private.

She turns around halfway into the living room, and I freeze in my tracks, taking a moment to just stare at her. My heart squeezes, and the butterflies in my stomach go wild. She's so fucking breathtaking in that white summer dress, and having her here, in this space we used to share, *fuck*.

"Wine?" I murmur, needing something to do, something to keep my hands occupied so I don't reach for her the way I want to.

She nods and follows me to the kitchen, the sound of her familiar footsteps bringing me a sense of comfort I never knew I needed. I missed every single thing about her. Everything.

My hands tremble slightly as I pour her a glass, acutely aware that she's barely looked at me since Tyra left us standing in front of her mural, our hands entwined. We stood there together for a while, just looking at each other, before I managed to murmur to her that we should talk.

Serenity takes a seat by my breakfast bar and knocks back half her glass. I refill it instantly before grabbing my own, my heart uneasy. I thought she'd be happier to be here with me, but she won't even look me in the eye.

Her body tenses almost imperceptibly when I move to stand to her side, facing her. My heart sinks when I read her body language, and I can't help but wonder if it's too late, if she's already moved on. I place my glass down beside hers and lean back against my breakfast bar, her knee brushing against my thigh. It's the closest I've had her in weeks, and it isn't enough.

"I've missed you," I murmur, my voice barely above a whisper.

Her eyes snap up, and her gaze softens, hope sparking in them. That expression of hers…it eases the worst of my fears, and I take a leap of faith.

"Not a single day went by without me thinking of you, Serenity. Every day, I wondered if we'd find our way back together and how long it'd take. It's been 108 days since you left, and every single one of those days was torture. My mind ran wild with thoughts of where you might be and who you might be with…" I run a hand through my hair and sigh, unsure what I'm even trying to say. I've imagined this scenario countless times, but now that it's happening, I'm stumbling over my words.

My breath hitches when she reaches for my hand, and I look at her, my broken heart undoubtedly written all over my face. "I still love you, Serenity Adesina. With all I am, all I've got. I still love you, and even if you don't feel the same way anymore, please…please give me a—"

My eyes widen when she wraps her hand around the back of my neck and pulls me in, her lips crashing against mine as she steals away my words. I groan as I grab her waist and push her legs apart with my knee, pressing her body against mine. *Fuck*. I've missed everything about her—the way her hair smells when I've got her this close, her soft curves against my chest, and the way her fingertips slide up my neck and into my hair as she kisses me. I missed feeling this alive, this *whole*.

We're both panting by the time my forehead drops to hers, and I cup her face, my gaze searching, drinking her in as she clutches the lapels of my suit jacket. "I missed you too," she says, her voice breaking. "It's been 108 days since we last saw each other, but it's been 33 days since we last spoke. I thought that…" She takes a shaky breath. "I tried to let you go, Archer, but I couldn't. I didn't want you to be trapped by the guilt you undoubtedly felt every time you spoke to me, and I didn't want to deprive you of a chance at the happiness you lost, so I stopped replying to your text messages…but I… You're all I thought of, all the time, everywhere I went. God, you have no idea how scared I was."

"Scared of what?" I ask, my hands roaming over her body, my need to touch her insuppressible. I missed this intimacy with her, the peace her proximity gives me.

"I thought that someday we'd come face-to-face, and you'd regret me, *us*. The idea of having to smile as you loved someone that wasn't me…"

"That would never happen," I tell her, leaning in for another kiss. This one is soft, lingering. "You're it for me, Serenity. I tried to be the man you thought I was and supported Tyra as best as I could, but my heart only ever beat for you."

She looks into my eyes like she doesn't believe me, and I smile, oddly reassured by her insecurity. Knowing I'm not the only one who feels this way, who battled these thoughts…it's such a fucking relief.

"You weren't swayed?" she asks. "If even a small part of you still wants to be with her, I need to know. I can't…I can't go down this road if—"

"No," I reply, cutting her off. "There isn't a single doubt in my mind that you're the woman I want to spend the rest of my life with, Serenity." I hesitate. "Were you? Swayed, that is. I saw the photos you posted with Theo."

She grins, not a single hint of guilt in her eyes, and the tension drains from my body. "No, Archer," she says. "As it turns out, you are the love of my life, and no one will ever take your place. Even when I couldn't have you, I didn't want anyone else, and that'll never change."

"The love of your life, huh?" I murmur as I lift her into my arms.

She gasps, a soft giggle escaping her lips when I carry her to my bedroom.

"I love the sound of that. Say it again."

She smiles so beautifully as I carefully place her down on top of my bed, loving the way her hair fans around her. She has no idea how badly I've missed this exact image, how desperately I wanted to see it again. "I love you, Archer Harrison. You're the love of my life, and you always will be."

My heart soars as I lower my body on top of hers, holding myself up on my forearms to look at her. "I love you more, darling," I murmur, kissing her forehead and then the tip of her nose, before moving to her cheek. "I will always love you, no matter what. If there's one thing I learned while we were apart, it's that I never knew what real happiness was before you, and I didn't know how much I cherished it until I lost you."

She wraps her hands into my hair, our eyes locking. "Is this really okay?" she asks, her voice trembling. "Do we truly get to be together?"

"Yeah," I whisper, kissing the edge of her mouth. "It might not be easy, and there might be an adjustment period, but, darling, we're going to be okay." I push myself up a little, my gaze roaming over her face. "We did the right thing, and in turn, so did she."

Sixty-Two

SERENITY

"Where are we going?" I ask as Archer entwines our fingers, and I frown when I realize his hands are clammy. He seemed nervous over the last couple of days, and I can't figure out why. "You've been acting super weird all day, Arch."

"It's a surprise," he says, his expression tense.

I frown as he pulls me through crowded streets, unable to figure out what he's up to. The last couple of weeks have been an adjustment, like he said it'd be. Tyra moved in with Ezra as all four of us try to figure out our new normal, and it hasn't been easy.

She and I don't talk as much as we used to, and I miss her, but I don't think either of us knows how to be around the other anymore. Every time we're together, Tyra still gravitates toward Archer. It's clear she's hurting and she still needs him, but she's trying her best to be respectful toward me, and I'm not sure how to handle it. I didn't want anything to change, but everything has, and I'm not sure if it's for the best. It feels a lot like Archer and I are being selfish at her expense, and it's hard not to let guilt consume me.

"Here we are," he says, pausing a few steps away from what appears to be an art gallery.

I raise a brow and smile. "You're taking me on a date?" I ask, laughing. "Why didn't you just say so?"

He looks into my eyes and smiles tightly. "Not exactly," he says, before guiding me into the building.

My breath hitches halfway through the door, when I realize that almost every single piece I've ever painted lines the walls, including some of the ones I painted as The Muse. This is a gallery that exclusively showcases *my* work, and it's buzzing with people dressed in incredibly expensive clothes, all of them admiring my art.

"There's a secret I've been keeping from you," Archer says, turning toward me and grabbing my shoulders, his expression filled with sincerity. "I bought every single one of your paintings…except for one that I couldn't get my hands on. I did it because…" He looks around, his smile becoming a little more tender, a little more intimate. "Because you painted memories of us that I wanted to collect and keep forever. I thought I'd lost you and that this was all I'd ever have, so I created this place for myself. It's where I'd go when missing you became unbearable, and for a few moments, I'd feel your presence all around me."

I place one hand over his heart, the other moving behind his neck. "Archer," I whisper, my voice breaking. I thought he'd been getting over me, but all the while, he was doing the exact same thing I was doing—losing himself in memories of us.

"I was scared that you'd find out I bought your work and you'd think that I did it for the wrong reasons. I know how your mind works and how you undervalue your work, so this…all of this…this is for you." He cups my cheek, his thumb brushing over the edge of my lips. "You see all these people here? I invited them because each and every one of them reached out to me in an attempt to buy your work off me when they saw it through the windows of this gallery. I wasn't willing to part with it then, but I think I am now—bar a few of my favorites, of course."

He leans in and presses a soft kiss to my forehead. "I don't need the memories when I've got the real thing, and I need you to see how well-loved your work is. I can't deprive you of your growth by hoarding your work when it should be out in the world, for everyone to enjoy. Your kind of talent? It only comes around once every generation. Those masters you admire? You're one of them, Serenity. You just don't see it yet."

"God, I love you," I whisper, rising to my tiptoes as I throw my arms around him and kiss him with all I've got, wishing my touch could convey my feelings and knowing nothing I can ever do or say will be sufficient to express how I feel about him.

He groans, his lips lingering as he pulls away. "I love you more, darling," he says, his eyes twinkling with equal parts pride and love. "Come on," he says, stepping back and grabbing my hand. "There are a lot of people who are dying to meet you."

I'm in a complete daze as Archer begins to make introductions, and dozens of people express their admiration for my work. I've always been anonymous as The Muse, and I mostly kept my identity hidden for the work I signed my own name on too, never using more than my first name. There's never been a face to either brand, nor have I ever spoken to anyone who's loved my art. I've even specifically stayed away from Muse fan groups, since my art was always just mine and I didn't want it to become anything more than that at the time.

Archer smiles at me as Ezra appears out of nowhere and takes the stage. "It is a true honor to be standing here today," he says, addressing the crowd. "Most of you might not know this, but Serenity Solutions was named after Serenity Adesina, my younger sister, and this auction is a true moment of pride for me. I convinced my business partner to name our company after my sister because I saw limitless potential in her, and I'd hoped to channel that. Seeing all of you in this crowd today, each of you appreciative of her work, fills my heart with unbridled joy. It means that she has done exactly what I always expected of her. Serenity exceeded my expectations and more than lived up to her potential, even if the road to get here wasn't as smooth as she may have wished."

I stare at my brother in pure disbelief, and he grins at me as he officially opens up the auction, one painting after the other being carried on stage. The room quickly becomes heated, and I look around in shock as my paintings are sold for prices ranging from thousands well into the seven figures. It's mind-blowing that people would pay that much for my work, but that's perhaps not the most shocking part. It's that the room is filled with celebrities. From where I'm standing, I can spot Elena and Alexander Kennedy, Silas and Alanna Sinclair, Raven and Ares Windsor, Sierra and Xavier Kingston accompanied by several other Kingston family members, and of course, Celeste and Zane Windsor. Some of the richest people in the world are standing right in this room, and they're all bidding for my work.

"Serenity?"

I turn around to find Tyra approaching us and instinctively move away from Archer, but he just pulls me back, his hand wrapping around my waist possessively. Tyra glances at the way he's holding me and pauses for a moment before looking up to meet my eyes. The awkwardness between us hurts, but Archer is convinced that dancing around her and being overly cautious won't help anyone. He thinks it's best for all of us to get used to Archer and me being a couple, but I don't have it in me to hurt her.

"I'm so proud of you," she says, stepping closer and gently pushing one of my curls out of my face. "Look at everything you've accomplished, Ser."

I smile and pull away from Archer to hug her, and she squeezes me tightly. I know it isn't easy for her to be here today, but she still showed up for me. Even if it hurts, she's trying her best to keep me in her life, to find a new normal that doesn't involve us losing each other.

"I hope you won't be mad at me," she says, pulling back. "But I brought guests."

She steps away, and my eyes widen when my parents turn the corner. Dad smiles, but Mom looks at me with a hint of reluctance blended with disdain. One look, and it's clear she's only here because Dad made her.

I'm so startled to see them that it takes me a moment to realize that my dad is holding a canvas. "It was you," Archer says, sounding somewhat aggravated. "You bought the one painting I couldn't get my hands on."

Dad holds it out and looks at it, smiling ruefully as he takes in the painting of a girl standing in a field of tulips, the sun shining down on her. It's a self-portrait, one that depicted me at my happiest. "I'm not willing to sell it," he says, his tone resolute. "But I brought it because I felt it deserved to be on display here."

One of the gallery employees takes it from him, and all the while, I just look at my father in disbelief. "You bought one of my paintings?"

He grabs my hand and nods. "Of course I did, honey. This may not be the career trajectory that I'd have chosen for you, but it's something you clearly excel at. It may take me some time to understand it all, but I'll do my best to be supportive in the meantime, like I should have been all along."

He looks at Mom then, his expression expectant. She looks into his eyes, and then she sighs. "Your father and I are on the same page in that regard," she says, her tone conveying her displeasure. "I do not understand your art, but it's clear you're successful at what you do, and ultimately, *that's* what mattered to me most. Financial security and independence, that's what mattered to me, and though I don't like to admit it, I was narrow-minded in my views of how to get there."

Dad smiles at her like he's pleased with her words, and I can't help but grin. It's more than I'd ever expected of them, and the relieved look in her eyes makes me suspect I owe a lot of it to Tyra. I have no doubt that she spent hours wearing Mom down.

Archer pulls me back to him, his hand wrapping around my waist like it was before, and Dad's eyes widen, pure confusion crossing his face. "What do you think you're doing, grabbing my little girl like that?"

Archer freezes and looks down, like he didn't realize he'd been touching me. It's so instinctive for him these days. He won't go more than a few moments without touching me if I'm anywhere near him, and I don't think he's aware of the quiet reassurance he's been seeking.

Mom tenses for a moment, looking between Archer, Tyra, and me, and then the edges of her lips turn up. "He's merely holding his girlfriend, Caleb," she says, shaking her head bemusedly.

"His *what*?"

Tyra chuckles and takes my father's arm. "*His girlfriend,*" she repeats. "I distinctly recall you once saying that he's a fine young man that you consider family, so I can't imagine it being a problem if he ever does become family, right?"

My dad stares at her speechlessly, and I burst out laughing, my heart overflowing with joy and contentment. I didn't think we'd ever fully recover the happiness we experienced months ago, but we did.

This is it.

This is the happiness I've always dreamt of.

Epilogue

ARCHER

THREE YEARS LATER

Serenity looks out of the window of my private jet, excitement radiating off her as we slowly begin to descend near Keukenhof, where we've gone every single year to see the flower displays and the endless rows of tulips.

This year, a whole field of flowers was planted to recreate one of her paintings from above. It's absolutely surreal what she's accomplished, and I couldn't be more proud of her. In a mere few years, she has become an international sensation, like I knew she would be.

"Oh God, I can't wait," she says, sounding giddy.

I grin and pull her onto my lap, my arms wrapping around her. "We've got about five minutes before they come tell us that we need to put on our seat belts," I murmur, my mouth caressing her neck.

She giggles, her head falling back on my shoulder as my hand slips underneath her dress. She turns her head slightly, her lips brushing against mine, and I grin when she reaches behind her, her hand wrapping around the back of my neck as she kisses me slowly, leisurely.

"I can't get enough of you," I murmur against her mouth, and she draws a shaky breath as she pushes off me long enough to straddle me.

"The feeling is entirely mutual," she says, cupping my face with one hand as she pushes the other up my neck and into my hair. It's unbelievable that I get to call her mine and that she still loves me the same. If anything, as time passes, our feelings just seem to grow deeper.

We moved in together very quickly, but now we've truly built a life together. She spends her days painting in the apartment below ours that she bought and converted into a fully equipped studio, while I go to the office and try to find every excuse I can to work from home instead, so I can watch her do her thing. I miss her terribly when she travels for exhibitions, and though I try to join her as often as I can, I love that we've both built our own careers while simultaneously building a home together. I didn't think life could get better than when we first started dating, but it did. I've never been happier, and judging by the way she still looks at me, neither has she.

I sigh as I pull her closer, kissing her right until the seat belt sign comes on, and she laughs when I struggle to let her go, my cock throbbing from one single kiss. She still does that to me—drives me wild with one single touch, and she knows it. "If you can wait for an hour or so, we can disappear in a field of tulips, just me and you," she whispers, before kissing my neck in that way she knows I can't resist.

I groan as she moves off my lap and back into her own seat, the butterflies in my stomach going wild as I watch her. I'd wondered if this feeling might fade someday, if it was just infatuation and the fact that our relationship was so new and thrilling, only I've eventually learned that what she made me feel back then was *nothing* compared to the way she makes me feel now.

Serenity frowns when we arrive at her favorite park only to find it empty. She glances at me in confusion. "Someone was supposed to meet us here," she says, reaching for her phone. "The park isn't meant to be closed today." I take her phone from her and hide it away in my suit pocket, earning myself a sexy little glare.

"Actually, darling," I murmur, nerves rushing through me. "I thought we could go for a walk."

Our eyes lock, and she studies me for a moment. "I'd love to," she says, her voice soft.

I bite down on my lip as I pull her along, worried that she's on to me. No one knows me like she does, after all.

I watch her gush over all the flowers, and fuck, I didn't think I could fall any deeper in love, but right here, right now, I do. She does this to me every single day, and I just don't understand how. How is it possible to love someone this deeply?

"Let's check out that cute little bridge," I tell her, my tone just a touch too nervous, but thankfully, she doesn't seem to realize. She's too taken with the beauty that surrounds her, not even realizing just how taken I am with *her*.

"Wow, look! Doesn't that look like words in between the flowers? Is it some kind of installation?" she asks excitedly as we walk onto the bridge. I watch her face as we reach the perfect vantage point for her to read what's spelled out underneath her in pink tulips amongst red ones, the message subtle but undeniably for her.

Serenity, will you marry me?

"Oh my God," she whispers as she places a hand over her mouth in shock.

I grin as I drop down to one knee in front of her and reach for the ring box in my suit jacket, my hands shaking as I pop it open.

Serenity turns to look at me, happiness radiating off her.

"Serenity Adesina," I begin to say. "You and I started off unconventionally, both of us thinking we wouldn't last longer than a stolen moment or two, but from the moment I first kissed you, I knew things would never be the same again. Before I knew it, I was enthralled, addicted to your smiles, your outlook on life, your generosity, and your heart, not to mention your beauty, your wit, and your incredible talent. You are so much more than I ever expected, so much more than I deserve. I'm well aware that I'm not worthy of you, Serenity, but I swear on all I hold dear that I'll never stop doing everything in my power to make you happy."

I take a deep breath when she smiles through her tears. "So give me a moment with you and then another. Grant me enough moments with you to fill up a lifetime because, darling, if you'll let me, I'd like to be yours every moment of every day for the rest of our lives." She inhales sharply when I take her hand, our eyes locked. "Serenity, will you please make me the happiest man alive and marry me?"

She nods, a tear running down her face. "Yes," she says. "*Yes.* Nothing would make me happier, Archer."

Relief rushes through me as I slip on the four-carat engagement ring that Laurier, a famous and highly exclusive jeweler, custom made for her.

She barely glances at it, unable to take her eyes off me, and I grin as I rise to my feet and sweep her off hers. I twirl her slowly, until she cups my face and leans in to kiss me, stealing away every thought but one.

I can't wait to spend the rest of my life with her.

Want more of Archer and Serenity? Access an exclusive bonus scene of their wedding day, plus a deleted steamy scene, via this link:

hi.catharinamaura.com/archerBONUSpb

or scan the QR code below

Acknowledgments

First of all, thank *you*, dear reader, for choosing to read *Mine for a Moment* when there are so many absolutely amazing books to choose from. I am beyond grateful for your support, and I hope you enjoyed Archer and Serenity as much as I've loved writing them.

Having said that, this book would not exist at all without my amazing team at Bloom Books—especially Gretchen, Christa, and Madison. Thank you for believing in me, for answering my millions of questions, and for always being there, no matter what I might need. You've moved mountains for me, and it doesn't go unnoticed. I am forever grateful that I get to work with you, and publishing this book alongside you has been a true honour.

Thank you also to Team Cat: Anna, Kenza, Vivi, and Bhavik. It's impossible to put to words just how much I value your constant support, and I honestly do not believe I'd have been able to write this book if not for everything you took on to help me meet my deadlines. I am incredibly grateful that I get to have you on my team. You're all absolute rock stars, and I appreciate you so much!

Last but not least, thank you to my sweet husband, for inspiring all of my heroes and for believing in me more than I've ever believed in myself. I wouldn't be able to write about love if you hadn't shown me what *true love* is. This book will be hitting stores almost exactly 10 years since you first asked me to be your girlfriend, so happy dating anniversary, darling. Thank you for being you and for choosing me, every single day for the last decade. I love you, Raj. More than anything.

About the Author

Catharina Maura writes angsty, fast-paced contemporary romance novels that break your heart before they lead you to a hard-won happily ever after. Cat lives in Hong Kong with her husband and a dozen houseplants that all have names, and when she isn't daydreaming about future characters, she's exploring the world and seeking out new adventures. You can find Cat's socials and latest updates here:

hi.catharinamaura.com/bio